EXES

BRANDON MASSEY

DARK CORNER PUBLISHING

Published by

DARK CORNER PUBLISHING

ISBN: 979-8-9854216-4-4

Cover design, illustration and interior formatting:
Mark Thomas / Coverness.com

"When you marry someone, you marry their entire family."
-- Kevin Jonas

BEFORE ...

Naomi had murder on her mind.

Austin Dash recognized the look in his wife's gaze, was intimately familiar with the chilly glint in her large hazel eyes. He even had a name for it: *the evil twin glare*.

He'd never shared that tidbit with Naomi, of course. She wouldn't have found it amusing.

They were at a steak house in downtown Albany called Robinson's, the most expensive restaurant in the southwest Georgia city. Robinson's had tables covered in starched white tablecloths, dark leather booths, oak-paneled walls, black-jacketed servers delivering cocktails and steaks, and a tuxedoed pianist playing jazz standards. It was a Saturday in late March, their monthly date night. Their five-year-old son was sleeping over with Austin's in-laws.

Austin had been anticipating a drama-free evening. A nice dinner out, a movie back at home where they could snuggle on the sofa, some foreplay that would lead hopefully to a rambunctious tumble in the sheets. The night was exactly on track—until Naomi was triggered.

The incident that summoned Naomi's evil twin: a former Albany State classmate of Austin's, a mahogany-skinned woman named Shavon, breezed past their booth and offered an innocent "hey there, haven't seen you in a while, hope all is well" greeting to Austin and briefly touched his shoulder. Shavon offered a hello and a smile to Naomi as well.

Naomi returned neither the smile nor the greeting.

The entire interaction had taken less than thirty seconds. But he could see Naomi was fuming. Her eyes narrowed to slits. Finely sculpted lips drawn into a firm line. A deep blush simmering on her golden beige face.

Tension twisted like a centipede through his stomach. Naomi looked like a Nubian goddess, but when the evil twin arrived, she could transform into something downright ugly, and nothing invoked the twin like her jealousy.

"Who was that bitch?" Naomi asked in a taut whisper. She slid aside her overpriced peach martini with her manicured nails, tucked a strand of her silky auburn hair behind her ear, and leaned forward.

She wore a form-fitting black dress with a deep V-neck. In the glow of the candlelight, Austin saw crimson bumps scattered across her cleavage.

She had broken out in hives. A stress response, he knew from prior experience. If he'd had any doubt about the gravity of the situation, the hives made it clear.

Underneath the table, he felt the sharp tip of one of her pumps press like a knife's point against his shin. He winced, edged his leg away from her foot.

I've got to talk her down, he thought. When his wife descended into one of these moods, nudging her away from the brink required him to exercise skills of persuasion that rivaled an FBI hostage negotiator's.

"She's only someone I knew from college." Austin shrugged. "I haven't seen her in over a decade."

"She touched you." Naomi glanced at the shoulder of Austin's button-down shirt as if his old friend's fingers had left behind smudges. "She's your ex-girlfriend—that's not a question."

"I haven't seen her in years, Naomi," Austin said.

"A marriage has to be built on trust."

"I agree. A hundred percent."

"I'm not feeling trusting right now. Watching my husband flirt with his ex-girlfriend."

Austin closed his eyes for a beat. Took a deep breath. Logical responses to these absurd accusations would not work. But emotional reassurances might.

"I've never cheated on you," he said. "Ever. Never will. No woman could ever compare to you. You're my queen."

"Daddy says, 'Never trust the quiet ones.'" Her red lips twisted. "They're so slick. They fool you."

"You're the most beautiful woman I've ever met," Austin said. "I'd never want to be with anyone else."

"But you were with *that* bitch." Naomi cast a dirty look over her shoulder. "That skank."

"Over. Ten. Years. Ago."

"Does she still look good to you?" Naomi turned around for another look, swiveled back to Austin. "Hmph. She and I, we could almost be sisters, don't you think? She's got that tiny waist, the perky titties, the nice round booty. She's a little darker than I am, but whatever—I know your type. *She's* still your type. My wifey instinct says so."

"She's not my type. You're my type."

"I want to believe you, Austie." She ran a slender finger along the rim of the martini glass.

"Why wouldn't you believe me?"

"You ought to know why. Don't force me to say it."

"I haven't cheated on you, Naomi."

"But I saw how you looked at her. How she looked at you. It was in your eyes. There's still something there, a spark. Like for a split second, both of you flashed back to the last time you slept together. You had a shared moment. I saw it as clear as I see this candle on the table."

Naomi picked up the glass candleholder and blew out the candle flame. In the absence of the light, a shadow darkened her features.

"There's absolutely nothing going on between me and that woman," Austin said.

"'*For out of the heart come evil thoughts.*' Or something like that. You were thinking about it."

"Can we get back to our dinner, please?" Austin asked. "We were having a nice time."

"We were having a nice time," Naomi said, mimicking him in a childish voice. She picked up her martini and downed the contents of the glass in one gulp, her gaze remaining on him as she drank. Carefully, she placed the empty glass back onto the table.

He saw her hands shaking. Coldness tickled his spine. She was like a geyser on the verge of eruption.

Not here, he prayed. *Please.*

When the server glided to their table, Naomi asked for another peach martini. Austin followed her lead and ordered another draft beer. Perhaps she was going to forget about this and let the evening settle back onto its prior, smooth track.

But she shut down. She set her purse on the table and dug inside the bag, and as she did, Austin glimpsed the pearl handles of the butterfly knife she carried and felt his breath catch in his throat, but Naomi only slipped out her iPhone. Instead of engaging with him or her meal, she swiped and tapped the screen and sipped cocktails.

Austin gave up and looked at his phone, too, in between bites of his steak. The evening had tanked, but he was relieved. It could have been a lot worse. Naomi's evil twin had been known to go nuclear in public sometimes.

Later, as Austin drove them back home in his SUV, Naomi finally broke her silence.

"You need to make amends," she said.

Here we go again. Squeezing the steering wheel, Austin glanced at her. "I haven't done anything."

"Think about how you're going to make this right. Instead of thinking about how you want to bang your ex. You're playing those memory tapes in your head, I know it."

He wanted to scream. Instead, he counted to ten and took a couple of deep breaths.

"I'm not thinking about my ex," he said. "All I'm thinking about is you. You're all I ever think about."

Naomi laughed. "Liar, liar, pants on fire."

"I'm not lying. You're the only woman for me."

She laughed again, a manic cackle that set his nerves on edge. Then she punched his arm.

"Hey!" he said. "Dammit, what's the matter with you?"

Reflexively, one of his hands clenched into a fist. The reaction was pure instinct, but Naomi saw it, and grinned like a snake.

"You wanna hit me, huh?" she asked. "Go ahead. Hit me back and I'll call the cops crying that my former athlete husband is battering me. How's that gonna work out for you, *Black* man?"

Austin relaxed his hand and rested it on the steering wheel. "Don't touch me again. I'm driving."

"You deserved that. Make amends."

Austin returned his attention to the road. His arm throbbed; she could hit hard. But he wouldn't allow her to see his pain. And he would never, ever strike her, not even in self-defense. Naomi was five-seven and weighed a hundred and twenty-five pounds. He was six-one, an ex–college athlete (track and field) and weighed a buck ninety.

He was a grown man, he reasoned. He ought to be able to handle whatever physical punishment she dished out when she got into these volatile moods. The kicks, the punches, the slaps. He could handle them.

Because of his childhood, raising his hand against any woman, for any reason, was unthinkable.

Austin had spent the first nine years of his life living under the draconian rule of his alcoholic, abusive father. Dad had been an athlete, too, had made it to the NFL as a wide receiver for the Miami Dolphins, but a torn ACL ended his burgeoning career after only two seasons. Dad never adapted to life off the gridiron, the derailment of his dreams, and he had taken out his frustrations on Austin, and Austin's mom.

Especially his mom.

Dinner delivered lukewarm could earn a vicious tongue-lashing—or a slap. A house not cleaned to Dad's exacting specifications might earn a shove across the room. And back talk, if you were foolish enough to let a cross word slip . . . well, back talk could bring out the fists.

Austin was nine when he saw his drunken father punch his mother so hard that she staggered, rapped her head against the oven door handle, and sank like an empty sack to the kitchen floor. He charged at his father, for what little it was worth, and Dad had grabbed him by his neck and flung him like a toy soldier across the room. Dad charged out of the house, leaving Austin there with his mother lying unconscious on the floor.

Mom died later that night from a traumatic brain injury. Dad hadn't been around to see it. When he had run out of the house, he'd climbed into his Corvette Stingray and, speeding over a hundred miles an hour and not wearing a seat belt, he struck a tree and catapulted through the windshield, bringing his own troubled life to a tragic end.

Yeah, Austin thought. *I can handle Naomi. I've lived through worse.*

He loved her, and he knew she loved him, but when she was triggered, she could lose control of herself for a little while. No one was perfect, right? You had to take the good with the bad, the bitter with the sweet.

That was what he told himself, how he rationalized these wild swings in their interactions with each other. It was complicated. Naomi was a good mother to their son, a fiercely protective mama to their little cub. She stood up for Austin when no one else did. Although he knew how to cook, she insisted on doing all the cooking, and she laundered his clothes, too, got annoyed if she caught him washing his own clothing. Living with her, in some ways, was like being a kept man.

And in the bedroom, she took his breath away.

Austin turned onto the private access road that led to their property and activated the gate via remote control. Actually, it was her family's property. The Xavier family owned an eighteen-hundred-acre pecan orchard on the outskirts of Albany, called Gold Crest Farms. Gold Crest Farms was one of the largest pecan producers in Georgia, shipping their prized product all over the world. Their success had earned them a feature story in *Black Enterprise* and nationwide acclaim.

Ten years ago, Naomi's father, Edward, had hired Austin as their lead accountant. That was how he had met Naomi. She worked in the family business, in the marketing department. Austin thought he had walked into heaven the first day he had seen her in the office, because she looked like an angel, bearing a strong resemblance to the classic Hollywood star Lena Horne.

Three years later, they were married. They moved into a house located on the family property. It was close to her parents (too close, a buddy had advised) but for the most part, her family kept their distance, though he knew Naomi told them almost everything that went on under their roof.

He envied her relationship with her folks, though. He didn't have any siblings, and after his parents died, he moved in with his mother's childless older sister. His aunt raised him in her southwest Atlanta home, and after high school, he snagged a track scholarship to Albany State, but his auntie died of a heart attack a year after he graduated college. He had a handful of distant cousins scattered across the country and chatted with them occasionally on Facebook, but that was the extent of things. The Xavier family had absorbed him into their clan, and while they had their idiosyncrasies, for the most part, he liked them.

He cruised past his in-laws' house, the largest residence on the property.

"I ought to tell Daddy what you did," Naomi said. "He would be worse than the cops, you know. He'll bring his rifle."

"Can we just get home and unwind? I'll open a good bottle of wine and we can relax."

Arms crossed over her chest, Naomi stared straight ahead. The evil twin hadn't yet retreated into her cave.

He pulled into their driveway. Their house was a three-bedroom brick ranch with an attached garage. Although the residence wasn't exactly what he had in mind as their forever home, they didn't carry a mortgage, and as an accountant, he could certainly appreciate the value of not having a loan hanging around his neck.

Inside, he unbuttoned his shirt collar and went into the dining room where they kept a wine refrigerator nestled in the corner. He opened the door, searching for a Riesling, Naomi's favorite. He would open a bottle of her favorite wine and offer to give her a massage. Those nonverbal tactics tended to work wonders whenever he needed to coax her into a better mood.

As he was bent over, looking in the refrigerator, turning through bottles, he heard her footsteps creak closer.

"Hey," he said without glancing up. "It looks like we've got your favorite bottle right here."

Naomi smashed a heavy object onto his head.

Austin collapsed to the floor. His vision blurred as pain flashed like a solar flare through his skull. Moaning, he rolled over.

One of his track-and-field trophies from college lay on the floor beside him.

She actually hit me with that thing?

He looked up. Naomi stood over him, chest heaving, the evil twin glare back in full effect. She gripped a sharp, shiny object in her hand.

It looked like the butterfly knife she kept in her purse.

Get up, he ordered his legs. *Move, move, move.*

He wobbled to his feet, dizziness sloshing through him.

Naomi screamed again, an animalistic cry of fury.

Austin ran.

But not before Naomi swung the blade.

1

Seven years later

On that Sunday in early April, Austin was running.

He sprinted on the indoor track at the local YMCA in Marietta. He ran as he'd been trained: shoulder blades tight, arms bent at ninety degrees. Hands relaxed and cupped, legs executing smooth strides, earbuds nestled in his ears as classic Run-DMC boomed through his brain. He was well off from the times he hit during his college days, but with two major knee surgeries behind him, he was willing to accept that he'd never hit the peaks he scaled in his youth.

The track was located on the upper level; beyond the waist-high railing on Austin's left, he had a view of the full-size basketball court on the first floor. As he ran, he periodically swept his gaze across the court. He was keeping an eye on his son, Khari, who was shooting hoops with friends.

Khari was twelve and the tallest kid playing down there in his group, which made it easy for Austin to watch him. One of the reasons Austin loved running there at the Y was because he could watch his son play ball and get in a run at the same time.

Some parents might have labeled Austin overprotective. He admitted that if it were possible to have a miniature drone that hovered around his boy twenty-four seven and broadcast live video to Austin's phone, he would have gladly signed up. As a young Black male, Khari faced threats from multiple sources—but only one kept Austin tossing and turning at night.

As Austin sprinted, he passed a very pregnant woman for perhaps the twentieth time. She walked as briskly as she could, perspiration glistening at the back of her neck. As he flashed past her, she playfully swatted his backside.

Austin muted the music on his phone, slowed to a walk, and waited for her to catch up.

"I'm getting an extra workout just from watching you, babe," Brooke said.

"I wouldn't be running at all if it weren't for you."

"You give me too much credit." She laughed, her eyes dancing. "I was only doing my job, man."

Three years ago, Austin had injured his right knee (again) while jogging on the road in his neighborhood. Arthroscopic surgery was required; after surgery, he needed eight weeks of physical therapy at an outpatient clinic. Brooke was the physical therapist assigned to his case. After that first appointment, he knew he wanted to ask her out to dinner.

She was beautiful, of course: she had russet, reddish-brown skin smooth as satin, big copper-colored eyes that sparkled with warmth and intelligence, a smile that made you want to grin along with her. She was smart. Most of all, she was funny. She'd kept him laughing so much as she put him through that first session that it made the pain much easier to bear. He found himself constantly daydreaming about how she might be outside of work, speculating about the fun they could have spending time together socially.

But he waited. As her patient, he didn't want to ask her out and put her in an ethically dicey position. But after his last session concluded, he said, "*Now, I can finally ask you out on a date. Interested?*"

Six months later, they were engaged; five months later, married. Now, pregnant, their baby boy due in May.

After his nightmarish marriage with Naomi, Austin had been doubtful that he would ever find happiness again. He'd worried there was something broken in him that attracted a certain kind of woman; that he had a sign hanging around his neck that declared, "*Kick Me and I'll Love You.*" But Brooke was everything that Naomi was not, in all the best ways.

He reached for Brooke's hand as she walked toward him. She took it, and they ambled together around the track.

"Did I interrupt your workout?" she asked. "I'm sorry about that."

"It's not possible for you to interrupt me, babe."

She grinned. "Sometimes we still sound like newlyweds."

This was also Brooke's second marriage. She was thirty-seven, four years younger than Austin, and had been briefly married in her twenties. As she described it, she and her ex had been high school sweethearts who evolved into an incompatible couple as adults, and after less than two years, they mutually agreed to an uncontested divorce.

Brooke knew all about his prior marriage. It was impossible to hide the knife scar on his back, the puckered old wound across his sternum, the faded slash on his right arm. What he'd lived through had horrified her.

In retrospect, with Naomi behind bars in a women's penitentiary, Austin found it hard to believe what he had endured at her hands. What had he been thinking? Why had he tolerated such abusive behavior? What had been wrong with him?

"After we leave here," Austin started, "we should—"

He glanced over the railing at the basketball court below, and his words sputtered in his throat.

"Babe?" Brooke asked. "What is it?"

Austin dropped her hand and hurried to the doorway.

She can't be here, he told himself. *It's impossible. She hasn't been released yet.*

But the auburn-haired woman who had led Khari out of the gym could only be Naomi.

His heart feeling as if it had entered his mouth, Austin flung open the door, nearly crashing into an older man entering the track area. He muttered an "excuse me," and pushed past the guy. He raced down the short hallway to the staircase that led to the first floor.

As he pounded down the steps, Khari and the woman rounded into view at the bottom of the staircase.

"Hey, Dad," Khari said, his eyes brightening. "Miss Darla wants to know if I can sign up for the boys rec league."

Austin halted on the stairs. He blinked, chest tight.

He recognized this woman. She was on staff at the YMCA, in charge of the various youth sports leagues. She looked only vaguely like his ex-wife. She gave Austin a tentative smile, but he could see the concern in her gaze.

"Is something wrong, Mr. Dash?" she asked. "You look like you've seen a ghost."

No, I didn't think you were a ghost. I thought you were my ex-wife, here to take my son and destroy our lives.

"I'm . . . I'm fine," Austin said.

But he felt light-headed, and barely made it down the remaining steps without stumbling. Finding a bench nearby, he plopped onto it. He dragged in deep breaths.

It took a while for his heart rate to slow.

But his thoughts kept racing. One of these days in the very near future, Naomi might show up.

What was he going to do then?

2

"What happened back there?" Brooke asked.

Austin pulled his Dodge Durango out of the YMCA parking lot. Brooke sat in the passenger seat, her gaze riveted on him. Austin glanced in his rearview mirror and saw that from the back seat, Khari watched him, too.

Khari had inherited his mother's hazel eyes and chiseled facial features, and like Naomi, his skin was several shades lighter than Austin's. His hair would have been auburn like Naomi's, too, if Austin hadn't agreed to let him color it with streaks of red, a lapse of parental judgment that Austin still regretted.

"It's nothing worth discussing." Austin shrugged.

"You looked like you had a panic attack." Brooke spoke in a muted tone, but her gaze never strayed away from his face.

Austin checked in the mirror again. Khari continued to watch him, anxiety reflected in his eyes. His son had witnessed his freak-out firsthand. Austin could only guess at his boy's thoughts.

"Can we talk about this later, babe?" Austin asked.

Brooke touched his leg, smiled to show she understood, and dropped the subject. That was another difference between Brooke and Naomi. Naomi never dropped anything, would demand an immediate accounting of every topic that attracted her attention. Talking to her often was like being on the witness stand under the thumb of a relentless prosecutor.

Austin headed straight home after they left the Y. Home was a two-story single-family residence in Marietta that he had bought five years ago. One benefit of living mortgage-free during his marriage to Naomi was that he'd stockpiled cash in his personal savings account. He'd applied a portion of that money toward a down payment on the house.

It was a modest place, located in a solid neighborhood attached to a quality school district. It was also only a ten-minute drive away from the mixed-use development where he leased an office for his small accounting firm.

But it didn't offer enough space for their growing family. He and Brooke were planning to purchase a larger home sometime that year. Moving on up, he liked to think.

When Austin pulled into the driveway and hit the button to automatically open the door of the two-car garage, he noticed a group of neighborhood kids in the cul-de-sac tossing around a football.

"Dad, can I play out here with the guys?" Khari asked.

Austin had known this request was coming. He saw familiar faces in the cluster of boys.

"You were balling at the Y for an hour," Austin said. "Don't you want to chill for a while? Maybe play some Xbox? I'll play with you. You up for some *Madden*?"

The truth—which he would never tell Khari—was that the incident at the gym had rattled him. He wanted to have his son close at hand, safely out of harm's way, for his own peace of mind.

"I wanna be outside with my friends," Khari said.

Austin noticed that Brooke was watching him closely. He realized that to her he probably sounded ridiculous. Most parents these days lamented that their kids didn't spend *enough* time outside playing in fresh air and sunshine, that their children kept their eyes glued to screens—now he wanted to hide his son indoors?

"All right," Austin said. "Stay where I can see you. Don't wander off."

Khari mumbled something under his breath. Austin thought he heard Khari utter the phrase *freak out*.

"What was that?" Austin looked over his shoulder. "We've talked about the mumbling, Son."

"Say it with your chest!" Brooke piped in.

That comment made Khari snicker. Austin laughed, too.

"I'll stay near the house, Dad, okay?" Khari said. "It's cool."

A short while later, Austin stood at the window of their second-floor master bedroom watching Khari play catch with the group of kids. Brooke entered the room. He didn't turn, but felt her arms encircle his waist, her bulging stomach nestled against the small of his back.

"I need to hit the shower," Austin said. "You might not want to be hugged up against me right now."

"You smell good to me." She buried her nose against the base of his neck. "Hmm. I could put this man funk of yours in a bottle and sell it on Amazon, make all the ladies swoon."

"He's growing up so damn fast." Austin nodded toward the window. "Have you noticed that he's almost as tall as I am?"

"Oh, yeah, I heard that's the thing about children. They tend to grow up."

"It scares the hell out of me, Brooke."

Brooke came around and faced him. Her arms still encircled his waist. Her gaze probed him, an unspoken question in her eyes.

"What is it?" he asked.

"Are we finally going to talk about what happened at the Y?"

"I'll be fine. It was only a blip."

"Don't shut down on me. You always minimize your feelings. That's why your blood pressure is up."

A month ago, Austin's annual physical exam with his primary care doctor had revealed an alarming increase in his blood pressure readings. His doctor had written him a prescription for Lisinopril. Austin had gotten the script filled (at Brooke's insistence) but was reluctant to take the pills; he figured he could manage his condition without medicine, that perhaps it wasn't a true condition at all, only a temporary situation.

"Come on, talk to me," Brooke said. "What're you really scared of?"

"Khari thinks I'm overprotective. He's probably right, but I can't help worrying about him. I want to keep him safe, always."

Brooke shook her head.

"Are you serious, babe? You are an *amazing* father. You don't give yourself enough credit." Brooke took one of his hands in hers, kissed his knuckles, then placed his fingers on her belly. "I couldn't imagine a better dad for Khari, or for our little one on the way."

"I worry about losing him."

"He's going to grow up," she said. "But he'll never forget that you're his daddy, that you raised him and loved him as best you could."

"What if that's not enough? There's so much trouble out there . . ." He let his words trail off.

"Whatever happens, you'll always be there for him." She pulled his head down, kissed him softly on the lips. "Go ahead and freshen up. I'll get dinner started, all right?"

Brooke shuffled out of the bedroom.

After she left, Austin shifted back to the window. He hadn't disclosed to Brooke the root cause of his worries. He had an almost superstitious fear—well, it *was* superstitious—about vocalizing things you didn't want to happen. As if speaking the words would, like a magical incantation, guarantee that the dreaded event would come to pass.

He pulled off his shirt. Studied his myriad old scars.

Before he went to shower, he cast another look out the window, making sure Khari was still there.

3

"Dad, can I get a phone for my birthday?"

Austin had stopped by Khari's bedroom to bid him good night when his son hit him with the question. Austin groaned. The topic of Khari getting a smartphone had been a point of contention between them for the past year.

Khari was sitting at the desk where he typically did his homework, played games on his iPad or laptop, or worked on his superhero drawings. He was a gifted artist, and Austin thought his son might have a future as a professional creative if he decided to pursue that path.

Khari pushed away from the desk, the tablet tucked under his arm. He clasped his hands together and gave Austin a pleading expression.

"Please?" Khari asked.

"Your birthday isn't until November," Austin said. "It's only April."

"I'm planning ahead," Khari said. "You always say: 'When you fail to plan, you plan to fail.'"

"You have a phone already, kid."

Khari rolled his eyes. It was one of those expressions that reminded Austin so much of Naomi that Austin's heart lurched.

"It's just some cheap phone that doesn't do anything," Khari said.

"It allows you to call me and your stepmom. That's the basic purpose of a phone. Making phone calls."

"You know those guys I was playing with outside?"

"Yeah, the neighborhood crew. What about them?"

"All of them have *smartphones*." Khari's gaze drilled him. "*Everyone* at school in my grade has a smartphone."

Of course, not everyone in his grade had a thousand-dollar phone, but the boy tended to exaggerate things. Khari already had challenges self-regulating his screen time, tended to get sucked into the digital world and forget about his homework and household chores. Austin worried that giving the kid a smartphone before he was ready would only worsen those tendencies.

"We've been over this before," Austin said. "When you turn thirteen, we'll revisit getting you an iPhone. I promise."

Shaking his head, Khari plopped onto his bed and positioned his iPad on his lap. He swiped the screen, his long, slender legs trailing over the edge of the bed.

He really is growing up fast, Austin thought. It seemed like only yesterday that he used to hoist Khari over his shoulders and carry him around the house. Where had the years gone?

"Time to hand over the iPad, too," Austin said. "You know the bedtime rules, buddy."

A house rule: Khari wasn't allowed to sleep with his tablet in his room. If he did, Austin knew he wouldn't sleep at all. He would be up all night playing *Roblox*, *Minecraft*, *Fortnite*, and whatever other digital obsessions the children his age pursued.

"I wasn't even playing games," Khari said. "I was looking up Mom."

Austin's spine tingled. "What do you mean?"

"There's this website—it lets you look up people who're in prison."

"Who told you about that?"

"Jahlil, from school. One of his cousins or something is locked up and he found him on that website and sent him a letter."

Austin's knees sagged, and he leaned against the doorway to keep his balance. He should have known this was coming. Khari was twelve, whip smart, thoroughly versed in technology. Eventually, he would figure out how to research Naomi online.

For the past seven years, Austin had been slow to share the background with Khari of why his mother had landed in prison. *Something bad happened between us, Son, and the law decided that your mother had to go away for a while, for her own safety, mine, and yours. It's not your fault.* Khari hadn't pushed too hard, much to Austin's relief. But the boy was getting older, more independent. Pat answers weren't going to placate him any longer.

"It says she's going to be free soon," Khari said. "Like, this month. Is that true?"

Why do you think I thought she was abducting you at the Y? Austin nearly responded. *Yeah, I know she's getting out, Son, and it terrifies me.*

"This is a heavy topic to discuss right before bedtime," Austin said.

"But she's really getting out?" Khari asked.

"Most people get released sooner or later. Yeah, she is."

"Can I see her? Do you think she wants to see me? What about the rest of my family?"

"Whoa, whoa." Austin made slow-down gestures. "You're broadsiding me here."

"I want to see my *real* mother." Emotion flashed in Khari's eyes.

Austin's stomach did a slow somersault. *Where is all this coming from?*

Austin glanced over his shoulder, then stepped deeper into the room and closed the door behind him.

"I thought you liked Brooke," Austin said. "She absolutely adores you."

"She's nice, I mean. But you guys are going to have your own family soon. What about me? What about my mom, my grandparents?"

Austin hadn't anticipated this flood of questions, but he realized he should have. Another lapse in judgment on his part. He shuffled to Khari's bed and sat beside his son. He put his arm around him.

"First of all, *we* are your family," Austin said. "That never changes, regardless of how many more children Brooke and I have together. Do you get me?"

Khari's shrugged his narrow shoulders. "I guess."

"Second, the situation with your biological mother and your mother's family is complicated. I need some time to think about it."

"How much time? I want to see her. She's gotta want to see me, too, right?"

Jesus, kid, you've no idea what we're getting into here, Austin thought.

"I haven't even talked to her this whole time," Khari said. "I haven't sent her a letter or anything. Have you talked to her, Dad?"

Austin shook his head.

"What about my grandparents?" Khari asked.

"I haven't been in touch with them, but it's sticky with them, too," Austin said. "Give me some time. I promise we'll make a decision about this."

"Whatever, Dad." Khari dropped the tablet into Austin's hands.

Austin went to kiss Khari on the forehead, but his son turned away and flopped onto the bed.

Good job, Austin.

4

The butterfly knife streaked like fire down Austin's back.

Austin was twisting away to flee when Naomi started swinging the blade. He could not have been more disoriented if he'd been blindfolded: she'd just smashed a trophy upside his head and he hadn't regained any sense of balance or his surroundings.

This can't be happening, *he thought in the back of his mind, but he knew full well that it was, that this vicious attack was the culmination of years of escalating violence his wife unleashed against him.*

He crashed into the dining room table and, like a pinball flicked by a paddle, he bounced against the wall. The collision left him exposed to another slash of the knife, a searing cut down the back of his right arm.

He flailed, screaming. He lunged at her, driven purely by instinct, wanting to rip the knife out of her hands.

She tore the blade across his chest, dangerously close to his heart.

Gonna kill me. She's really gonna kill me . . .

Austin awoke with a shudder. Cold sweat saturated his face and T-shirt.

The knife scars on his body felt as if they were burning, and when he pulled away the bedsheet, he half-expected to see a luminescent glow outlining each old cut.

Beside him, Brooke slumbered; an assortment of pillows propped her up, an arrangement she had figured out would allow her to sleep during these last weeks of her pregnancy. He envied her. He rarely slept an entire night without waking from a terrible dream of some kind. The mornings when he woke without remembering a dream at all were the best ones.

He swung his legs off the mattress. It was almost two o'clock in the morning. He badly needed to sleep—it was Monday, and he had a full week ahead of him—but after dreams such as those, sleep was out of the question.

He padded down the hallway to the spare bedroom that doubled as his home office and booted up his computer. He clicked on one of the links he had bookmarked in his browser: "Find an Inmate."

He had saved the page featuring Naomi's inmate profile. It included a photo: her mug shot from seven years ago, when she was convicted of aggravated assault with a deadly weapon.

Naomi glowered at the camera with her evil twin glare.

At the bottom of the profile, her release date was listed. Khari had been right: her release date was that month.

She was getting out tomorrow.

5

When Brooke awoke sometime later that night, she reached across the mattress and felt an empty space where Austin should have been.

What's really going on with him? she thought, the question breaking through her drowsiness. The elevated blood pressure, the panic attack (yes, it was a panic attack, despite his denials) at the YMCA, the darting gaze, as if he were on the lookout for an impending threat . . . There was something important weighing on his mind, and he wasn't talking.

Brooke maneuvered out of the bed. Getting out of bed while heavily pregnant required agility and careful movements. She thought her background as a physical therapist would make it easy, but nothing had prepared her for the actual experience. Back pain, heartburn, and insomnia had been her recent companions.

Her maternal sleep gown billowing around her like a giant ship's sail, she wandered out of the bedroom. In the dimly lit hallway, she noticed the door at the end of the corridor was closed, but light glowed underneath.

She padded across the carpet to the door, knocked, tried the knob. It was unlocked, so she opened the door.

Austin glanced away from the computer monitor and gave her a thin smile, his eyes dark hollows.

"I know what you're going to say," he said. "I can't sleep. But *you* need to be sleeping."

"What're you looking at?" Brooke edged closer, tried to get an angle on the screen.

Austin clicked the mouse. Whatever he had been looking at vanished.

"I was researching houses," he said.

"It's past two, babe. Come to bed."

"I didn't realize it was so late. Time must've slipped away from me." He turned in the desk chair. "But again, you need your rest."

Brooke couldn't deny the truth of his words. This pregnancy had been an experience fraught with tension. With her first husband, she had experienced two miscarriages. She was convinced it was a major factor in their divorce.

Now she was thirty-seven, an advanced maternal age, and trying to have another baby. Yeah, she was nervous. She wanted to do everything perfectly. They had made it this far, and the plan was for the baby to be delivered via C-section, yet those two failed pregnancies loomed in her mind like a bank of storm clouds on a dark horizon.

If something happened and they lost this new baby, would Austin blame her?

In her most private thoughts that she would never share with anyone, she wondered if part of what had attracted her to Austin initially was that he already had a son. That if she failed to give birth to a child, it might be okay. His son was a safety net, of a sort.

She reached for his hand. "Come to bed with me."

"I'll be there in a few minutes." He yawned. "Don't wait around for me."

Brooke returned to the bed, rearranged her pillows in the pattern that enabled her to sleep.

She tried to wait up a few more minutes for Austin, but he didn't come back.

She drifted into slumber, alone.

6

When Naomi walked out of Pulaski State Prison on that sunny Monday morning in April, she felt like dancing.

Seven years of crappy food and sharing a cramped cell with other women. Seven years of being told what she could do and when she could do it. Seven years of sheer hell.

When she cleared the gates and strutted into the sunshine, she screamed, and she didn't give a damn who heard her.

They gave her back her old clothes, the outfit she had been wearing when she was booked. Jeans and a red blouse and sneakers. The only item that fit were the sneakers. The jeans and the blouse both sagged off her body, several sizes too big on her.

Some women went to prison and got chunky on junk food and the slop they gave you. Naomi got ripped. She'd shed about twelve pounds, replacing softness with hardness, flab with muscle.

Compared to when she had been convicted, she looked better than ever. She'd always been a dime, with a face pretty as a doll's and a body that made men (and not a few women) swoon. It had seemed inconceivable to her that she could come out of that hellhole looking better than when she had been dropped in there, but there it was.

Wait until Austie sees me, she thought. *He'll be begging me to take him back.*

Her mother, Karen, and her older sister, Charlotte, were waiting beside a white Cadillac STS in the inmate pickup section of the parking lot. They cheered and waved when they saw Naomi coming.

Naomi had always heard that she and her mother looked a lot alike. They both had that glowing, natural beauty that time seemed only to enhance rather than steal. Charlotte wasn't so fortunate in the looks department: she had a short, blocky body and bad skin prone to rashes and acne breakouts despite her age. But she was a sweetheart, a true ride or die sister.

Mama and Charlotte had visited regularly during her incarceration, a couple of times a month. But today was different. Naomi was going home with them.

Naomi hugged them hard. Mama was crying, and Charlotte wiped tears from her eyes, too.

"Where's Daddy?" Naomi peered inside the shadowed sedan looking for her father. She didn't see him.

"Oh, you know Daddy." Mama's eyes were downcast. "He ain't been feeling too hot lately. You know what the doctor said the last time I dragged Daddy in there."

Health issues had plagued her father since her incarceration. Six years ago, he'd suffered a major heart attack. As if that weren't bad enough, a few months ago Daddy had been diagnosed with late-stage prostate cancer, the cancer that afflicted Black men more than all others. He wasn't too keen on the treatment options, either, from what Naomi had heard. Like her, Daddy could be stubborn sometimes.

"I was hoping to see him, Mama. This is a special day."

"I know, Peach." "Peach" was her family's nickname for her. "You'll see him when we get back home. He sends his love."

"We figured you'd wanna get something to eat first," Charlotte said. "You were always talking about how much you hated that dump food in there."

"Girl, you ain't never lied. I need some real food. Take me to Waffle House."

A half hour later, Naomi and her family slid into a booth at the nearest Waffle House they could find. Naomi didn't need to look at the menu. She had fantasized for years about her freedom and knew exactly what she wanted to order.

"Three scrambled eggs, a waffle, hash browns scattered, smothered, covered," she said to the server. "And get me a side of bacon and some coffee with lots of cream and sugar."

"You lost a lot of weight in there." Mama gave her a critical appraisal. "Look like you intending to gain some of it back, eh?"

"I'm not gaining nothing back. I'm gonna go on a run when we get home and burn it all off."

Charlotte and Mama exchanged a look.

"I told y'all when I was in there how much I used to exercise," Naomi said. "That's not changing now that I'm out."

"I gotta admit, you look good, Sis." Charlotte nodded.

"I'm a married woman," Naomi said. "I gotta keep it tight for my man."

Charlotte and Mama exchanged another look.

"Austin's gone, Peach," Mama said. "You *know* he's been gone. You getting out ain't gonna bring him back."

"Yeah, I know he filed for a divorce, Mama. I saw the damn papers. I didn't sign them. He got away with it 'cause he had some sheisty lawyer. I didn't agree to none of it."

"We still don't know where he is," Charlotte said. "He took your boy, too. How old would he be now?"

"Twelve," Naomi said. "He's got a birthday coming up in November."

One of the only personal items she was allowed to keep in her cell was the photo of her son. In the picture, he was only five. She had looked at that picture every day, done age progression of his appearance in her own mind. The promise of seeing him again kept her sane.

Their food arrived. Naomi dug into her meal, but snapped up when the door opened. That was a habit she had picked up from prison: always being aware of your surroundings, on edge, waiting for something to go down. Being rousted by a CO for no reason. Dealing with other inmates trying to make moves. She had learned she had to be ready within a blink.

But it was only a mother and her son. Seeing the boy brought her own child to mind. He looked to be the same age as her son. Naomi's heart clutched; this moment felt like a preview of her reunion with her baby.

The two of them headed for a table right in front of Naomi and her family. As they sat, Naomi said, "That is a good-looking boy you have there, ma'am. So handsome."

The woman glanced at Naomi, and something in her dark face soured. As if Naomi had said something dirty; or as if Naomi had the word "convict" tattooed on her forehead.

Hell is her problem? Does she think she's better than me?

"I gave you a compliment, ma'am," Naomi said, in a louder tone. She clutched her fork, her knuckles white as bone.

"It ain't worth getting into." Mama touched Naomi's arm. "Hell, you just got out, Peach."

Naomi nodded, but she was fuming. She finished her food in relative silence. Charlotte and Mama understood that when she got into this mood, it was best to allow it to run its course, like a storm that needed to shed its rain and thunder.

After they finished their meals and walked out of the restaurant into the sunshine, Naomi nudged Charlotte.

"Lemme hold your blade, Sis."

When they were teenagers, Daddy had gifted them butterfly knives and ordered them to keep the weapons in their purses always. Because you never knew when you might have to cut someone—or something.

"What you gonna do, girl?" Charlotte unzipped her purse and handed over the blade.

"Gimme a minute."

Naomi remembered that the woman had been wearing a Georgia Southern hoodie. The white Honda CR-V parked in the corner of the parking lot had a Georgia Southern sticker on the bumper. It had to be hers.

After a quick glance around to ensure no one was looking, Naomi flicked out the blade. She stabbed the rear left tire and twisted the knife around. Sour air escaped the ragged rupture with a soft hiss.

Charlotte and Mama chuckled.

"You haven't lost a step, Peach," Mama said.

"I gave that skank a compliment on her kid," Naomi said. "She'll mind her manners next time."

The drive home to their family farm took about an hour and a half. Naomi kept looking around as they rolled down the state highways, taking in all the sights of everything that had changed in the years since she'd been locked down. She felt like Rip Van Winkle, waking up into a whole new world.

But when they approached the sign for Gold Crest Farms, the home of their family's pecan empire, Naomi felt her stomach curdle.

"Is the business still open?" Naomi asked. "That sign is crooked and dirty."

Driving, Mama sighed. "Things ain't been the same since Daddy's been sick."

"Business done took a turn," Charlotte said. "We still open, technically, but things ain't like they were before you got locked up. Daddy's been ailing, and you know that hurricane came through a few years back and wiped out a bunch of our trees."

"Y'all never said anything about that," Naomi said. "All the times you visited, not a word about how the business was suffering. Daddy didn't say nothing in his letters, neither."

"What was you gonna do about it from inside that place?" Mama glanced over her shoulder at Naomi. "You ain't no mafia don, gonna run things from a prison."

She had Naomi on that. It wasn't as though Naomi had ever been involved in the overall management of their pecan orchard. She worked in the marketing department, coming up with glossy flyers and pretty pictures, and when she went to agriculture conventions all she was ever asked to do was to dress sexy and smile. Daddy had handled the operations side of things.

Mama turned onto the main road that cut through their property and they passed through the gates. The road was bumpy, full of more potholes than Naomi remembered. She bounced around in the back seat, stuck out her hands to brace herself.

The primary residence, her parents' home, came into view. By then, Naomi was expecting the house to have fallen into disrepair, too, and her expectations were amply met. The rambling Colonial-style house needed a fresh coat of paint and a thorough power washing. A couple of shingles hung loose, flapping like bird wings in the wind. Kudzu vines climbed the exterior walls like mutant arteries. The lawn was choked with weeds and the flowers out front were begging for a pruning.

"Good Lord," Naomi said under her breath.

The luxury Winnebago RV parked in the driveway sat on two flat tires, and every side was mantled in a layer of pollen so thick the whole vehicle might have been painted egg-yolk yellow. Her parents had the motor home on order right before the incident that landed her in prison, and it looked as if once they had taken possession, they hadn't driven it at all.

"Guess y'all haven't taken that camper out on the road," Naomi said.

"We had big plans for it, but nope," Mama said.

Mama parked in the driveway beside the motor home and her daddy's Ford pickup. Naomi got out and stretched, enjoying the feel of the sun on her skin. It felt amazing to be out, to be home, to be free. She whirled around like a schoolgirl and laughed.

"Ain't you something?" Mama seemed amused.

"I'm glad to be home is all," Naomi said. "I feel like clicking my heels and whistling."

Naomi raced to the front door. She pushed it open. A musty odor hit her in the face like a backhanded slap. The windows needed to be opened, the carpets steam cleaned, the whole house dusted thoroughly.

"Where's our cleaning lady?" Naomi asked her mother. "The Hispanic lady, Rosita?"

"We had to cut back on some things, Peach," Mama said. "I do the best I can, but this is a big house, you know. I got my hands full taking care of Daddy."

Sounds like a bunch of excuses to me, Naomi thought, but she kept her lips buttoned. She didn't want to get into it with Mama, not then. This was supposed to be a happy time, a joyous reunion.

"Daddy!" Naomi cried. "Daddy! I'm home!"

She didn't hear any response. She would have expected to hear her father's distinctive booming baritone coming down the hallway, but she heard only the clink and clatter of the A/C.

"Daddy's down in his den," Charlotte said. "That's where he tends to be now, Peach."

"Lemme go see him."

Naomi hurried through the house, taking note of the disarray. She trailed her finger across a side table and damn near an inch of dust cleared in her finger's track. She scowled to herself.

A short staircase led into the den. It was like descending into a dungeon. There were deep shadows everywhere, and the sour odor of sickness permeated the heavy air despite the spinning ceiling fan.

Naomi's eyes slowly adjusted to the gloom. In the middle of the low-ceilinged room, her father, Edward Xavier, sat tilted back in a threadbare La-Z-Boy recliner. He wore denim overalls but he was barefoot; the way his long feet were stuck out reminded her of a corpse lying on a cold table in a morgue. He looked like a mannequin in a museum of horrors. She remembered him as a towering oak tree of a man, but he was down here withering away.

Tears pushed out of her eyes. She sniffled, wiped the wetness away with the back of her hand.

"Daddy?" she said. "You awake?"

He didn't answer. But she heard him breathing, his breaths rattling in his lungs like grit in a busted air conditioner.

Lord, he's in a bad way, she thought.

The flat-screen television in front of him was on, the screen so dusty the images were obscured. But she recognized the show playing: *All in the Family,* that old sitcom that her grandparents used to watch all the time. It was as if Daddy had aged thirty years during her incarceration and taken up the ways of his own parents.

It was hard to look at him in this condition. He used to be the ultimate model of a man, in her mind, the one against whom she measured all others—and no one had ever stacked up to Daddy, pound for pound, Austin included. In Daddy's youth, he was a dead ringer for Harry Belafonte.

But now, Daddy had drool sliding down his chin in a ropy thread. Approaching him, she found a box of tissues sitting on a side table, plucked one out, and used it to dry his face. When she touched him, his eyes fluttered.

He had hazel eyes, like she did. But his eyes were as clouded as the bottom of an empty milk bottle, the edges rimmed with crimson.

Naomi's paternal great-grandfather was a wealthy European who bought vast swaths of land in southwest Georgia and married one of his house servants, a Black woman. He had founded the pecan farm, too, and passed it down to the eldest son she bore for him; in turn, that son passed down the land to his oldest boy, Naomi's daddy. Who was next in line to take over? Naomi had some clear ideas about that.

Slowly, Daddy blinked.

"That you, Peach?" he whispered in a raspy voice. He coughed, the sound like a death rattle in his chest. "You home now?"

"Sure as hell ain't here on furlough, Daddy." Grinning, she took one of his big hands—the roughened hands of a man who handled dangerous machinery for a living—and squeezed. "I'm home at last, dear."

"I'm sorry." A tear slid down his wrinkled cheek. "I never came to see you."

"You hush now." Clasping his hand, she kissed his knuckles. "You wrote me letters. Every month. They helped me get through."

"I couldn't take seeing you in there, Peach."

Naomi knew her father assumed responsibility for her conviction. She didn't blame him. He had hired the best lawyers they could afford, but in the end, none of it mattered. They still threw the book at her. In her fantasies, she hunted down the judge and every member of the jury and slit their throats like she'd gashed that tire earlier.

"Now I done went and got sicker," Daddy said.

"You talk like you went to the store and bought your condition off the shelf."

She dabbed away his tears with the tissues and held his hand again. "It's not your fault, Daddy."

He squeezed her hand back, but weakly. The sight of him, wasting away like this, made her heart burn.

Austie's fault, she thought. *This is all his doing. He ruined everything for our entire family.*

Would Daddy be suffering if she hadn't gone to prison? And why was she in prison anyway? Because Austin had decided to make their private affairs a matter of public record. The only reason she went off on him in the first place was because he was acting shady about his feelings for other women. Everything, all the tragedy that struck her family, could be traced back to Austin, and Austin alone.

"I'm home now, and we're gonna get you back to health," Naomi said. "When I was locked away in that awful place, I learned that the important thing you need to be healthy is a crystal-clear purpose."

"Huh?" Daddy squinted. He probably didn't follow what she was saying, but that was okay. In time, she would make it plain.

She spotted his favorite rifle resting in its steel rack on the wall above a sagging sofa. He had plenty of other firearms in a closet on the other side of the room, but the Ruger was his favorite. He had literally chased some of her past suitors out of the house with that gun.

Naomi stepped to the wall and lifted the rifle out of the rack. She brought it to her father, laid it across his lap like a gift, and put one of his hands on the shaft.

"I wanna get my family back," she said. "My son and my husband. They've gone astray and we need to bring them home. I know you had that heart attack and now you got the cancer and all, but I need your help in this, Daddy. I need *you*."

Hands trembling, Daddy slid his fingers along the weapon's cold, dusty shaft. He looked up at her, and it was as if he was seeing her for the first time since her return.

"We really missed you, Peach." His voice sounded a little stronger, too.

"There was a man we used to work with—he'd run background checks on folks before we'd hire them, dig up all their dirt," Naomi said. "I need his information. We got a nice project for him."

Nodding, Daddy's grip tightened on the barrel. She kissed him lightly on his cracked lips.

"Let's get to it then," Daddy said.

Here I come, Austie, Naomi thought with a grin. *Ready or not.*

7

Two weeks later

On a Tuesday afternoon, Austin and Khari accompanied Brooke to her perinatologist appointment at a medical center in Buckhead. Although Brooke was due to give birth in only a few weeks, the doctor wanted a final ultrasound. Three months ago, the physician had discovered water in the baby's kidneys—a condition known as prenatal hydronephrosis—and wanted to keep close tabs on the child's development.

Normally, only she and Austin would have visited the doctor, but Austin wanted Khari to come along with them. He signed his son out of school early.

He hoped that bringing Khari would help him feel more connected to the upcoming addition to their family, especially because the ultrasound was the highlight of the visit. Seeing his little brother-in-utero on the screen, Austin reasoned, ought to pay dividends in Khari's relationship with his new sibling.

The ultrasound went well, the baby's kidney condition trending toward a non-issue at birth. Khari was appropriately fascinated by the child on the display and remarked that he and his brother had similarly shaped ears.

"They're called Dumbo ears," Austin said, drawing chuckles from both Brooke and the doctor. Austin indicated his own prominent ears. "You're in good company, kid."

It was half-past three in the afternoon when they walked out of the multistory brick building. The day was warm, the clear sky the color of a tranquil ocean. Austin usually hated fighting Atlanta rush-hour traffic, but he was in such a buoyant mood that the prospect of facing slow-moving cars on the interstate didn't overly concern him.

He had parked his Dodge Durango in the main parking garage of the medical center complex, an ugly cement monument of five stacked parking decks teeming with vehicles. From the ground level, they took an elevator to the fifth floor, the uncovered top level, and strolled into the sunlight.

There were only a few vehicles still parked up there. Austin had snagged a spot only a short walk from the elevators.

"I hope this visit made ditching school worthwhile," Austin said to Khari.

"Seriously, Dad?" Khari said. "Any excuse to miss school is a good one."

"I can't believe you're encouraging juvenile delinquency," Brooke said with an exaggerated roll of her eyes, but of course she had been on board with Austin's plan from the beginning.

"It's going to be cool when the baby is really here," Khari said. "I'll have seen him when he's still in your stomach. Like I can always tell him that. Seniority over him forever."

"You'll have one up on him for life," Brooke said.

Austin pressed the key fob button to pop open the SUV's doors. Khari hopped into the back seat and grabbed his iPad and earbuds out of the seat pocket before he even reached for his seat belt. Austin had to bite his tongue against making a critical remark. The appointment had gone well. He didn't want to ruin it with yet another parental lecture about screen time.

Austin reached to open the passenger door for Brooke when he heard the elevators ding behind him.

Purely out of habit—or maybe, on some instinctual level, he knew all along what to expect—he glanced over his shoulder.

Naomi walked out of the elevator.

Austin's hand froze on the door handle as if he had been trapped in a state of suspended animation. Noticing his hesitation, Brooke turned, too. He heard her breath catch in her throat.

The reaction from his wife was proof that he wasn't experiencing a hallucination. Brooke's response was evidence that it was all real.

She's really here.

Naomi strutted across the parking deck with that distinctive hip-swinging stroll of hers, that arrogant sashay that trumpeted to the world, *I look good, I know it, and so do you.* She looked leaner than the last time Austin had seen her seven years ago at the county courthouse wearing the ugly orange inmate jumpsuit. She wore a tight black blouse, black jeans that looked shrink-wrapped on her long legs, and black leather boots that she had once called "my ass-kicker boots." Her formerly straightened auburn hair had been wound into braids that flowed in wild abundance to her shoulders. She wore a crimson scarf around her neck.

Her face was as beautiful as ever, the visage of a goddess. She wore blood-red lipstick and light blush.

"You look surprised to see me, Austie." Naomi spread her arms. "I'm back."

She smiled, but the smile didn't reach her hazel eyes. The old evil twin glare was in full effect.

Austin started to speak, but the words, whatever they might have been, died on his dry lips. His heart felt as if it were about to swell and burst like a boiled peach.

Naomi had been released from prison two weeks ago. He knew that. He had been logging onto the "Find an Inmate" website regularly for *years,* and knew the date of her release as well as he knew his own birthday.

What he didn't know was how she had tracked him to this place, at this moment.

As he stared at her, thunderstruck, Naomi strolled up to him, invading his personal space as if nothing had ever changed between them, took him in her arms, and gave him a full-on kiss on the lips.

Austin broke his paralysis and stepped back. Naomi flipped her braids over her shoulder and laughed, a high-pitched squeal.

"Excuse me," Brooke said, clearing her throat.

"Excuse *you,* Miss Thang." Naomi looked Brooke up and down, and her face wrinkled like a prune. "Oh, you're the baby mama, huh? Got the bun in the oven. Didn't Austie tell you that we're still married?"

Brooke looked at Austin. He saw confusion cloud her gaze.

"I served you divorce papers when you were in prison," Austin said. "I know you got them. I ran a notice in the newspaper. It's over. If you don't have the papers, my attorney will be happy to send them to you again."

"I don't wanna talk to your lawyer," Naomi said. She pressed a slip of paper into Austin's palm; he saw a phone number scrawled on it. "This is between me and you."

"We need to go." Brooke turned away toward the vehicle to get in, but she wouldn't meet Austin's gaze.

Austin opened the door for her, but he wondered: Did Brooke believe Naomi's lie? Did she really think he was still married to a woman who had tried to kill him?

"Where's our son?" Naomi said. "I saw him. He's in the car? You let me see my baby boy right now, you hear me?"

"I can't do this here." Austin couldn't have felt more cornered if he had stuck his foot in a bear trap. He had envisioned what he might do if ever confronted with Naomi again, and in his imagination, it had never played out like this. Their reunion had played out in a courtroom or in the quiet office of a family law attorney. Not in a parking lot in broad daylight with Naomi eager to raise hell.

Does she have her knife? he wondered, and he knew it was a silly question. She carried her knife on her person like people carried their smartphones.

"Get in the car, please," Austin said to Brooke.

"Yeah, you better get in the car if you know what's good for you, *skank,*" Naomi said, wagging her finger. "Me and my husband, we're gonna have a private conversation."

"He's not your husband anymore," Brooke said, her tone rising. "*You* need to accept that."

"Brooke, please." Austin tried to nudge her aside. "It's not worth it."

Brooke didn't argue further, and Austin was grateful. She was slow to anger, avoided confrontations unless necessary. Seeing someone like Naomi probably was a shock to her system, like unexpectedly encountering a rabid dog waiting on your front porch when you stepped outside to take out the trash.

But Austin worried about Khari. Khari probably had slipped on his earbuds and was immersed in his tablet, or else he would have been out here. Was he oblivious to everything going on?

Austin heard a door swing open on the other side of the SUV.

"Dad?" Khari asked. "What's going on?"

Austin's stomach plummeted. *Not now, God. Please, not now.*

"My baby!" Naomi opened her arms.

Austin grabbed Khari's arm before Naomi could embrace him. "Get back in the car, Son."

"Is that my mom?" Khari tugged against Austin. His voice cracked like fragile crystal. "Hey, is that Mom?"

Austin never exerted any physical force to control his son, or anyone for that matter. But something instinctual in him did not want his son touching this woman, whether she was his mother or not. He had kept Khari safe for seven years. Naomi represented the destruction of everything he had built.

"Get back in the car!" Using his full strength, Austin wrangled his son back into the SUV. "Sit in here and be quiet! Now is *not* the time, boy!"

Against Khari's protests, Austin shoved him inside and slammed the door. Naomi was crying, causing one hell of a scene, and Austin realized in a flash of insight that she had planned it to play out exactly like this: to put him on his heels, keep him off balance by sideswiping him when he least expected it.

She'd always known how to push his buttons better than anyone.

"You can't keep him away from me!" Tears streamed down her face, ruining her makeup. "I have rights. I'm his mother, goddammit!"

"We're not having this conversation right here, right now." Austin grabbed the handle of his own door, yanked it open.

Naomi shrieked. It was an awful, bloodcurdling cry. Austin felt something inside him shrink, and he glanced around the upper level to see if anyone else was in earshot. Thankfully, they were alone.

Hives had broken out on Naomi's neck and face. Austin hustled inside his SUV and slammed the door. He snapped the locks down.

Inside, Khari was crying. "I wanna see my mommy, I wanna see my momma, I wanna see my . . . my . . . my mother . . ."

Brooke, too, was sniffling, dabbing at her eyes with a tissue. Austin punched the ignition button.

Naomi slapped the palm of her hand against his window. She pressed her face against the glass, her eyes comically distorted and huge, rashes glowing on her cheeks and throat.

"You can't leave me!" she screamed. "We're married!"

Austin rammed into Reverse, the engine bellowing. Naomi leaped back, but waved her arms wildly.

"He's taking my son!" she cried. "Someone, help! He's taking my son!"

"Jesus," Brooke said.

Austin drove across the parking lot, nearly colliding with another vehicle coming around the curve ahead. He looked in the rearview mirror and saw Naomi flailing her arms and wailing.

As fast as he could manage, he got out of the parking lot and on the highway. He half-expected to see the blue lights of a police cruiser in his rearview mirror, but it never happened.

They had escaped.

But he knew it was only the beginning.

8

The instant that Austin pulled out of sight, Naomi stopped crying so abruptly it was as if a movie director had yelled "Cut!"

She wiped her eyes with the heel of her hand, her breaths coming in short bursts. Her hands weren't getting the job done, so she dug in her purse and pulled out a few tissues.

It had felt amazing to see her son. He was so big, so handsome, exactly how she had dreamed he would be. A spitting image of her and his father.

And Austin . . . well, her husband had always looked so fine, even when under distress. He had picked up a few gray hairs, but he still looked fit, like the athlete she had fallen in love with all those years ago.

As far as the skank that he was "married" to, Naomi didn't have anything good to say. She sounded weak. Why that wasn't clear to Austin was a mystery to Naomi. The woman wasn't fit to carry Naomi's makeup case.

Naomi's cell phone buzzed. She slipped it out of her purse and answered the call.

"He's gone," Charlotte said. "We saw him pull out and take off down the road. Did you talk to him?"

Walking down the stairs to reach the ground level of the garage, Naomi narrated what had happened.

"That's what you expected, ain't it, Peach?" Charlotte said.

"That's about right." Naomi stepped away from the staircase and strutted down the sidewalk. "I see y'all. I'm gonna be there in a few minutes."

Her family's camper was too big for the parking garage. They had parked on a street adjacent to the medical center. The motor home's roof was mashed against the boughs of a nearby elm tree.

Naomi rapped on the door. Her mother opened it, and Naomi climbed inside.

Since Naomi's release, she had worked to rejuvenate her family, to give them a sense of purpose again. A key aspect of that was getting back her *own* family, both Austin and her boy. It was a mission that everyone—Mama, Charlotte, and Daddy—could all get behind.

The RV had been sitting on flats when Naomi got out of prison, and that was an easy repair. All the rest of it had needed was some detailing and a tune-up, and it was ready to hit the road.

She found Daddy in his little "den" they had installed in the camper. He had a comfortable chair and a flat-screen TV where he could watch his old movies they streamed via their internet connection. He was starting to look like himself again, the father she remembered before her lockdown. The pain meds obviously helped—she had convinced Daddy to get back on the opioids his oncologist had prescribed—but Naomi attributed his newfound vitality mostly to their shared mission.

Purpose, Naomi thought. *That's all anyone ever needed. A reason to draw breath and get out of bed. Cancer be damned, Daddy.*

"How'd it go, Peach?" Daddy asked. His baritone that she loved was back in effect.

"He was happy to see me." Naomi giggled.

"Was he now?" Daddy smiled, his hazel eyes twinkling. "That's why he pulled outta there like the hounds of hell were after him, eh?"

"I think he was a little *surprised* to see me, sure." Naomi sat on her father's lap, like she did when she was a little girl, and wrapped her arm around his shoulders. She let her fingers play in his thin patch of gray hair. "But he's gonna come around to seeing things my way."

"You sure about that?" Daddy squinted at her.

"I know my Austie," Naomi said. "Deep down, he's weak when it comes to me. Always has been, from the moment he saw me. He can't help but melt in my hands."

"You know him," Daddy said. "Still think we oughta just take our grandson and head on back to the farm, but you're running this."

"Thanks for trusting me, Daddy." She kissed him atop his forehead. "You'll see. I'm right. I always am."

9

Austin drove home, and the drive was awful. Traffic was a nightmare. Worse, Khari was crying, Brooke was sniffling, and he felt warm water in his own eyes, too, tears that he refused to shed.

The questions circling his thoughts put a lock on any crying that he might have done. How had Naomi tracked him down? She had known exactly where they would be, and when. To the minute.

If she had known they were going to be at a doctor's appointment, then she obviously knew where they lived. It was a reasonable assumption. Had she already driven by his house? Watched him drive back and forth to work? Seen Khari board the school bus, followed the bus to school, been there when he got on the bus in the afternoons, trailed it back to their home?

The Naomi he remembered was capable of obsessive attention to detail for matters that interested her. He'd thought he had prepared for the day when she would return. But he realized that he wasn't prepared at all.

He didn't even know what to tell Brooke, or most of all, Khari.

None of them had spoken almost an hour later when Austin finally pulled into the driveway and opened the garage door. But Khari had stopped crying. Brooke had been staring out the window, avoiding meeting his gaze.

They were both angry at him, he assumed, and he had no idea why.

"I didn't do anything wrong," Austin said, breaking the silence. "I didn't expect her to show up and say any of those things."

Khari didn't respond, but Brooke wiped the back of her hand across her bloodshot eyes and said, "Is it true?"

"Is what true? Trust me, if Naomi said it, then it's probably not true."

"Are you still married, Austin?" Brooke asked. Her gaze was as direct as he had ever seen it.

"She is *lying,* Brooke. She's a chronic liar."

"I never asked to see the papers, you know." Brooke laughed, but it was a hollow sound. "Should I have done my due diligence, asked for proof of your divorce?"

"I never asked for your divorce papers, either," he shot back.

"Hmph. Well, I have them. Want to see them?"

"No." He shook his head. "No, I don't want to see your divorce papers, because it's not necessary."

Suddenly, Khari opened the back door and hustled out of the SUV. Without a word, he rushed into the garage, disappeared in the shadows.

Both Austin and Brooke watched him go.

"What are you going to tell him?" Brooke asked. Her tone was softer.

Austin looked at the square of paper that Naomi had pressed into his palm, the phone number scrawled in her distinctive slashing handwriting.

"I don't know," he said.

"You can't keep Khari away from her forever."

"But she's dangerous. It's like inviting a rattlesnake into your house."

"But she's his mother."

Austin clenched his hand into a fist, crumpling the note. "This isn't how I imagined this would turn out. I knew she'd come back, but not like this."

"You *knew* when she was getting out of prison? That's what you've been stressed about lately, isn't it?"

"I didn't want you to worry." Austin shrugged. "I screwed this up."

"You should have been honest with me from the start. I'm a part of this, too."

"I'm sorry." He shrugged. "Let me go get those papers."

"Austin—" she started, but he raised his hand.

"You asked," he said. "I want to settle it. It's the one part of this mess that I can settle."

He pulled into the garage and went inside. He should have called for his son, but he didn't. What would he tell him? He didn't yet have the words to address everything that needed to be said to the boy.

Upstairs, he noticed that Khari's bedroom was shut. He turned away and entered his office.

In the filing cabinet, he found the folder that contained his legal documents. One of the papers therein concerned his custody of Khari. Another set detailed the finalization of his divorce.

Brooke was changing clothes in their bedroom. He brought the sheaf of papers to her.

"Here," he said.

"I don't need to see it."

"We need to settle it. I don't want this hanging over us like some dark cloud. Please look at it."

"I don't want to look at it, baby. I believe you. I never should have doubted you. I'm sorry."

Austin set the document on the bed. He sank onto the mattress. He wished he could lie down, close his eyes for a couple hours, and wake to find none of this had ever happened, that it had all been a bad dream.

Brooke had slipped on an oversized T-shirt and loose-fitting pants. She slid aside the paperwork and eased onto the bed next to him. She reached for his hand.

"Your hand is clammy." She touched his wrist. "Your pulse is racing, too. You need to take your blood pressure meds. Especially now."

He waved away her concerns.

"I don't know what to say to him," Austin said. "Naomi totally blindsided me. She's good at that."

"How did she track us down?"

"Someone's helping her. She probably hired a private investigator, I'd guess. It's not as though I'm living under a fake name. With a little digging, anyone could find me, follow me."

"Are you going to call her?" Brooke asked.

Austin had tucked the note into his pocket. He felt the warmth of it there, like a simmering coal.

"I need to talk to Khari first," Austin said.

10

Khari's door was not only closed—it was locked, too.

"Son?" Austin rapped on the door. "Open up; we need to chat."

There was no response. Austin knocked again. Harder.

"Khari, open the door," he said, his voice louder.

His son didn't reply, and didn't open the door. Austin punched the door so hard it rattled in the frame.

"Open the damn door!"

But still, nothing.

Perfect. Now the kid won't even speak to me.

"Give him some time," Brooke said, from the doorway of their bedroom.

Austin massaged his throbbing knuckles. He didn't usually react with any level of physical forcefulness, against anyone, in any circumstances. But Khari was his world, and Naomi threatened to crash them all into ruin. It triggered a ferocity that Austin didn't realize he had.

"I need to clear the air between us," Austin said to Brooke. "He needs to understand that I'm doing the right thing here. He needs to be on my side."

"It's about sides now?" Brooke asked.

Austin brushed past her, headed back into their bedroom. In the nightstand on his side of the bed, he found a set of keys; the keys that unlocked every interior door in the house. He returned with the keys to Khari's room.

"I'm coming in," he said.

He unlocked the door.

Khari's room was empty. But the window that faced their backyard was open, curtains fluttering in the breeze.

"Shit." Austin crossed the room.

He stuck his head out the opening. The patio was underneath Khari's bedroom window, a large outdoor sofa sitting right under the windowsill. A couple of the pillows had been displaced and lay on the concrete pad.

"He actually jumped out the window?" Brooke asked.

Austin's heart slammed. Khari was a runner—that had always been the boy's nature. He ran away from conflict. He hated to argue, hated uncomfortable situations.

In that respect, he and Austin were a lot alike.

"I've got to find him." Austin rushed past Brooke. She reached for his arm.

"Do you need me to do anything?" she asked.

"Wait here, please."

Austin hurried outside. He looked back and forth down the road. It was full of houses like his; it was a community of about two hundred homes, all of them built according to five or six floorplans and elevations. Khari had known some of the children there for years, had developed friendships. He could have gone to ground with any of them.

But Austin didn't want to start texting the parents of Khari's friends, not yet. People would stick their noses in his business, would want to know what happened, and why. All these people knew about him was that he used to be a single father, now was recently married with a child on the way. They didn't know about Naomi and what had brought him there, two hundred miles away from literally the scene of the crime.

He would keep his own counsel. He would find his son on his own. The boy didn't have a car, and if he had leaped from a window, he didn't take his bike, either. He was on foot.

Austin started running at a moderate pace. He had a sense of where Khari might have gone. He raced toward the community's recreation area.

The rec complex included a playground with a slide and swings, a tennis court, a swimming pool (*Residents Only!* a sign warned) . . . and a basketball court.

Austin spotted Khari on the basketball court long before he reached him. His son was shooting baskets, alone, and there were no other players around. He attacked the rim as if it owed him something. If he were tall enough—and he nearly was—Austin was certain Khari would have slam-dunked the ball hard enough to make the entire goal sway.

Austin thought about leaving him there, watching from a distance, then catching him when he started to come home. He would come home, eventually. He was angry, but his anger would pass.

But even as Austin considered that approach, his feet carried him forward. He realized that he worried what Khari was thinking, that he didn't want him making assumptions about his father, about his mother, about anything. Austin needed to squash this and get his son on his side.

It's about sides now? Brooke had said.

Damned right it's about sides, Austin thought. He'd worked too hard to give Khari a stable life to lose it all.

"You didn't need to jump out of the window," Austin said, reaching the court. "You could have just walked out the front door."

Khari ignored him, kept shooting baskets. His next shot was wildly off and the ball bounced in Austin's direction.

Austin plucked the ball off the ground and fired a pass back to Khari. Khari caught the ball deftly and avoided meeting Austin's gaze.

But Austin could see his son's eyes. They were reddened from tears.

Austin's heart twisted. Christ, he hated to see his kid sad. It felt like a failure of parenting whenever he saw his child teary-eyed, though Austin knew he couldn't take on responsibility for every emotional peak and valley of his son's life.

"For the record, I didn't have any idea that Naomi would show up there," Austin said. "It's not as though she gave me any advance warning."

Khari bricked another shot, muttered under his breath, chased down the ball, and raced back toward the rim. He flipped up an underhanded shot that went in.

"Naomi has issues," Austin said. "We need to go about things the right way, for everyone's safety."

Dribbling, Khari mumbled something, cut a sharp glance at Austin.

"What did you say?" Austin said. "Please, no mumbling."

Khari stopped dribbling and glared at Austin.

"I said, you didn't even let me speak to her!" he shouted. "I haven't seen her in seven years! You didn't even let me speak to her!"

Austin sighed, lowered his head.

"I could have handled it better," Austin said. "I'm sorry."

Khari stopped dribbling. He clasped the ball between both of his hands—hands almost as large as Austin's—as if he wanted to crack it like a walnut.

"I wish you'd stop treating me like a baby. I'm twelve. What I think *matters*. You don't get to force me to think whatever you think."

"I'm not trying to force you what to think."

"Yeah, right." Khari started dribbling again. He launched a shot and swished it.

Austin retrieved the ball this time. He shot a jumper from the baseline and it was an airball, not even close to touching the rim.

"There's a right way and a wrong way to do things," Austin said. "You want to talk to Naomi—fine, I get it."

"She's my mother. Can you call her that?"

"Okay, you want to talk to your *mother*? I get it. You haven't seen her since you were five years old. I understand. But—"

"Can I talk to her or not, Dad?" Khari said. He held the basketball in his hands, his muscles clenched. "Are you going to let me talk to her or not?"

"It's not that simple, Son. We need to discuss conditions, boundaries, supervised visits. We need to talk to a lawyer."

Khari hurled the ball in Austin's direction and turned away with a sneer. He walked off the court.

Austin watched him leave. He could have tried to stop him, but he knew it wouldn't have made any difference. He wasn't going to tell Khari what he wanted to hear.

He followed Khari, from a distance. His son was heading back home.

Austin went back home, too.

11

Brooke met Austin when he came back into the house. She was in the kitchen putting away dishes.

"You didn't come in together," she said. "I guess that means the chat didn't go so well."

"Where is he? Upstairs?" Austin leaned against the island in the middle of the kitchen.

"Went right up there without a word and slammed the door loud enough to shake the whole house."

"I can't give him what he wants, not how he wants it." Austin clasped his hands together.

"He wants to talk to his mother, obviously."

"It's not safe. I don't think he understands."

"Stalemate," Brooke said. She came over to him, rubbed his arm. "How can I help?"

"I need time to think," he said. "There's a lot to consider here, legally. I don't want to get sucked into a custody battle—I got full custody when she went to prison. Her family didn't fight me, and she didn't have a leg to stand on at the time."

"Considering Khari's age, a family law judge is going to want his input," Brooke said.

"Christ." Austin opened the refrigerator and found a bottle of beer. He twisted off the cap and took a long swig.

"How was she, as a mother?" Brooke asked. "Honestly."

"Honestly?" Austin lowered his voice, worried that Khari would eavesdrop. "She was really good with him. Adored him. She saved her evil twin outbreaks for me."

"Evil twin outbreaks?"

"Her mood could change, literally like flipping a switch. Anything could set her off—you never knew what might do it. She could go from pure sweetness to a monster just like that." He snapped his fingers.

"But she never lost her temper with Khari?"

"I don't recall seeing it. But he was only five. He's almost a teenager now. It's going to be different." He took another swig of beer. "But that's not what I'm most worried about."

"What are you most worried about?"

"I'd rather not discuss it. Don't want to speak it into existence if you know what I mean."

Brooke cocked her head, gave him a curious look. "Not bringing up something for discussion doesn't exactly prevent it from happening."

"It's a superstition thing with me." He drank more beer, but the unspoken words churned through his mind.

I'm worried that Naomi will use Khari to try to manipulate me into going back to her. She hasn't accepted the divorce, babe. She's going to keep pushing. Getting Khari on her side is only the first step. And I hate dealing with pressure—I hate saying no to people. I hate saying no to her.

Brooke closed the last cabinet, shut the dishwasher door.

"Are you going to call her, then?" she asked. "Or are you going to wait for her to make the next move?"

"Is there an option three?" he asked.

"What would that be?"

"Ignore her and hope she goes away."

Brooke slid her hands around her bulging stomach and glanced toward the ceiling.

"I don't think your son will like that decision."

"Right," Austin muttered.

"Sleep on it. See how you feel about things in the morning."

Austin sipped beer. "I like that plan."

But when he awoke the next morning, he had a bigger problem on his hands.

12

When Austin stepped outdoors at seven o'clock that morning for his morning run, he discovered a gigantic motor home parked in the cul-de-sac, the vehicle's nose blocking his driveway.

He stopped in his tracks at the front door, his breath bottled in his chest.

He couldn't have been more shocked if an alien spacecraft had landed on his front lawn. He had expected Naomi to do something after yesterday's confrontation at the parking garage—but he hadn't anticipated *this.*

He knew the camper belonged to Naomi's family based on one telling detail: the RV had a stunning mural along the side that faced Austin's house. The painting depicted an immense pecan orchard basking in golden sunrays, the sky as clear and blue as the ocean. Austin vaguely recalled that Naomi's dad had ordered the customized motor home shortly before his marriage to Naomi had imploded, but he had never seen the behemoth until now.

Condensation obscured the vehicle's windows. How long had it been parked there? Overnight?

On feet that felt weighted with stones, Austin moved forward.

His neighbor, a middle-aged woman named Becky, was out walking her male Labradoodle along the sidewalk. Austin passed her most mornings when he was running, exchanged a greeting or a wave, and she always smiled at him.

She wasn't smiling this morning.

"Do you know who *this thing* belongs to?" Becky asked as she drew near.

She indicated the RV with a sharp look. Her dog wagged his tail and sniffed Austin's leg.

"It's my in-laws," Austin said, and then he corrected himself: "I mean, *ex* in-laws."

"Hmph." Becky's eyes dwindled to dark points. "As the HOA president, I must inform you that parking a recreational vehicle overnight in the neighborhood is a violation of the CC&Rs. This isn't a campground."

"I didn't ask them to come," he said. "They showed up, unannounced."

"How long are they planning to stay?"

"They'll be leaving today." Austin swallowed and looked toward the camper's dark windows.

"I certainly hope so, or else I'll be calling the police. This is a parking violation."

"I'll take care of it." He gave her a level look. "I promise."

13

Austin approached the motor home's front passenger door. He couldn't see anything through the tinted windows. He knocked.

In his mind, he had rehearsed what he was going to say regardless of who answered. *Good morning. You can't park your RV in the neighborhood. Someone's going to call the police. Leave now and we'll discuss the situation with Khari later.* A reasonable but firm statement. He needed to say it like he meant it. Delivery was everything.

As soon as he rapped on the door, it opened immediately, as if whoever was on the other side was waiting for his knock.

It was Naomi.

Involuntarily, he drew in a breath. He wanted to say that after their violent history as a couple she would always be ugly to him. Rationally, perhaps that was true. But on a primal level it was impossible to ignore how good she looked. She wore a green tube top designed to display her chiseled six-pack. A pair of pink yoga pants hugged her narrow waist, shapely hips, and long legs. She looked as if she had recently applied makeup because every detail of her face was picture perfect. Even her braids seemed lustrous, freshly woven.

"Hey there, handsome." She batted her eyelashes, reached toward him, and touched the sleeve of his hoodie. She had long, manicured nails, and he noticed, much to his chagrin, that she wore the wedding set he had given her. "Still an early riser, aren't you? Stepping out for your morning run? Before you ask, we pulled in last night."

We, she had said. That meant her entire family had joined her. Lovely.

"Naomi, what in the hell are you doing here?"

"Why don't you come inside? You need to check out Daddy's Winnebago—it's top of the line. You remember he talked about getting it?"

She spoke as if the two of them had parted on amicable terms and were merely needing to get caught up. He remembered how she would behave like this during their marriage, ignoring her prior misdeeds and insults as if they had never happened. Living with her had often made him feel as if he were being perpetually gaslighted.

"You can't be parked in the neighborhood like this." He hated the tone of his voice; he sounded like a whiny teenager. This wasn't going at all like he had rehearsed. "You're blocking my driveway."

"We got off on the wrong foot yesterday. Let's have a cup of coffee and chat like grown-ups, sweetie."

Austin turned and glanced at the window of the master bedroom. He saw, between the parted blinds, Brooke standing at the glass. Her presence both comforted and terrified him. What was she thinking about what he was doing? Did she trust him to do the right thing? After their argument yesterday, he wasn't so sure.

"I promise not to bite." Naomi nodded toward the house. "I'll give you back to the baby mama up there when we're done. I know she's watching."

"Ten minutes," Austin said.

Naomi took his hand. She rubbed her thumb across his palm. Austin felt a tickle at the base of his spine. She often used to touch his hand like that right before they'd have sex, her signal to him that she was ready to get it on.

He pulled his hand out of her grasp, followed her up the steps and into the vehicle's cab. She slipped around him to close the door behind him, her breasts pressed against his shoulder, perfume clouding his nostrils. He recognized the fragrance, Yves Saint Laurent. He'd once given her a bottle as a birthday gift.

He exhaled. She was pouring it on thick. *Keep it together, man.*

As she moved back in front of him, he felt her hand creep across his butt.

"Naomi, knock it off." He showed her the platinum wedding band Brooke had given him. "I told you, I'm married. *Legally. Happily.*"

"Where's the ring I gave you?" She pouted. "Did you pawn it?"

"Does it matter?"

He hadn't pawned it, in fact. After their divorce was finalized, he had flung the band into the Atlantic Ocean while on a beach trip to Florida with Khari. It had been liberating, like tossing off a set of shackles.

The spacious cab contained two padded leather chairs. A heavy curtain separated the cab from the remaining sections of the camper. Naomi slid it aside.

A dinette area lay ahead. There was seating on either side, like a booth in a restaurant, with a table in the center. On his right, an electric range, and cabinets. One of them he assumed contained a refrigerator. It was an amazing display of efficiency and utilized the limited space to a startling degree.

He saw a pot of coffee standing on a warmer. Naomi lifted a coffee mug out of one of the cabinets.

"A touch of cream?" she asked.

It was how he had always taken his coffee. "Sure, thanks."

"Go ahead and have a seat wherever you want. It'll be only a minute."

He took the seat nearest to the front door. Another curtain separated the dinette area from other sections of the motor home.

"Where's the rest of your family?" he asked.

"Sleeping." She gestured toward the area beyond the partition. She winked. "If I decide to give you a little nookie, don't make me holler or you'll wake them."

Blood flushed his cheeks. Naomi put a dollop of cream in the mug and handed it to him, bending over so that her cleavage was directly in front of his face.

"Thanks." He accepted the cup and looked away.

She picked up her own mug and settled onto the seat across from him, crossing her legs underneath her. He noticed a one-inch scar on the side of her neck, nearly hidden by a strand of braids. She noted his observation of her and frowned.

"Prison life," she said. "The bitches inside weren't used to seeing someone like me in there. Me coming in got all the ugly hens clucking and clawing."

Austin didn't know how to respond to the comment. Was he supposed to apologize? She went to prison because she had sliced him up like Zorro.

"But you know what, I made it." She sipped her coffee, flashed a hard smile. "I'm a survivor, Austie. I do whatever it takes. By the time I left, I had those starving bitches eating out the palm of my hand . . . and other places." She giggled.

He sipped the coffee. It was good coffee, flavored exactly how he liked it. He found it discomfiting that she remembered so many details about him.

"But I see you've done well for yourself," she said. "A new house in a new city. A new lady, bless her heart. A new bun in the oven."

He cleared his throat. "How did you find me?"

"How did you find me?" She mimicked his voice—something that had always annoyed him—and laughed. "You weren't hardly hiding, honey. Doing your CPA thing out of your own office now. We set our guy on you and he dug up *everything* I wanted to know."

"You hired a private investigator, like I thought." He stared into the cup. "I started over, Naomi. I've given Khari a new, stable life. He's doing well in school. He's happy. He adores Brooke."

"You're calling him by his middle name now?" Her eyes sharpened into beady points. "His name is Warren."

Austin lowered his voice. "You know I never wanted to name my son after your father."

Her father's full name was Edward Warren Xavier. Naomi had decided that their son would take her father's middle name, and she didn't budge.

Naomi sneered. "I ain't calling my son some quasi-African boom-chakalaka bullshit. You know my feelings on that. He needs to use his proper Christian name. You're damn lucky I let you give him that ghetto-ass middle name."

"When he's grown, he can call himself whatever he wants, but I'm calling him what I intended to name him from the start. That's how it is."

"That's how it is." She mimicked him again. She cocked her head and studied him. "You need one good fuck, Austie. I can see from looking at you that Miss Thang in there hasn't been plucking your cords right. You look like your dick is constipated."

"Everything's good." He put the coffee mug on the table. "We've got a baby coming, don't we?"

"Hmph." Smirking, Naomi rose from her seat and crossed the short distance between them. Austin started to get up, but she pushed him back onto the chair. She straddled him.

Despite himself, Austin felt his body respond as if she had toggled a switch.

"It feels like your friend Mr. Peabody is happy to see me." Naomi ground against him. "Oh yeah, Mr. Peabody's really happy right about now. Mama's home."

Austin closed his eyes. He could have let it happen. God knows, his body had no argument with lying there and enjoying the ride. Naomi had always been an unbridled animal in bed, was willing to do things no woman had ever done before to him, back then or since.

"I got a couple tattoos when I was in the joint," she whispered, her breath smelling of sweet cream. "Got my baby's name on my left boob, here." She touched herself, added: "And I got *your* name on my ass. Wanna see it?"

Brooke's face glowed in Austin's mind like a beacon on a hill. His wife. The woman he loved, effortlessly. The woman with whom he was building a life, a future worth having. If he gave in to Naomi, she would destroy it all, just as she had shattered his life before.

I can't do this. I won't *do this.*

"Get off, Naomi."

She laughed in his ear, her breath hot against his cheek. "What do you think I'm doing?"

"I mean it. Get off me."

He grabbed her arms. She stopped grinding against him and glared at him, her nose inches away from his.

"You're starting to piss me off now," she said.

"I'm going back to see my wife. You're going to pull this monster motor home out of my neighborhood. Or I'm calling the police."

"Bullshit."

"I don't think your parole officer would want to hear about the cops getting called on you already," he said.

"You fucking asshole." The evil twin had returned. She put her index finger on his chest, jabbed him with her tapered nail. "I should have cut out your goddamn heart. 'Cause that's what you're doing to me."

"Off," he said.

Tears dampened her eyes. She wiped the back of her hand against her eyes and got off him. A crimson scatter of hives had broken out at the base of her neck.

Austin stood.

"I want to see my boy," she said, fists on her waist.

"I'll take it under consideration."

"Dammit, I have rights! You can't keep him from me!"

Someone swept aside the curtain separating the dinette area from the rest of the camper. Naomi's father, mother, and older sister sat clustered in chairs, as if they had been watching the scene unfold through a pane of one-way glass.

Austin hadn't seen his former in-laws in seven years and couldn't say that he missed them. They were an oddly clannish bunch, intensely loyal to one another and distrustful of everyone outside their circle. He had gotten along well enough with them when he and Naomi were married, but he'd never truly felt like he was a part of their family.

"Austin," Edward said, with a nod of his large, mostly bald head. "Been a while."

"Edward," Austin said.

"That's *Mr. Xavier* to you now, son," Edward said. "I never fought you on my grandson, and you know I could've wrangled you up in the courts, made it rough on you. I respected you as the boy's daddy, but what you're doing now ain't right. You know my girl deserves to see her baby."

"I'm not having this conversation with all of you," Austin said. "You all need to go back to picking your pecans and I'll settle this with Naomi in court."

Redness flushed Edward's face, an emotion that seemed transmitted to every member of his family via a telepathic link. All of them glowered at him.

"And move this damn RV out of my neighborhood," Austin said. "I meant what I said, and I know all of you heard me. I will call the police and report you for blocking my driveway."

Naomi squeezed her hands into fists, her toned muscles standing out like cables on her arms. Austin's heart knocked so hard he thought he might pass out, but he didn't offer an apology or a compromise. He had to stand his ground with her, with all of them.

He backed out of the dinette, and into the cab. He opened the door and stepped out of the motor home.

If Naomi's and her family's eyes could have shot bullets, they would have sprayed him with a thousand rounds as he walked back to his house to his wife, to his life. But he didn't slow, and he didn't turn back.

14

"Well, shit," Daddy said. He looked as if he wanted to spit on the polished vinyl floor. "That boy done went and got himself some balls, ain't he?"

Naomi opened her mouth—and screamed. She had to let it out. A cry of rage had been boiling in her, and she couldn't hold it back any longer. Her scream went on for at least five seconds, until her throat got choked up and her lungs were empty as deflated balloons.

Her family watched. They knew how she was. Some things had to run their course.

Charlotte gave her a fistful of tissue. Naomi muttered a thank you, dried her eyes and dabbed at her nose. She was so pissed that snot dribbled from her nostrils.

How could Austin have turned her down? The Austin she remembered had been completely incapable of rejecting her. She used to get him whenever she wanted him, like she did with any man, as easily as taking cookies out of a jar. It bewildered her that he'd possessed the willpower to push her away, especially with her looking hotter than ever.

"He's acting," Naomi finally said. "He thinks he's a big bad man in there now with his new woman greasing his pipe. She's got his head all wrapped up in the clouds and he's lost."

"You think he's gonna call the police, Peach?" Mama twirled a strand of her hair in her fingers, a nervous tic of hers. "That wife of his might. We don't know her."

"She's *not* his wife," Naomi said. "I told y'all, I'm not accepting that. It's illegitimate."

"What're we gonna do now then?" Charlotte asked.

Naomi peered through the camper's side window at Austin's little cottage. She could imagine him in there, bragging to his skank about how he put her and her family in their place. *I told them to pull out or I'm calling the police, honey. Yeah, I handled them, baby.*

Stone pavers lined the walkway that led to his house. Back in the day, Naomi would have grabbed one of those stones and fast-balled it through the window. She'd done that very thing with one of her exes, pre-Austin, a slick talker who she discovered was married. The brick she'd hurled through his window had shattered the glass and clipped old boy in the head, opening a gash that required fifteen stitches. The philandering lowlife had pressed charges and she had been locked up in the county jail for three months. That felony on her record was why the judge presiding over her case with Austin threw the book at her.

But her extended bid in real prison had taught her patience. You couldn't help but learn patience when you were locked up for seven years. You learned how to wait, and you learned how to scheme. She had known inmates who had waited for *years* to get the drop on somebody—another inmate, or maybe a troublesome CO. Naomi had pulled off such an act of vengeance herself: the bitch who had cut her on the neck soon after she got in would never put her hands on anyone else again.

"Don't y'all worry," Naomi said. "I've got plenty of cards left in the deck. It's gonna be fine."

"We oughta roll in there and get our boy," Daddy said. He had taken his rifle out of its case and started cleaning it. Ever since Naomi had put the gun back into his hands, he seemed to want to keep it close by, like that *Peanuts* character Linus and his blanket. "Sometimes when you want something bad, you gotta take it, Peach. Ask forgiveness but don't ever ask permission."

"We gotta play it smart," Naomi said. "I'm not going back to prison, not ever. Y'all gotta trust me on this. All right?"

15

It took tremendous effort for Austin to walk back into the house without stumbling. He was so drunk on adrenaline, on elation, on anxiety, that he was dizzy.

Once inside, he shut the door and leaned against it. He was shaking. Cold sweat coated his face and shirt.

The nerve of Naomi. The nerve of all of them, her entire family. Who did they think they were?

He wasn't going to allow them to have their way. Not this time. He would not be bullied into submission. He had raised Khari for seven years and the boy was doing great.

None of them needed this.

He heard Brooke come downstairs, a slow, careful walk down the staircase.

Austin straightened. "Hey."

"Is everything okay?" Brooke asked. "I was worried I might have to call a search and rescue team to pull you out of there."

"Is Khari awake yet?" Austin checked the time on his phone; it was twenty past seven. It felt as if he'd been in the camper for hours. "He should be up getting ready for school."

"I heard him bumping around up there before I came downstairs. He's going to want to know what's going on, too."

"Okay." Austin abruptly felt exhausted. Confronting Naomi had always taken a lot out of him. He had forgotten how draining it could be to deal with her.

Brooke came closer, her gaze weighted with concern. "Are you going to tell me what's going on? I saw Naomi in the RV."

Austin summarized the encounter, omitting Naomi's attempted seduction. Telling someone else about it, someone well-grounded like Brooke, immediately made him feel better. Brooke was as flabbergasted as any rational person would be when someone shared that their former in-laws had parked an RV in front of their house to try to demand compliance.

"This is crazy," Brooke said, after Austin had finished.

"I don't want you to worry." He rested his hands on her shoulders. "We don't need you getting stressed out over this situation. I'll handle it."

"I'm not going to shatter like an egg," Brooke said, her eyes like steel.

"We've got to think about the baby. You don't need to get sucked into this."

"I'm sucked into it because we're married. What do you need me to do, Austin?"

Austin sighed, bowed his head. He traced his hand across the swell of her stomach. Their future.

"I'm going to hire a lawyer," he said. "I was dragging my feet on that earlier, but it's obvious now. I can't delay."

"A family law attorney?" Brooke asked. "I know someone. A friend of the family—she's great."

Austin nodded. "Then we need to call her today and tell her what's going on."

"What do we do right now?" Brooke gestured toward the front of the house. "They're blocking our driveway. Are they leaving?"

"I told them I'd call the police if they don't pull out of here."

"Did you mean that?" Brooke's gaze searched him.

Suddenly, he heard Khari coming downstairs, with the clamor of a boulder rumbling down a mountain.

"Hey, what's going on?" Khari asked. "Who's parked in front of the house in that big bus?"

"It's called a motor home," Austin said.

"Whatever." Khari shrugged. "Is that my mom? I thought I heard you guys say something about my mom."

Khari came toward them. He was already dressed for school and should have been sitting down to grab breakfast about then, and by eight, he needed to be on the corner to catch the school bus. Would he even want to go to school now? Austin remembered that his son had a test today. Was he going to be able to concentrate?

"I want to see my mom!" Khari said. "Is she really out there?"

Before Austin could answer, the doorbell rang.

16

Khari reached for the door. Austin nudged aside his son's hand.

"I'll open it," Austin said.

Khari squeezed his outstretched hand into a fist, a challenge in his eyes.

If he were the same size as me, I think he'd try to knock me flat right about now, Austin thought.

The visitor knocked, five frantic raps against the wood. The doorbell rang again.

She won't be denied. But he couldn't avoid dealing with her, not with Khari glaring at him.

He unlocked the door and pulled it open.

Naomi stood on the threshold. A large, gift-wrapped box with a bow on top lay at her feet.

She grinned at Austin and indicated the package. "I wanted to give this to my baby."

"Mom?" Khari rushed past Austin. Austin was about to reach out, hold him back, but he felt Brooke's hand on his arm.

Let him, she lip-synced. Austin dropped his hand.

"Oh my Lord," Naomi said. She rested her hands on Khari's shoulders. Tears streamed down her cheeks. "You're taller than I am! Oh my Lord."

Khari was weeping, too. Naomi pulled him into a bear hug embrace. They rocked in each other's arms.

"I thought about you every day, every hour," Naomi said. "Every *minute*."

Austin's chest felt tight. Had he done the right thing by keeping Khari away from his mother during her incarceration? No doubt, it had been the best move for *him*—he didn't want to see Naomi ever again—but had keeping the boy away from his mother been a mistake?

Watching them hug, he wasn't so sure anymore. He felt like mud on the bottom of someone's heel. Would Khari ever forgive him for this?

"Love you so much," Naomi said, and finally slid her arms from around Khari. Khari clasped her hand. He looked like a five-year-old again, not a boy of twelve who was nearly as tall as his father.

"All right," Austin said. "Khari's got school today. We'll resume this again, later." He touched Khari's shoulder. "Your mother and I will work out an arrangement, Son."

"We'll work it out, baby." Naomi sniffled. "Go on to school now, you hear? Remember your mama loves you, always."

Tears trickling down his face, Khari picked up the gift-wrapped box and came back inside the house. He didn't look at Austin. He brushed past his father as if they were strangers and raced to the staircase.

"I can't believe how he's grown," Naomi said, almost to herself.

"I need y'all to move that camper now," Austin said.

"Morning, lady." Naomi peered around Austin, at Brooke. She winked. "I'm going now, y'all. We're gonna work this out, Austie."

"Legally," Austin said.

"You can't keep a boy from his mama forever." She blew a kiss at Austin and spun around.

Austin shut the door and sighed.

"It's not even eight o'clock and I'm exhausted," he said.

"I feel you." Brooke gave him a weak smile. "You're doing the right thing, babe. But you need to call that lawyer friend of my family's *today*. I'll reach out to my mom and then text her info to you."

Austin heard Khari upstairs. What had Naomi given him? He still didn't trust her.

He heard the loud grumble of an engine. He stepped to one of the front windows.

"They're leaving." He felt a palpable sense of relief. He hadn't really wanted to call the police.

"Involving cops would have been messy," Brooke said. "I'm glad they saw reason."

Austin went upstairs. Khari's bedroom door was closed. Austin knocked and tried the knob.

It was locked. This was becoming a new trend with his son, and he didn't like it at all.

"Khari, you've gotta get ready for school," Austin said. "Open up for a minute."

He knocked again.

Khari didn't answer.

17

Khari couldn't recall the last time he had felt such excitement. He had gotten to see his mother, finally. After seven years. It felt amazing.

She looked like him. Or rather, *he* looked like *her*. It was sort of like looking in a mirror.

But Dad had to ruin everything. It was as if he were determined to make Khari miserable and to poison Khari's ideas about his own mother.

Yeah, he knew his mom had been in prison because she got into a fight with Dad. She had attacked him with something. That whole situation confused Khari, though. Did his mother have a reason for fighting Dad? Was she protecting herself?

Dad had never really talked about it and his silence let Khari's imagination cook up all kinds of scenarios.

He put the big box Mom had given him on his bed and tore it open as if it were Christmas morning. He ripped open the top flaps.

Wow, she had gotten him a pair of Jordans? They were the right size, too.

There was a Nintendo Switch in there, too, the latest model. It was amazing that she had spent all this money.

But the item he discovered at the bottom of the box blew his mind.

It was an iPhone. The absolute newest edition, still in the manufacturer's box.

An envelope was attached to the top of the box. His name—his birth name, Warren—was written on the letter, along with the directive: "*Read this now.*"

His hands trembling, Khari tore open the envelope and slid out the single sheet of paper.

"This is your phone, baby. Don't tell your father I gave it to you. It will be our little secret. The phone's activated and my number is already in it. Call me whenever you want, baby."

Khari's heart felt as if it were going to explode. In a single day, his mother had given him the one thing that he wanted more than anything else in the world, while all Dad had done was deny it to him.

His father knocked on the door and said he had to get ready for school. Khari hid the phone and the letter, too. He smiled to himself.

Our little secret, Mom.

18

Austin was deliberating whether he would again use the master key to unlock his son's bedroom door when Khari finally opened it. He wore a sullen expression, as if Austin were the last person in the world he wanted to see.

Seeing me used to make him grin, Austin remembered. Granted, that was a long time ago. But Austin missed those days of parental bliss. Now it seemed he and his boy were constantly at odds over some thing or another. This latest row over Naomi promised to be the war to end all wars.

"Are you ready for school?" Austin asked.

"Do I have to go to school?" Khari asked.

"You don't have any reason to stay home."

"Don't you and Mom need to work out stuff about me or something?" Khari's gaze was hopeful. "The custody thing?"

"That's between me and your mother." Austin looked over his son's shoulder and into the room. "What did Naomi give you?"

Khari shrugged. Austin brushed past him and went inside the bedroom. He saw the open gift box lying on the bed amid torn ribbons of wrapping paper.

"It's only clothes and stuff," Khari said. "I'm going to the bus stop. Are we done?"

Austin looked at him. His son stared back.

Why do I feel like such an asshole? Austin wondered. *What did I do wrong?*

"How about I drive you to school?" Austin said.

"Nah, I can take the bus."

"I insist. I'll be downstairs shortly."

"What are you looking for in here?" Khari asked.

"Should I be looking for something?"

Khari muttered under his breath.

"What was that?" Austin asked.

"Nothing."

Right. "Go on downstairs, Son."

Khari shuffled down the hallway and pounded down the stairs. Austin turned back to the open box.

He found an envelope lying inside with his son's official first name scrawled on the front in Naomi's handwriting, along with the directive: "*Read this now.*"

Austin picked up the envelope. It was open, and empty.

What was Naomi up to? He felt as if he were losing control of the situation. For seven years, he had closely managed both of their lives, and for the first time ever, their smoothly running existences had been disrupted, and he wasn't sure what he could do to right the ship. Call the lawyer, work out a new custody arrangement? That was a start. Nevertheless, things weren't going to be the same anymore.

I should have moved us out of the country, he thought wistfully. *Somewhere with a non-extradition treaty or something.*

It was a silly idea, of course, and running away from Naomi and her family was no longer a viable option. He needed to muddle his way through this situation somehow.

Downstairs, he kissed Brooke goodbye and loaded up in his SUV with Khari. Khari normally sat in the front when it was only the two of them traveling, but Khari slid onto the back seat.

"You can sit up front with me," Austin said.

"I'm good," Khari said.

"Sitting in the back seat like a five-year-old, huh? Should I get you a booster seat?" Austin chuckled.

"Whatever, Dad."

Austin pulled out of their driveway. He steered out of their neighborhood. The school was only about an eight-minute drive from their house, and he had about thirty minutes before he needed to drop off Khari.

"Do you want me to swing by Chick-fil-A and get you some breakfast on the way?" Austin asked.

"That's not on the way to school," Khari said.

"We'll make a detour then. How about a chicken biscuit? You love those."

"I'm not hungry."

Austin squeezed the steering wheel. He wasn't getting anywhere with this kid. A wall had risen between them, and it felt insurmountably high.

"What do you want me to do, Son?" Austin asked. "I don't like this new rift between us."

"You don't listen to me anyway."

"I'm listening now. I want your thoughts. Please."

"I already said what I wanted, Dad. Like I said, you never listen."

"Tell me again, Khari."

Austin navigated through traffic, glanced in the rearview mirror. Khari was looking out the window, but his jaws were clenched as if he wanted to spit.

"I want to spend time with Mom. I want to get to know her."

"We'll be working on that, like I said. I promise."

Khari glanced toward the front of the SUV. Briefly, their gazes met in the rearview mirror.

Khari hesitated. "Maybe I want to move in with her, for a little while."

Austin felt as if he had swallowed a fish bone.

"*Move in* with her?" Austin asked.

"She's my mom, right? I've been with you all these years. Maybe I need to be with her, too, and get to know her for myself."

"That's not going to happen." Austin looked at him in the mirror. "It's a terrible idea."

Khari glanced away. "Don't I get to say what I want?"

"You're only twelve. You don't know what's best for you, not in a situation like this."

"I read online that in a custody case or whatever, a kid my age gets to say what he wants."

This keeps getting better, doesn't it? He wasn't ready to entertain these ideas. Khari moving in with Naomi? In Albany? Sharing custody over weekends or perhaps the summer was one thing, and neither of those appealed much to Austin, either, truth be told—but living with her full-time?

"I can move in with Mom," Khari said, "and then you and Miss Brooke can raise your new baby. You guys are gonna be busy doing that anyway. You won't have time for me anymore."

It sounded as though his son had it all worked out, in his own mind. He and Austin were so far apart in their thinking that Austin didn't know how to respond. He drove for a couple of minutes in silence.

"Let me make this clear: I'll always make time for you," Austin said. It was all he could think of, but he meant it. "Nothing changes between you and me, kid. *Nothing*."

"It's already changed, Dad."

19

Later that morning, Austin arrived at his office. He leased a small commercial space in Westside Village, a live-work-play community in Smyrna. His spot was located between a frozen yogurt shop and a spa.

It was a relief to unlock the door and flip on the lights. His office felt like the one place in the world where he was in control, where things proceeded according to sensible, well-defined rules.

He brewed a cup of coffee and settled behind his desk. He worked alone there, with no staff. Brooke had recently helped him redecorate so the space didn't look like an institution, by adding new furniture in soft tones, several live plants, paintings, and a splash of accent colors here and there. Admittedly, he could have worked from home, saved on rent, and met with clients, when necessary, at a neutral location, but he liked having his own spot with his name above the door: *Austin Dash, C.P.A.* Folks seemed to take him more seriously and there were fewer distractions versus working from home.

Tax season—by far the most hectic time of year—had ended last week, and his business had slid into that temporary post-filing lull. He didn't have any appointments scheduled today. He had received a couple of inquiries from prospective business clients overnight via his website, and he needed to follow up on those leads, but otherwise, his day was blessedly free.

Brooke had texted him the contact information for the family law attorney, Sharon Randall. Austin looked her up online. She was a sweet-faced Black woman who looked to be in her mid-fifties. She reminded Austin of his late aunt.

He slipped on his Bluetooth headset and called the number. A woman answered on the second ring in an upbeat tone.

"Good morning, this is the Randall Firm. How may I assist you?"

"I was referred by Brooke Stephens-Dash. She's a friend of Ms. Randall. May I speak to her?"

"Of course, Brooke!" Warmth flooded the woman's voice. "How's Brooke doing? Has she had the little one yet?"

"I'm her husband, Austin, and no. She's due next month. Are you Ms. Randall?"

"Call me Sharon, honey." Austin recognized a South Georgia accent. "Brooke's parents always have such wonderful things to say about you, Mr. Dash. How can I help you this morning?"

Austin hadn't expected the attorney to answer the phone herself. He had expected he would have to leave a message with an assistant. But he was glad to reach her directly and get things moving.

"It's concerning the custody for my son." He summarized, as succinctly as possible, what was going on, but he spared no details when it came to Naomi's incarceration. He hoped that Naomi's felony conviction would give him the edge in legal matters.

As he talked, his gaze circled to a photo on his desk: a framed shot of Khari from his school's Picture Day last year. Khari wore a snazzy dress shirt paired with a tie that Brooke had picked out for him. Depending on how you looked at it, Khari resembled either a young man in his late teens—or a young child eager to grow up too fast. Austin felt heartburn coming on as he looked at it.

"I've got news for you, Mr. Dash," Sharon said when he finished. "I know you may not want to hear this, but your ex-wife has parental rights."

"Of course." Austin groaned. "I had a feeling that you were going to say that."

"It's also relevant that her conviction, as problematic as it may be, was a crime against *you*, not your son."

"She's emotionally unstable," Austin said. "I'm convinced she's a sociopath, that she's got antisocial personality disorder. She's got all the traits—I've looked them up." He ticked them off on each finger, from memory: "A total disregard for right and wrong. Superficially charming, to manipulate others for her own gain. Totally impulsive behavior. Extremely arrogant. Violent tendencies."

"Has she been diagnosed as sociopathic by a mental health professional?" Sharon asked. "To your knowledge?"

"She'd never agree to talk to a therapist. That's part of the problem. She thinks everyone else has the issue and that she's fine, that you need to get with her program or get the hell out of her way."

Sharon clucked her tongue. "I understand your concerns. But in the eyes of the court, she's still his mother."

"And she has rights," Austin said, shaking his head.

"Unless she proves herself unfit for parenting by specific behaviors that jeopardize your son's safety, she'll have custodial rights. You'll need to agree on a joint custody arrangement."

"Perfect." He couldn't keep the sarcasm out of his voice.

"How does your son feel about this? He's twelve, yes? The court will want his input."

"Khari says he wants to move in with her. I don't think he means it, though. He's confused."

"The court will take his opinion into consideration. But he can't solely decide that he's moving in with her. You're still his father."

"So being a father still counts for something, then."

"If you hire me, I'll do the best I can to craft an agreement that satisfies everyone," Sharon said. "But there's going to be some compromise, on both sides. I expect your ex-wife will hire a lawyer if she has the means."

"Her family is wealthy," he said. "They own a major pecan orchard down in Albany, Gold Crest Farms."

Sharon paused. "I assume they're supporting her?"

"One hundred percent."

"I've worked in family law for thirty-three years." Sharon hesitated. "But I won't lie to you, Mr. Dash. If she's got strong legal representation, this can get tricky. They're going to try to influence the court to take a close look at you as well."

"At me? I've raised Khari since he was five, with no support from anyone!"

"In custody battles, both parents get scrutinized. If you've been the model father, and it sounds as if you have, you've nothing to worry about. But her lawyer will try to muddy the waters. It can turn into a character assassination, to be frank."

"Then I've got that to look forward to then," he said. "Getting raked over the coals by a shady attorney."

"I'll do my best to ensure that doesn't happen. That we stick to relevant facts." She cleared her throat. "Mr. Dash, the court is primarily concerned with what's best for your son. We need to make the case that minimizing drama is in his best interests."

"It sounds good, and I'm going to hire you," Austin said. "But the honest truth? All Naomi knows is drama."

20

Brooke decided to take her lunch break at her usual spot: a cozy café a couple of doors down from the physical therapy center where she worked. A few minutes past one o'clock, she told the center's admin assistant that she'd be back in half an hour, and then she pushed through the glass door and went outdoors into the overcast April afternoon.

Her work location was based in a large strip mall off busy Cobb Parkway. Hundreds of vehicles occupied the vast parking lot.

But she immediately spotted, on the far side of the lot, the Xavier family's camper. With its immense size and the distinctive pecan orchard mural on its side, the RV was as impossible to miss as a circus tent in a corn field.

She felt a lurch in her belly, and it wasn't her baby boy shifting about.

Had they followed her from home? Or did they already know where she worked?

Maybe it's a coincidence, she thought. She worked about fifteen minutes away from the house she shared with Austin. Had they come there looking for somewhere to park their gargantuan motor home for a while? It wasn't as though the camper could be parked on a residential street without risking a traffic citation.

Yes, it had to be a coincidence, she hoped.

Nevertheless, she was going to share this with Austin. He'd already texted her and said he had talked to Sharon Randall, that she was taking on his case. They needed to keep Sharon in the loop on anything that happened that could impact what promised to be a nasty custody battle.

Inside the busy café, the familiar aromas of baking bread and freshly brewed coffee tickled Brooke's appetite. She placed her normal order—a chicken salad sandwich on whole wheat bread and a cup of vegetable soup—and snagged her usual spot at a table in the corner. She had brought a paperback with her, *What to Expect the First Year*, and was starting the chapter on sleep training when she happened to look up and see Naomi stroll into the café.

Brooke's heart skipped. Coincidence? Yeah, right. In the back of her mind, she had been on the alert for Naomi's appearance, had positioned her chair to allow a clear view of the door.

She had to give credit to Naomi: she looked fantastic, not at all like a woman who had spent seven years in lockup. She had changed clothes from that morning, but still wore an outfit that displayed plenty of skin. A two-piece stretch ensemble in eye-catching orange, the zipper top cut to show off her sculpted abdomen, the pants hugging her hips and slender legs.

Every man in the café looked up at Naomi's entrance, and their gazes lingered.

Naomi's lips curved in a smile as she basked in the attention. She flipped her braids over her shoulder, and her gaze found Brooke. Her smile broadened.

What does she want anyway? Brooke shifted in her chair. *Might as well get this over with.*

Naomi sashayed to Brooke's table. Brooke put down her book and her fork.

"Hey there, girlfriend." Naomi took the chair across from Brooke. "It's time we had ourselves a chat."

"How long have you been watching me?" Brooke asked.

"I like to do recon on my competition."

Competition? Is this woman completely insane?

Austin had given him a rundown of Naomi's tendencies. He believed she was a sociopath. Brooke was a physical therapist, not a psychiatrist, but Naomi's track record supported Austin's story.

She always carries a butterfly knife, he had said. *It's a thing in her family. Her mother, and her sister—all of them carry knives. Like a gang of street thieves.*

Naomi had put her purse on the table. She unzipped it and slipped her hand inside. But she didn't retrieve a knife—she pulled out a compact and checked her face.

"You and I, we almost look like we could be sisters." Naomi snapped the compact shut and slid it back into her purse. She giggled. "Have you noticed, girl? Your complexion is a tad bit darker than mine, but Austie *definitely* has a type. I bet when he saw you, he thought he was looking at my long-lost twin."

"What do you want, Naomi?" Brooke asked.

"How does it feel to be a home-wrecker?" Naomi stared at her, hazel eyes seething. "Hmm? You're living with my husband, my son. My whole world. Playing house. But you're only a baby mama."

"Whatever is going on between you and Austin has nothing to do with me," Brooke said. "And this conversation is over."

Brooke put her food items on her tray and started to get up. Naomi shook her head.

"Sit your fat ass down, girl." She smiled sweetly, but her voice was cold as a January ice storm. "Or do I need to start talking about Robert and Anita?"

Brooke froze. "My parents have absolutely nothing to do with this, either. Nothing. Don't you dare—"

"Sit." Naomi pointed to the chair. "Down."

Her heart knocking, Brooke sat.

"You're going to file for an annulment." Naomi slid a business card out of her purse and pushed it across the table to Brooke. "This is our family's attorney. You'll call him today and tell him you had a sham marriage to Austie and want to dissolve it. He'll take care of everything."

"You're crazy." Brooke trembled.

"You don't want to tangle with me, sweetie," Naomi said. "Stress is a terrible thing for a pregnant lady."

"If I see you again, and if you *dare* to go near my parents, I'm calling the police."

"Call him today." Naomi tapped the business card with a perfectly lacquered fingernail and rose from the chair. With a dramatic flick of her wrist, she tossed her braids over her shoulder. "Enjoy your lunch, baby mama. We'll be in touch."

Naomi strutted out of the restaurant. Brooke let out a deep breath and blotted perspiration from her brow with a napkin.

She needed to talk to Austin, but more urgently, she had to check on her parents. She sent her mother a text message.

It's me. Is everything ok with you and Dad?

Thankfully, her mother responded within a minute. *Hey, sweetheart. We're fine, working outside in the garden. Why?*

Brooke closed her eyes. Had that encounter with Naomi actually happened? It felt like an episode from a bad LSD trip.

She opened her eyes. The business card lay in the center of the table, an uncomfortable reminder that Naomi really had been there, had made those ridiculous demands.

Brooke picked up the card, but she didn't read it.

She ripped it in half, then into quarters, and tossed it into the trash.

21

"Now that we can speak freely, I've got to get this off my chest," Brooke said to Austin. "I've been thinking about this all day. I want to file an order of protection against your ex-wife."

They were home, sitting at the dinette table, and had finished dinner: Thai takeout, since neither of them had been in the mood to cook. After barely speaking to them and picking at his fried rice, Khari had retreated to his bedroom. Austin was confident his son was out of earshot, but he winced at Brooke's comment.

He was concerned about Naomi, too, obviously. But he wasn't surprised that his ex-wife had appeared at Brooke's job and tried to intimidate her at the café. It was a classic Naomi tactic: outright bullying to get her way.

Austin rose from the table and started to clear away dishes and take-out containers.

"I'm handling this," he said. "I've already hired your lawyer, like I said earlier. Leave all of this up to me. You don't need to get involved."

"Don't you get it?" Brooke glared at him. "I'm *already involved* because I'm your wife."

"You know what I mean."

"She threatened to hurt my parents," she said. "My *parents*."

"She's selling wolf tickets," Austin said. "She only wanted to rattle you. That's what she does. It's how she manipulates people to make them do what she wants."

"Why the hell are you minimizing this?" Brooke asked. With effort, Brooke rose from her chair. Austin reached for her plate, but she snatched it out of his hands. "I'll do it myself."

Austin let his hand drop to his side. "You have every right to be upset. I get it. It pisses me off, too. But how is Khari going to react if we get an order of protection against his mother?"

Brooke met his gaze. "She needs to be held accountable. I'm not going to sit back and enable this crap."

"Do you think I've been enabling her?" He stared at Brooke.

"Did I say *you've* been enabling her? Interesting that you've made this all about you."

"That's what you were suggesting. That somehow this is my fault."

Brooke was shaking her head. "Clearly, we're not on the same page. At all. But I promise you that if your ex-wife crosses my path again, or if I hear a peep from my parents about some strange lady following them, I'm getting an order of protection."

"Brooke, please."

"There's nothing left to discuss." She glowered at him, and then she pointed. "You need to get clear on your priorities."

"You said something earlier about picking sides. Sounds like you want me to pick a side, now."

In silence, Brooke loaded the dishwasher, and she wouldn't look at him. He knew from experience that when she got into these moods—which was extremely rare—that further debate was pointless. She wasn't going to engage him on the subject. She said her piece and that was that.

It made him want to gnash his teeth. He was already at war with Naomi, on the skids with his own son. Did he have to fight a battle with Brooke, too? Why did it feel as if everyone was aligned against him?

He pulled the trash bag out of the bin—it was full—and turned to Brooke.

"After I dump the trash I'm going on a run," he said. "I've got my phone. Text me if you need something."

Brooke didn't respond, but he knew she heard him. He headed outside with the trash bag dangling from his hand.

It was about a quarter past eight o'clock; the sun had just set. The evening was cool, with a soft breeze.

Austin deposited the trash in the large bin on the side of the garage and turned to the sidewalk. He started jogging.

Ever since he was a child, running had always had a soothing effect on him. It helped him clear his thoughts. Some people preferred meditation, but for Austin, nothing centered him like a nice, brisk run outdoors.

He raced past homes, flashed by the stand of mailboxes. At an intersection, he made a right, heading toward the community's recreation area.

From a hundred yards away, he saw the motor home. It was parked near the community swimming pool, angled so that it blocked off half of the parking lot. Muted light glowed at the tinted windows.

He felt a swelling sensation in his throat, as if he had choked on a golf ball.

The Xaviers were back.

22

Keeping an eye on the RV, Austin slipped out his phone and sent a text message to Brooke. A troubling thought had struck him. It superseded their still-fresh argument.

Hi, is Khari in his room? Can you pls check?

Ten seconds passed, and then he saw the three dots signaling that she was replying.

Going to look now.

Reason number eight hundred and ninety-seven why he loved that woman. She knew, innately, when to set aside their differences and focus on a more critical goal.

He squeezed his phone so tightly that his knuckles crackled like breadsticks. He knew what Brooke was going to say before her next words appeared on the screen.

He's gone. Bedroom window is open. Where do you think he's gone?

I know where he is. Will be back soon.

Be careful, she responded, as if via some kind of telepathic spousal link she realized what lay ahead.

Hands shaking, Austin shoved the phone into his pocket. He squared his shoulders and took his time approaching the motor home, his feet feeling as heavy as cement blocks.

When he reached the front door, he didn't knock. He grabbed the latch and pulled the lever.

It opened.

He ascended the steps into the darkened cab. The curtain had been drawn between the cockpit and the other sections of the camper.

Light glowed at the bottom of the curtain. He heard voices. His son, talking excitedly. Naomi laughing. The rest of her family chattering and chuckling.

They sounded like ordinary people enjoying a family gathering. Except nothing about this was ordinary. These people had invaded his life and sucked his son into their whirlpool of dysfunction. They had no right to be here, stealing his son.

No right.

Austin gripped the outer edge of the curtain and snatched it aside so hard it nearly popped off the tracks.

As one, they turned and looked at him. They were clustered on the various chairs. Eating pizza and ice cream, as if they were at a child's birthday party.

Khari's eyes flew open, and his mouth clapped shut with an audible snap. Naomi and the others grinned at Austin.

"We've got plenty of pizza left, Austie," Naomi said. She lifted a greasy slice. "Pepperoni, your favorite."

"Ice cream, too," Edward said. He had a bowl heaped with vanilla ice cream drenched in chocolate syrup and pecans. "Have a sit and let's talk, like civilized folk."

Austin's heart pounded.

"Khari," he said, and his voice cracked on his son's name.

"His name is Warren," Naomi said.

"Khari!" Austin shouted.

His son flinched. He shot to his feet, plate flipping off his lap and onto the floor.

Austin pulled in a breath. He had to keep control of himself, though he felt on the verge of an eruption.

"Go home," he said, in a softer tone. "Now. Please."

Khari looked from Austin to Naomi.

"You ain't gotta listen to him, sugar." Naomi stood, lifted her chin. "I'm your mama. I say, you stay. You're getting reunited with your family."

Tears glittered in Khari's eyes as his attention swiveled from Naomi to Austin, back and forth.

"Go home!" Austin shouted.

Khari stepped toward Austin. Naomi grabbed Khari's arm. Austin strode forward and took Khari's other arm.

Caught between them, Khari shook. His face was puckered, and Austin knew his son was struggling not to cry.

Austin glared at Naomi. She smiled at him, but the evil twin shine was in her eyes.

She's enjoying this, Austin knew. *She's loving every second of it.*

"How 'bout we cut the boy in half and y'all can share him?" Edward snickered.

"Wish I had made some popcorn," Karen said. "Y'all so entertaining."

"All of y'all so silly," Charlotte said.

"Shut up!" Austin yelled. "Son, come home with me. Please. We need to do this the right way, like I promised we would."

Tears spilled down Khari's cheeks. A sob escaped him.

"All right." Naomi released Khari's arm. "Go on, sugar. But you remember what we talked about, you hear?"

"Okay, Mama." His Adam's apple bobbed as he swallowed.

"Come on." Austin yanked his son toward him, probably a bit too forcefully. Khari stumbled and dropped to his knees. Austin bent to help him up.

"Don't touch me!" Khari screamed. He pushed away from Austin and staggered out of the motor home.

Austin watched him go, tightness lodged in his throat. He felt like either crying or screaming. Maybe both.

"You're tearing his heart in half," Naomi said. "Look at him. The boy's a mess."

Austin raised his finger. It quivered. "You stay away from us. *All* of us."

"He's my son, too," she said.

"I don't want to see you again until we're in family court. I'll get a restraining order against you, Naomi. I mean it—"

The slap came in a blur. His head snapped sideways so quickly it was a miracle he didn't get whiplash. It was like being struck by a grown man. Naomi always had hit *hard*.

"Don't you dare threaten me," she said. "I will whoop your ass from one end of this damn camper to the other."

Austin clenched his hands into fists. It would be easy to hit her back. To literally punch her lights out. But she always counted on him never hitting back. That was her power over him. She knew he believed, deep in his core, that a man hitting a woman was wrong, that because of the violence he had witnessed as a child he would never raise his hand against her.

And she knew he hadn't changed.

He relaxed his hands. The side of his face burned as if seared with a clothes iron, and he tasted warm blood.

"All right now, y'all," Edward said. He chuckled like a grandfather amused at watching children wrestle in the yard. "Play nice, kids."

"Don't you ever lay hands on me again," Austin said.

"Oh, I'm so scared." Her grin was savage as a barracuda's smile. "What are you gonna do, huh? Hit me back? A big, strong Black man like you beating down a pretty light-skinned sister like me? How's that gonna work out for you when I call the cops, huh? You know what would go down. They'd shoot your ass on sight, brotherman."

It was the same threat she always tossed back at him. Hit her back and she'd call the police. Was there any doubt that her family would back up her story?

"I meant what I said," Austin said. "Get out of here. I'm calling the police in five minutes to report a parking violation."

"I'm calling the police in five minutes . . ." Naomi mimicked him in a childish, high-pitched voice. "You sound stupid, Austie. Really."

Austin backed away, to the front of the cab. He turned to reach for the curtain.

"Hey, Austie," Naomi said.

He glanced at her, and wished he hadn't. Naomi snatched up her top and flashed him. She wasn't wearing a bra or any other clothing underneath.

Could this woman be any crazier? he thought. But that quick look at her made his mouth go dry.

"Sweet dreams." Naomi winked.

23

Outside, Austin watched the RV from a distance. After about ten minutes, the engine rumbled awake. The camper pulled out of the neighborhood.

If he had a brick in his hands, he might have hurled it at the motor home's rear window as it pulled off, and if he were lucky, it would have shattered the window and clipped Naomi upside the head.

Actually, he would not have done such a thing, but thinking about it was satisfying. His face felt swollen from Naomi's vicious slap. He expected he'd show a nasty bruise by morning.

As always after these violent encounters with Naomi, Austin wondered why he let it happen. He didn't consider himself to be a weak man, a punk, yet he tolerated her abuse, justified it by rationalizing that he was physically superior to her and could endure her slaps and punches. Allowing her to slap him sure as hell didn't feel good, but he outweighed her by seventy pounds and could subdue her if he really wanted to. It didn't seem worth the trouble to fight back. Dealing with her was like handling a child prone to temper tantrums, he reasoned. Better to let it run its course.

But there was something wrong with that viewpoint, he realized. And look how she had cut him up seven years ago. She would have killed him if he hadn't gotten away.

Still, he was more worried about Khari. How had his son known to hook up with Naomi and her clan? Had she given him instructions that morning in that envelope to meet her this evening?

His son had a lot of explaining to do. But it was a delicate situation. Clearly his boy wanted to spend time with Naomi and her family, a natural impulse that Austin understood. His late aunt had done an amazing job raising him, but she couldn't replace the parents he had lost. It was a void in Austin's life that would never be filled.

His son believed Austin was the enemy now. Austin hated how Naomi was turning Khari against him, and he wasn't sure what to do about it except try to pull him back, away from the brink. Like a tug-of-war.

As Austin shuffled back to his house, his phone vibrated. It was a message from Brooke.

Khari's back. He went right to his room. Where r u?

He responded: *On my way back.*

When he arrived at his house, he circled around to the backyard. Khari had left the gate open when he'd made his escape. Austin stepped to the patio and looked up at the window to his son's bedroom. Light glowed from within.

Austin's gaze traveled down to the sofa sitting on the patio underneath the window. On impulse, he grabbed the sofa and hauled it across the concrete slab, dropped it on the edge of the grass.

That'll put an end to this jumping out the window nonsense, he thought. It was a small step to take, but it was *something.* He had to reassert control, establish boundaries again.

He dusted off his hands and headed inside through the front door. Brooke met him in the hallway.

She gasped. "What happened to your face?"

"I'm fine." He turned toward the powder room on the edge of the hallway.

"She hit you?" Brooke asked.

"I told you, I'm fine. It's not a big deal."

He switched on the bathroom light and examined his face in the oval-shaped mirror. The side of his face was a hideous crimson. He could see the imprint of Naomi's hand on his flesh, as if she'd had paint on her palm when she struck him.

"Austin, listen to me." Brooke stood in the doorway, her jaws rigid. "We cannot bring our baby into a home where your ex-wife physically assaults you, and you shrug it off like it's business as usual. It's not normal!"

"Did you want me to slug her like Mike Tyson? If I lay a hand on her, she'll call the cops."

"*We* need to call the cops. We need to file a police report. This was an assault, for God's sake."

"I'm fine. Really. Don't make too much of this, okay?"

Brooke's face turned to a deep shade of red. She closed her eyes and pulled in a deep breath.

"You've told me about the terrible things you saw as a kid," she said, her gaze fixing on him again. "You don't want to raise a hand against this woman because of how your dad used to abuse your mother, but that doesn't mean you've got to *allow* her to abuse you."

"Don't bring my dad into this. Please. It's got nothing to do with him."

"Do you honestly believe that?" She gaped at him.

"Listen, I'm sorry I pulled you into this. But try to relax, all right?"

"We're filing for the restraining order tomorrow. Tomorrow *morning*."

"Brooke, come on."

"I'm not asking for your permission. I'm not going to allow this woman to hurt you anymore." She shook her head. "This ends here, and now."

Hands on her hips, Brooke gave him a stare that penetrated him so deeply he could only nod.

"Whatever you want," Austin said. "I'm going to check on my son."

"Let me give you an ice pack. It'll help with the swelling."

"In a minute." He brushed past her.

Upstairs, Khari's bedroom door was closed, and locked. Austin knocked, but his son didn't answer.

"Khari?" Austin knocked again. "Open up. We need to talk."

Khari didn't respond. Austin didn't have the energy to push matters any further. All he wanted to do was swallow a couple of ibuprofen, lie down, and try to get some sleep.

He turned away from the door.

When he dropped into bed, sleep didn't come easy. A single thought whirled through his mind like the spinning ceiling fan in their bedroom.

I'm losing my son, and there's nothing I can do about it . . . losing my son, and there's nothing I can do about it . . . losing my son . . .

24

The next morning, Thursday, Brooke got out of bed determined to prevent Austin from backing out of her plan to file a protective order against his ex-wife.

It was Austin's nature to avoid conflict. But Brooke knew from experience that when dealing with a bully, you couldn't back down; you couldn't bury your head in the sand and hope the bully went away. You had to stand up. Sometimes, you had to bring the fight to them.

They saw off Khari to the school bus stop—the boy was barely talking to Austin, an unfortunate fact that made Brooke almost physically ill—and she herded Austin back into the house and sat him down at the dinette table.

"Now let's take a photo of your face." She lifted her phone.

He groaned. "You took a photo last night."

"The bruise looks worse this morning. We need to add it to the record."

"Can you believe that Khari didn't ask how I wound up with a jacked-up face?" Austin was shaking his head. "I'm not sure he noticed or gives a damn."

"He's going through a lot right now."

"He acts like he hates me. What did I do wrong? Why do I feel like the bad guy?"

"I don't know, babe. But we're going to work it out. Sit still, okay?"

Brooke snapped a series of photos. She found it difficult to look at him without feeling a twinge of anger. His face looked as if he'd been on the losing side in a barroom brawl.

"Are you done now?" he asked.

"Yep, this is good." She scrolled through the pics. "I've got a nice package now to send to Sharon."

"The same lawyer I'm hiring for the custody case?"

"Dealing with situations like this is part of her practice, too. She helped me file a restraining order a long time ago, against a stalker ex-boyfriend."

"I never knew about that." Austin probed the side of his face. "So how many other photos do you have?"

"I took a photo of them blocking our driveway with their motor home. Then, after Naomi bum-rushed me at lunch, I took another pic of their RV in the parking lot outside my job."

"You've been preparing for this?" He scratched his head and seemed to regard her with a newfound respect. "I've never had anyone help me when it comes to *her*. I'd muddle through it on my own."

"I'm helping you whether you like it or not. Get used to it."

He smiled, his first genuine smile in days, she thought.

"Thank you," he said.

Brooke smiled back at him, but his comment saddened her. He was such a good guy. How had he wound up in a seriously dysfunctional, abusive marriage with a toxic woman like Naomi? He hadn't deserved to be treated so poorly. No one did.

He had brought those same low expectations into their marriage. He often seemed awestruck by a simple kindness or comment that she shared with him, that to her felt as natural as breathing. He had once confided to her that "after years of walking on eggshells, I feel like I can breathe again."

Brooke wasn't going to allow Naomi to pull him back into that terrible place. He wasn't on his own this time, and she wasn't going anywhere.

"I need you to give me all of Naomi's information," Brooke said. "Full name, date of birth, phone number, where you think she's living. We'll need it to file our petition with the court for the protective order."

"Right." Austin nodded. "But how can she get served with an order if she's not home? They're driving around like nomads in that RV."

"I've got the motor home's tag number and the Winnebago make and model. We'll include that info in our petition. The court can handle it from there."

"Probably they can come right to our neighborhood and find them," Austin said. "I think Naomi and her folks will keep coming back. She's never respected anyone's boundaries."

"Guess what?" Brooke said. "She'll respect them this time—or she's going back to jail."

25

"There he goes," Daddy said.

That morning, Naomi was sitting in the Winnebago's cab with her father. Daddy was behind the wheel. They were waiting in the parking lot of a Waffle House that was located within half a mile of Austie's house, and along the route that he took to work each morning. Their camper was angled to give them a view of the adjacent road.

She watched Austin drive past in his gray Dodge Durango.

"He's late." Naomi glanced at her phone. It was half past ten. "He's up to something with that skank of his, you wanna bet?"

"Could be." Daddy fired up the engine. He navigated onto the busy thoroughfare. "If she's worth anything at all, they're gonna do something after that little altercation y'all had last night, Peach."

"He knows better than to trigger me," Naomi said. "He brought it on himself."

"I'm only saying, girl. Action and reaction."

"Just follow him, Daddy, please."

They were too far behind to keep Austin in their view, but Naomi knew where he was going anyway. He was going to his office. Her Austie had always believed that putting in a hard day's work was a husband's duty.

As they drove, she thought about her daddy's warning about this new woman of his and what she might influence him to do. Naomi wasn't overly concerned. She knew how to break Austin. And she certainly knew how to break another woman—spending seven long years in a women's prison had been like a masterclass on the topic of shattering a woman's spirit.

About fifteen minutes later, Daddy pulled into the parking lot across the way from Austin's office. They got there right on time. Austin shuffled toward the building.

Naomi giggled and put up her feet on the dashboard.

"This is gonna be good," she said.

26

Austin was so deep in thought when he got out of his SUV and shuffled toward his office that he didn't notice the shattered window until he was a few feet away from the door.

He stopped, his breath snagging in his throat. It looked as if someone had hurled a brick through the large pane of glass that fronted his office. Shards littered the pavement, glittering like tinsel in the morning sunshine.

"It's a damned shame," someone said from behind him. "What kind of person does this?"

Austin turned. The owner of the business next door had come outside. She was a blonde-haired, svelte lady in her early sixties. She had sea-blue eyes and a perpetually bronzed complexion that could have been maintained only with regular visits to a tanning bed. Her name was Laura; the name of her establishment was Spa Rejuvenate.

When she saw Austin's face, her dyed eyebrows bunched. He had forgotten about the Ace wrap that Brooke had applied to his bruise, with a typical Brooke zinger: *Babe, if you don't cover that up, your clients might think you're a bookkeeper for Nino Brown.*

"I know who did it," Austin said. "It was my ex-wife."

"Oh." Laura's eyes glimmered. "A messy divorce, hmm? I know how *that* can be, honey. My first husband and I had a helluva fight in the courts."

Austin sidestepped the mess and unlocked the front door.

"Are you gonna call the police and report it?" Laura asked. "I was gonna call if you hadn't showed up."

"I guess I don't have a choice. My insurance company will want a police report."

"Good luck, honey," Laura said. "My son-in-law does glass repair. I can give you his number if you want."

"I'll stop by later and get it, thanks."

He switched on the lights. A brick was indeed the culprit. It lay on the carpet in a puddle of broken glass, a few feet away from the front window. He plucked it off the floor.

There was no message attached; a note wasn't necessary. The broken window *was* the message. It was classic Naomi behavior, wreaking havoc on things that he valued. Once, after a particularly nasty argument, she had taken his watch—a graduation gift from his late aunt—and driven her car over it. On another occasion, she had stolen one of his prized track-and-field medals and dumped it in the trash, and he didn't realize it until it was too late. Yet another time, she had swiped his most expensive Armani suit and donated it to the local Goodwill.

You made me do it, was always her justification. *You triggered me. You should know better.*

But his son wanted to *move in* with this woman. To live what he thought in his youthful naivete would be a fantasy life with his mother.

It was unthinkable.

Austin took his phone out of his pocket and snapped photos of the damage. It was additional evidence he could provide to their lawyer. It would help with the protective order, and the custody case.

As he was outside on the walkway taking the last photo, he caught a glimpse in the corner of his eye. He spun.

The Xavier family's Winnebago was cruising out of the parking lot.

Austin took a photo of the RV, too.

"Got you," he said to himself. "Try to deny you had anything to do with this."

27

Brooke got off work after her last therapy appointment for the day. She couldn't wait to get home and get off her feet for a while. It had been a full day, both inside and outside of the therapy center.

They were keeping their lawyer busy, that was for sure. First there was Naomi's attempt to intimidate Brooke at the café; then her assault against Austin last night; and then again, that morning, the vandalism she'd committed at his office.

Throwing a brick through the window, straight out of the hell hath no fury like a woman scorned playbook. While they had no evidence that Naomi had done it—she wasn't caught on camera or seen in the act—any judge with half a brain would know she was responsible for the damage. Her record spoke for itself.

Pulling her roller case alongside her, Brooke ambled across the parking lot to her car, a white Acura SUV. She had a prime spot—one of the perks of being pregnant, she supposed. Once she gave birth, she'd have to give up the rock star parking slots.

She saw the damage as soon as she rounded the sedan parked next to her vehicle.

Oh no, she didn't, Brooke thought.

The rear left tire was completely flat. What looked like a metal skewer that you might use for cooking kebabs jutted from the rubber, like a pin sticking out of a cushion.

Brooke did a quick look around the parking lot, but she didn't see the motor home.

Slowly, she circled her vehicle, looking for other signs of damage. The back right tire had been skewered, too.

The front tires were intact, for all that was worth. She wouldn't be able to drive home on two punctured wheels. She had to call a tow and get the SUV hauled to the shop.

Keep it up, Brooke thought to herself, and she took out her phone and started snapping pictures. *Keep it up, girl, and I'll have your ass stuck* under *the damn jail.*

28

It was well past seven o'clock by the time Austin and Brooke arrived home and settled around the dinette table. They had picked up dinner from Zaxby's, hardly their idea of a wholesome meal, but Austin knew they were both far too exhausted to bother with cooking. He had picked up Brooke from work after she discovered the punctured tires and he had followed the tow truck to the auto repair shop. Tomorrow, they would pick up her car, and their pockets would no doubt be several hundred dollars lighter.

Austin had required Khari to ride with him when he went to get Brooke. His son sat in the back seat with his headphones on as he swiped and tapped his iPad, his face drawn in a sullen look that had become his only expression lately.

Austin had felt like screaming at him: *Son, do you have any idea what your mother is out here doing? This is the woman you want to live with?* But he had bitten his tongue. He knew his words would fall flat, that Naomi would twist every unflattering truth he spoke about her into a self-serving myth that Khari wanted to believe.

When they settled at the table, Khari grabbed his box of chicken tenders and French fries and turned to leave the kitchen.

"Hey," Austin said. "Where are you going? We eat dinner as a family, Son."

"I've got homework to do." Khari shrugged. "Unless you want me to flunk, too?"

Khari wouldn't meet his gaze, and Austin was convinced his son was lying.

He didn't have homework. He didn't want to be around them.

"Go on," Austin said with a wave. He was too weary to fight Khari on every little point. "We'll talk later this evening."

Without a word, Khari disappeared. Austin heard him pound up the stairs.

Beside him, Brooke stabbed her chicken salad with a fork. "It's going to be okay, babe."

"I'm glad you think so. This was the day from hell."

The doorbell chimed.

"And clearly, it's not over yet." Brooke started to push away from the table.

"I'll get it." Austin touched her shoulder. "It's probably only a delivery."

The doorbell chimed again as Austin circled around the table and left the kitchen. Couriers didn't usually ring twice, he noted to himself. His jaws clenched, and he felt the bruised side of his face throb dully.

He wasn't in the mood to deal with Naomi again. As he entered the hallway, he pulled up the security camera app on his phone. He saw, in real time, that his visitor was neither a courier nor Naomi. There were two people, a man and a woman, young and well dressed. From a church, perhaps, evangelizing in the neighborhood?

He wasn't in the mood to listen to preaching, either.

Austin activated the intercom function on the app. "Who's there?"

"Mr. Dash?" The woman tilted her face toward the camera. "I'm Quinita Davis, from the Cobb County Department of Family and Children Services."

DFCS? Austin felt a chill come over him as if a nor'easter had gusted through the house.

"I'm here with my colleague Javier Mendoza," Quinita said. "May we come in, please?"

Brooke had entered the hallway behind Austin. She was shaking her head, her face in an expression Austin recognized as disbelief.

He swallowed, and opened the door.

29

The social workers gathered on the upholstered chairs in the living room. Quinita was a pixie of a Black woman who Austin guessed was in her late twenties. Dressed in a smart navy-blue business suit, she had shoulder-length ebony braids decorated with multicolored beads. Her partner, Javier, was Latino, also twenty-something, and so tall and slender he resembled a human version of a daddy longlegs. He wore a dark suit, no tie.

Unable to sit still, Austin circled the perimeter of the living room. He felt as if he had plummeted into new depths of the rabbit hole that had become his life lately. What were these people doing here? What had brought them there?

He had an ominous feeling about the answers to those questions.

Quinita had taken a manila folder out of her bag, along with a pen and a notebook. She opened the folder.

"Our office had a report filed recently, Mr. Dash." She studied him with her dark brown eyes. Although she was young, he had the impression that she had deep experience in these matters.

"Is your son, Warren, here?" Javier asked, using Khari's first name.

"Hold on a minute, a *report*?" The word tasted like a poison pill in Austin's mouth. "A report about what?"

"There was an incident yesterday evening." Quinita consulted her notes. "The child's mother reported that you struck him."

Austin stared at her. She met his gaze forthrightly. Her words didn't click. *Struck him?*

"Jesus." Brooke settled onto a chair across from the social workers. "This is too rich for words."

"Naomi hit *me*!" Austin shouted. He ripped away the bandage on his face and pointed. "Look at this! She slapped me!"

"Did she strike you in retaliation for you hitting the child?" Javier asked.

"I've never hit my boy, ever." Austin crumpled the bandage in his fist and tossed it onto the table. "We're in the middle of a custody fight with his mother—who was just released from prison, by the way. She served seven years for cutting me up with a knife. Do you have *that* in your precious file?"

Quinita and Javier traded a meaningful look that Austin couldn't decipher.

"It may be easier if we can speak to your son privately," Quinita said. "With your permission, of course."

Austin was prepared to say, *hell no*, but he heard Khari come down the steps. He suspected Khari had been eavesdropping from the moment he heard the doorbell ring.

"I'm right here," Khari said.

"Can we have privacy, Mr. Dash?" Quinita asked. She glanced at Brooke. "Mrs. Dash?"

"Dad didn't hit me," Khari said. He looked quickly at Austin, then lowered his gaze.

Austin could have kissed his son, right then.

But Quinita said, "Five minutes, family? Please?"

Reluctantly, Austin filed upstairs, Brooke following close behind him. He was tempted to hang out at the top of the steps and try to overhear the discussion, but Brooke took his hand and tugged him toward their bedroom. She closed the door.

"Am I dreaming right now?" Austin asked. "Do these people actually think I'm abusing my son?"

"She's so wrong for this." Brooke sat on the edge of their bed. She pulled her fingers through her hair. "Wow. I'm speechless."

Austin stepped toward the window that overlooked the street. Night had settled in. He saw the social workers' car, a green Honda Accord, parked in his driveway.

And the motor home was parked in the cul-de-sac again, a stone's throw from his front door. Lights glowed at the windows.

"They're parked outside," he said.

"The Xaviers?" Brooke asked.

"Who else?" Austin trembled. Naomi would be relishing every second of this new melodrama she had fabricated. "I should have seen this coming. This is another tactic out of her playbook. I saw her do this kind of crap to other people when we were married—when she wasn't taking out her anger on me."

"We need to let Sharon know," Brooke said. "Something like this, her filing a false report with DFCS, will help your case, even though it might not feel so good right now."

"As long as Khari doesn't lie."

"He said you didn't hit him, Austin."

"He said that when I was standing there in the room. I don't know what he'll say in private to these people."

"He doesn't hate you." Brooke clasped her hands across her stomach. "But he's conflicted."

Austin paced again, hands deep in his pockets. After a few minutes, he heard heavy footsteps on the staircase, the distinctive tread of his son. Then a knock at the door. Austin opened it.

"They want to talk to you guys now," Khari said.

"What did you tell them?" Austin asked.

Khari shrugged. "The truth, Dad."

"I hope so." Austin glared at him. "Did you know your mother was here again, parked outside?"

"No," Khari said, too quickly for Austin to believe him.

"We'll discuss this later." Austin stepped past him.

Together, he and Brooke returned downstairs. The social workers waited in the hallway by the front door.

"Are we done here?" Austin asked.

"Your son supports your account," Quinita said. "But I'll be honest, Mr. Dash, this situation is concerning on several levels. I sincerely hope that you and your ex-wife can settle your issues peacefully in family court."

"That's what I've been trying to do," he said.

Brooke let the visitors out. As she was locking the door behind them, Austin touched her arm.

"Don't lock up yet," he said. "I'm going outside."

"Hmm." Brooke frowned. "I don't think that's a good idea."

He found the folder that contained copies of the protective order documents their lawyer had filed with the court earlier that day.

"It's time for her to get served," he said.

30

Austin banged his fist against the camper's front door. In his other hand, he gripped the folder full of legal documents. While their petition hadn't yet been reviewed and approved by a judge, and they had to attend a hearing in court, he couldn't wait to shove these papers into Naomi's face and let her know they meant business.

It would make her angry, but after the stunt she had pulled, he didn't give a damn. She could smack the other side of his face for all he cared.

The door opened. Edward, her father, stood in the stairwell. He wore a plaid shirt, overalls, and scuffed boots, as if he'd just arrived back from his pecan orchard. A toothpick dangled between his lips.

"I need to talk to her," Austin said.

Edward stared back at him, his deep-set hazel eyes boring into Austin's brain. His face was expressionless. Austin had often found it difficult to guess what this man was thinking; he had the ultimate poker face.

"Please," Austin said.

"Peach is resting," Edward said in his lazy drawl. A chuckle slipped out of him. "Young lady has had herself quite the day, uh-huh."

Throwing bricks through my office window, puncturing my wife's tires, calling DFCS and making up lies about me? Right, she's had a lot on her plate today.

"Can I come in?" Austin asked.

"Everyone else is resting, too." Edward slid his toothpick to the other side of his mouth and smacked his lips. "The wife cooked up a storm in here, her famous fried chicken, remember that? We're lounging 'round in here with a serious case of the itis."

"Don't get too comfortable. You can't park here overnight. We've been over this before."

"That so?" Edward scowled. "You gonna call the police on me? You've been selling wolf tickets all around, son."

"Does this look like more wolf tickets?" Austin thrust the folder at him.

Frowning, Edward opened the folder. He squinted at the papers, slipped on a pair of reading glasses he fished out of his overalls' front pocket, and held the documents up to the overheard light in the cab.

"You're sending this to court?" Edward's voice rose a couple of octaves. "A petition . . . for protection? From Peach?"

"It's already done. We'll be getting the hearing soon, and she better be there. How about those wolf tickets?" Austin grinned. "Keep those papers. I have copies."

"You've done it now, son. *You've done it.*" Crimson flushed Edward's cheeks. Muttering to himself, he slammed the door in Austin's face.

Austin waited for a beat. He half-expected Naomi to explode like a demonic jack-in-the-box out of the RV and attack him on the spot, but after about a minute, the camper's engine came alive with a rumble.

Austin retreated to his driveway. As he watched, the motor home pulled out of his neighborhood.

He wanted to pump his fist in the air. He felt as if he had stood up to the schoolyard bully, bopped him in the nose, and sent him away crying.

When he went back inside the house, Brooke said, "You're smiling—and they're gone. What did you do?"

"I slapped the documents on her dad. They're scared now. They know we're not playing games anymore. She could go back to jail."

"You're sending my mom to jail?"

Khari had appeared at the bottom of the staircase. Austin hadn't heard his son approach. The kid had been lurking around all night eavesdropping.

"No one's trying to send Naomi to jail," Austin said. "If she goes to jail, it's by her own choice. Do you have any idea—"

"You're an asshole!" Khari pounded up the steps. Austin heard his door slam shut with a boom that echoed like a cannon shot through the house.

Hands on her hips, Brooke turned to Austin. "I don't know what to say about what I just heard."

"No words here, either." Sighing, Austin ran his fingers through his close-cropped hair. "But I can't dress this up and make it sound good."

"It is what it is." Her eyes were steely. "Naomi has to deal with the consequences of her actions."

"I feel as if I need to offer him hope. Like it's my duty to find a positive spin on this. Right?"

"Your duty?" She made a tsk-tsk sound. "Babe, it's your duty to tell him the truth. His mother is breaking the law, and if she keeps it up, she's going to jail—again."

"Let me go talk to him."

31

Here he was again, facing his son's closed bedroom door. Austin knew the door would be locked. Was Khari climbing out of the window as well, despite Austin having moved the sofa off the patio? Would he take off into the night and force Austin to track him down and bring him back home?

This had become the new dynamic in their relationship, and Austin hated it.

I could leave him alone, he thought. *Talking to him isn't helping anyway. He's not listening to me.*

Austin had the master key in his palm already, but he paused, mulling over his next move. Suddenly, he heard muted voices coming from Khari's bedroom. Someone snickered.

Austin felt the hairs rise at the back of his neck. He knew that laugh.

Naomi's in my house now?

Spurred to action, he unlocked the door and shoved it open.

Khari shot up in bed. He had tossed something underneath the bedsheet like a tweaker scrambling to hide a meth pipe. But Austin saw a familiar silver glow through the sheet's thin cotton, and he heard Naomi's voice coming from the device.

"Baby, is everything okay? What happened?"

Austin stalked toward the bed. Khari rose from the mattress.

"Hand it over." Austin extended his hand.

"It's *mine*. Mom gave it to me." Khari pulled away the bedsheet and grabbed the iPhone.

Naomi continued chattering like a bird: "*Hey, is your daddy in there? Is he hurting you?*"

"Give it to me, Khari. Now."

"But Mom gave it to me," he said again. But he dropped the phone into Austin's hand and then crossed his arms over his chest, his hands squeezed into fists.

Austin looked at the screen. Khari had a FaceTime call going with Naomi. Naomi leered at Austin.

"I am *not* in the mood to talk to you, Austie," she said. "Put my baby back on the phone."

Austin terminated the call. He drew a deep breath, regarded his son. Khari glared back at him so savagely that if he could have fired lasers from his eyes, Austin would have been vaporized.

In the calmest tone he could manage, Austin said, "This explains a lot of what's been going on lately."

"She's my mother," Khari said. "She has the right to talk to me. *She has rights.*"

The phone buzzed in Austin's hand. The caller ID said: *Mom.* Austin hit the button to ignore the call.

"She gave this phone to you without talking to me about it," Austin said. "Obviously, she told you to hide it from me. She doesn't have the right to do that, Son."

"I could have had you arrested," Khari said. "I could have lied to those people who came here. They would have sent me to live with Mom."

The phone buzzed again. Again, he ignored Naomi's call.

"She's my family, Dad." Khari's voice broke, and he bent over as if staggered by the power of the emotions storming through him. "I want to be with them . . . I want to be with my family . . ."

Austin pulled his son into his arms.

"Please, Daddy . . ." Khari sobbed. "Wanna be with my family . . ."

Austin held him close, rocked him.

The phone kept buzzing.

32

Before going to bed, Austin settled onto the sofa in their bedroom and checked his blood pressure, per the twice-daily schedule his doctor had recommended. The reading was so high that he blinked with surprise and checked it again. The numbers didn't improve.

"This says I'm on the verge of a hypertensive crisis," he said to Brooke.

Brooke was sitting upright in the bed, her back supported by an elaborate configuration of pillows. She glanced away from the book she was reading, her eyebrows creased.

"Deep breaths," she said. "Try that, please, right now. Rhythmic deep breaths."

"My lungs feel like I swallowed a bowl of broken glass." But he tilted back his head, closed his eyes, laid his palms flat on his lap, and sucked in deep breaths.

His mind wandered as he tried to settle his body. He had taken away the iPhone from Khari, of course, and shut it off, but not before Naomi had called probably fifteen times. He wanted to say he couldn't believe what she had done, giving Khari a phone without telling him, but that was a lie.

Once again, she had outflanked him in this new competition to win their son's loyalty. It angered and baffled him. He had taken care of Khari to the absolute best of his ability, without any assistance from her or her family, for *seven years*. But Khari seemingly didn't care about any of the history he and Austin shared. *What have you done for me lately?* seemed to be his kid's motto. Brooke cautioned him that Khari was young, too immature to fully understand the impact of his actions and words, but it wounded Austin regardless.

Hearing Brooke climbing off the bed, Austin opened his eyes. She shuffled to the sofa and eased onto the cushion next to him.

"Better?" she asked. "Try it now."

He checked his blood pressure again. After the machine beeped, he sighed and showed her the numbers on the display.

"Much better," he said. "Almost normal. I wouldn't have wanted to close out the day with an ER visit."

"You'll be okay." She touched his arm.

"But seriously, things have to improve now, right?" he asked. "I took away the phone, she knows we have the order pending in the court. Do you think we'll finally get some peace?"

"If we don't, I think I'm having this baby early." Brooke rubbed her stomach. "We've done everything we can, babe."

"Thanks for being here, supporting me in this. I couldn't do it without you."

"No thanks necessary. Come to bed."

She tugged his hand, and he let her lead him.

For the next week, their lives returned to a semblance of normality. They went to work, Khari went to school, and there was no sign of the Xaviers' motor home, no damage to their vehicles or property, no lies reported to DFCS, and no contact whatsoever from Naomi. They had a court hearing scheduled for the order of protection, and a custody hearing was in the works as well.

On a Thursday morning near the end of the month, Austin was in his office working on a tax report for a new client when the door opened with a soft chime. Austin looked up from his computer, and suddenly felt as if the floor had popped open like a trapdoor underneath him.

It was Edward. He wore a navy-blue suit that looked a size too big for him and clasped a gray fedora in his big, gnarled hands. Edward had long struck Austin as one of those men who always seemed more comfortable in blue-collar work clothes—which, for him, was a plaid shirt, denim overalls, and work boots—than he did in a suit and tie.

"We need to chat, son," Edward said.

33

"They want to come over tomorrow night for dinner," Austin said. That same day that Edward had come to his office, he met Brooke for lunch at the café she favored near her work. "Edward, Karen, and Charlotte. Naomi's *not* on the guest list. Edward said she's back in Albany and they're going back, too—he's been handling business matters here, he says—but they want to see Khari before they leave. They even want to bring the food, too, to make it easy for us."

"Hmm," Brooke said. It was what she always said when she was reluctant to commit to a request. She dipped a bag of mint tea into a steaming mug of water. "Do you trust them to behave?"

"Naomi won't be there."

"But they're her family. They've always taken her side, yes?"

"He said their lawyer drafted a custody proposal that would, in his words, be *very favorable* to me." Austin took a sip of his unsweetened iced tea. "He said they'll bring it to dinner so I can review it, take it to our lawyer."

"It doesn't sound like I need to be a part of this dinner," Brooke said.

"Edward specifically asked for you to be there. And I quote, 'Make sure that lovely wife of yours is there, too, son.' Sounds like they want to get to know you."

"And they'll bring the food? That's tempting." Brooke lifted her cup to her lips, hesitated. "What do you think, honestly? Do you trust them to stay civil?"

"I feel as if I owe it to Khari," he said, remembering how, only a week ago,

Khari had broken down sobbing in his arms: *Daddy . . . wanna be with my family . . .* "This is mostly for his benefit, not mine, though I'm curious about this custody proposal."

"All right." Brooke nodded. "I'm in. But if they start showing out, we show them the door. I can't handle any more drama."

"No drama," Austin agreed.

Later that evening, when Austin shared the news with Khari, his son grinned at him for the first time since all of this had started.

"See, I'm not a bad dude." Austin ruffled Khari's hair. "I think about what you want, too."

"Can I get my phone back?" Khari smiled. "Just kidding."

"Yeah, don't push it, man."

"I think I'm going to draw something new for them," Khari said. He rushed to the staircase, turned, and beamed at Austin again before he went upstairs. "Thanks, Dad!"

Finally, my dad game's back on track, Austin thought, and he allowed himself to smile.

34

The next evening, the doorbell rang at precisely seven o'clock.

Austin was already standing at the door when the guests arrived. From the front window, he had watched a silver Ford transit van park in front of the house and drop off the Xaviers; he tracked them as they filed out of the vehicle carrying bags and dishes, and then the van drove out of sight. Although he genuinely wanted Khari to spend time with his mother's family, he couldn't help anticipating a last-minute surprise such as Naomi popping up out of nowhere wearing a devious grin and bearing a sweet potato pie. *Hey, Austie, I thought I would drop in, too! Look, I brought pie!*

But he didn't see his ex-wife. Possibly, she was hiding out somewhere in the area and had never retreated to Albany like her father had claimed. She might have even been driving the van that dropped them off. Austin frankly didn't care so long as he didn't see her, and she kept off his property.

Khari and Brooke stood behind Austin as he adjusted his shirt collar and stepped forward to the door. Khari looked ready to pop from excitement and had changed into a dress shirt and nice pants that he wore on those occasions when they attended church. He knew Brooke was exhausted from a long day at work, but she looked fresh and beautiful in a green, pleated maternity dress. Austin wore a maroon long-sleeve polo shirt and a new pair of Levi's.

"Here we go, gang," Austin said. He pulled the door open.

"Evening, folks!" Edward said in his booming baritone.

Edward towered in the doorway behind his wife and daughter. He wore his fedora from yesterday, a plaid shirt, and khakis. Karen and Charlotte wore modest dresses in bright springtime colors, and each of them had put on makeup and jewelry.

"Welcome," Austin said. "Come on in, y'all."

They exchanged handshakes, hugs, and greetings.

"We appreciate y'all having us over," Edward said. "It's nice for folk to set aside differences and understand that we all want the same thing."

"Where's the motor home?" Austin asked.

"Left that behemoth in Albany." Edward shrugged. "We got a driver taking us 'round. They'll be back to scoop us up later."

Karen asked to be directed to the kitchen so she could "warm up the good stuff." Austin detected tempting aromas swirling from her bags and dishes as she breezed past him and followed Brooke.

"All you've gotta do is show me where things are, honey, and then you go on and sit your pretty little self down, you hear?" Austin overheard Karen saying to Brooke. "You look fit to pop right here and now, but this is your night off, sweetheart. I'll handle *everything*."

Later, when Austin dissected how the evening had veered off the rails, he would realize that allowing Karen to occupy his kitchen, alone, was the grave error. She had brought dinner, as promised, a fantastic homemade lasagna. But most importantly, she had prepared their respective servings, too, had brought their plates into the dining room, insisting on knowing exactly who was sitting where at the table, because she had cut individual portions for each person.

As they settled around the table, Khari offered to say grace. Austin was startled by his son's offer, but urged him to proceed while the Xaviers nodded. They bowed their heads and Khari offered a short but moving prayer about "getting to know family and learning how to all get along and be happy." To his credit, he didn't mention Naomi by name, but the topic of his mother was the elephant in the room.

Dinner was delicious. Austin remembered that Karen had always been a formidable home cook. When he indicated interest in a second helping, Karen insisted on getting it for him, whisked away his plate, and vanished into the kitchen.

Later, Austin would realize that by allowing Karen to fetch his food, again, he had been compounding his initial error.

At dinner, Edward, a colorful storyteller, regaled them with comedic tales of growing up on the pecan orchard and working in the family business. Austin had heard many of those same stories before, but his son was riveted.

"You used to ride around the farm with me on my tractor," Edward said to Khari with a wink. "You were a wee bit of a thing back then, son. You interested in another visit?"

"Yeah!" Khari said. To Austin, his son looked ready to leap out of his chair and go right then.

"I got something to give your daddy after we're done eating." Edward inclined his head toward Austin. "I think he will find it quite acceptable, yes sir."

Austin glanced at Brooke. She found his hand underneath the table, squeezed. He squeezed back.

From her body language, he knew she was glad they had agreed to this gathering. It was, so far, refreshingly drama-free.

For dessert, Charlotte had prepared a pecan pie. "I'm the baker in the family, y'all. And you know we grow these pecans in our own orchard. Y'all ain't getting a pie any fresher than this."

The pie was heavenly. Charlotte served each of them their respective slices, bringing the plates in from the kitchen. Probably another mistake, Austin would figure later, but it had likely been too late by then anyway.

Once they had wrapped up dessert, Edward rose from the table.

"Got somewhere we can chat in private, son?" he asked Austin.

"Sure," Austin said.

"Grab us a couple whiskey glasses, too, if you got 'em."

Austin looked at Brooke, but she was engrossed in an animated discussion with Karen. *You keep such a clean house, honey! Looks like our grandson is in good hands with you, for sure.*

Khari was a chatterbox with his aunt Charlotte. He had brought out his art portfolio, and Charlotte was gushing over his drawings. *You are so talented, boy! We ain't never had an artist in the family!*

Pleased with the atmosphere amongst their little group, Austin retrieved a pair of rocks glasses from the kitchen and led Edward into the living room. Edward had retrieved the battered leather bag he had brought with him. He unzipped it and fished out a legal-size blue leather folder, and what looked like a bottle of whiskey.

Grinning, Edward showed the bottle's label to Austin.

"Whoa," Austin said. "Is that Pappy's?"

Pappy Van Winkle was a rare, highly prized bourbon, literally impossible to get in a liquor store that didn't have a special arrangement with the parent distillery, Buffalo Trace, and when they did offer it for sale, you'd better expect to pay four figures. Austin enjoyed good liquor, but he was much too frugal to plunk down that much cash for a bottle of anything.

"I got a business partner at Buffalo Trace," Edward said. "I only crack this baby open on special occasions."

Edward gave each of them a generous pour. They settled onto upholstered chairs across from each other, the table between them with the bourbon and the folder sitting atop it.

Austin sipped the whiskey. "Wow, now this is a bourbon. Damn."

"Worth every penny." Edward sipped whiskey, pointed at the folder with his glass. "Check out what we drew up there."

Austin yawned—he was, suddenly, starting to feel quite drowsy—but he opened the folder and slid out the stapled, typed pages. He scanned the legalese. The font was small, and it was difficult for him to focus as he grew increasingly sleepy at a rapid pace, but he thought the proposal requested for Khari to spend one weekend per month in Albany; additionally, it provided for Austin (and his spouse) to be present as well, with their lodging at a local hotel comped by the Xavier family.

"Am I reading this correctly?" Austin asked. He tried to stifle another yawn but failed. "He has a supervised visit at your house once a month while you put us up in a local hotel for free?"

"Not some fleabag motel, either," Edward said. "We got a Hilton in town. Owner is a buddy. You and your pretty lady will get a suite."

"I'm floored." Austin yawned again, tears leaking from his eyes. "I'll have our lawyer review this, but honestly, this looks great."

"That's good to hear, son. I knew you'd like it."

"One thing, though." Austin tapped the document. "Is this what *she* wanted?"

"You *know* what Peach wanted, son." Edward gave him a knowing look. "Had to twist her arm a spell to bring her 'round. What she wants most of all is to get to know her boy. That's what we all want. Young man needs to know his roots. You can understand that, better than anybody."

"True," Austin said. He had once confided to Edward the tragic story of his parents.

He took another small sip of the bourbon. His head whirled. *I need to slow down,* he thought. *This is hitting me hard.*

As he leaned forward to place the glass on the coffee table, it slipped out of his fingers, spilling the precious liquor onto the tabletop. But such a powerful spell of drowsiness had swept over Austin that he had lost all coordination.

"I feel like . . . I've . . . been . . . drugged . . ." The words slipped out of him in a whisper. Unable to sit up, he lay on his side on the sofa.

"That's 'cause you have been, son." Edward chuckled. He rose from the chair, dipped his finger in the spilled whiskey, tasted it, sighed with pleasure. "Bourbon's clean, though. My wife's lasagna and Char's pie laid it on you good."

As the meaning of Edward's words washed over him, Austin struggled to get up, to keep his eyes open, but it was like fighting against an ever-increasing weight of sand pouring over him while he lay in a deep pit. He thought about Brooke and Khari, wanted to see if they were sedated, too, but he lacked the strength to turn his head and look. He groaned.

"Everything'll be better in the morning," Edward said. He took his phone out of his pocket and winked at Austin, and the last thing Austin heard before he spiraled into the blackest depths of sleep was, "*We're ready for you, Peach.*"

35

In Naomi's opinion, she had precious few flaws, but she would openly admit that she was an impatient woman. Whenever she wanted something, she *wanted* it, and every second she spent waiting for her desire to be fulfilled was sheer agony. She often mused, proudly, that she was like the character Veruca Salt from one of her fav movies from childhood, *Willie Wonka & the Chocolate Factory.* I want it now!

Waiting for their brilliant plan with Austie to reach fruition had been absolute torture. Allowing an entire week to pass during which she didn't have any contact with him or their son. Sitting in the transit van she had parked on the other side of the neighborhood while the rest of her family yukked it up in Austie's house that evening. Not taunting his baby mama. It was pure agony.

But the payoff was worth it.

As she stood in the middle of Austin's living room, looking at him lying unconscious on the sofa as if he'd knocked back way too many drinks, an uncontrollable bout of the giggles came over her. Tears flooded her eyes as she laughed.

"It really worked!" Naomi said. She high-fived Mama, Charlotte, and Daddy. "You guys did it!"

"I hope you didn't give the lady there too much," Daddy said, with a nod toward Austin's skank, Brooke. They had hauled her to the love seat across from Austin. She was heavy as a damn hippo, but what did you expect with a woman so pregnant that she might go in labor at any minute?

Her son was asleep, too. She had argued with her family about sedating the boy. She didn't want him ingesting some prescription-strength sleep drug. But Mama had counseled her that he might ask too many questions if they let him stay awake while Austie and the skank dozed, and might even cause problems. Naomi had been working on swaying him to her side, but he was still under Austin's influence, to a large degree. For his own good and the welfare of their family, he needed to be sedated, too. He was sprawled in the chair next to Austin, snoring like a grown man.

"All right, we got work to do," Naomi said. "Let's clean up in here, pack whatever we need to pack, and get back on the road."

The logistics of their plan were simple. Naomi had backed the rented transit van into the driveway, parked it right up against the garage door; they had also brought a wheelchair. They would open that garage door and use the wheelchair to transport their human cargo out of the house and into the van, and none of the neighbors would be the wiser. Once loaded up, Char would get in Austie's SUV, their little group would travel a couple of miles to where they had left the Winnebago, they would load up some stuff, and then their convoy would hit the interstate.

At Naomi's urging, Mama and Charlotte snapped into action as if they were soldiers in Naomi's private army, but Daddy sat on a chair, lit one of his Cuban cigars, and proceeded to nurse the rest of his bourbon.

"Daddy, we need to get moving," Naomi said. "We gotta be on the road in fifteen minutes."

"I done my part for now, Peach." Daddy exhaled a ring of sweet smoke. "I gotta catch a breath 'fore we get on the road. We got a good piece ahead of us heading back to the farm."

Naomi didn't argue with him. Out of all of them, Daddy had the most to lose by his participation in this felonious scheme of hers. He was the public face of their pecan empire. What would people think if they found out he played a key role in an act like this?

On the other hand, she reminded herself, Daddy had the late-stage prostate cancer, and it wasn't as though he was following his doctor's orders and pursuing all available treatments. She believed that was the real reason why he had agreed to participate in her plan. It saddened her to think about it, but Daddy's days were numbered, and he said he wanted to spend his last days on this earth doing something to bring her joy, God bless him.

She had told him that nothing would make her happier than reuniting her family.

I'll make it happen, Peach, he had said. *You suffered for seven years and I've never forgiven myself for that. I'll do whatever you want, sweetheart.*

She kissed Daddy lightly on the lips, tasting tobacco and whiskey. He grinned up at her.

Then she got to work.

36

Sometime later, Austin awoke. He had only a delicate grasp on consciousness, the effects of the sedative still strong.

His mouth was bone-dry. It was dark. He heard the low grumble of a large engine.

Dreaming, he thought. But he felt a soft bump, as if he were traveling in a vehicle.

"Where . . . ?" he said, and the word came out in a whisper.

"In my arms," Naomi said, and that was when he knew it had to be a dream. Slender yet strong arms encircled his waist. He felt a hand on his groin, stroking and caressing as though playing with a favorite toy.

I'm in bed with Brooke, he thought. The idea comforted him like a warm blanket.

"Hey, babe," he said, and drifted back into sleep.

37

Later, Austin awoke to stripes of gray morning light painted across his face. He groaned, raised a hand to his eyes to block the brightness. The movement stirred the remnants of a headache that lay in the back of his head like broken pottery. He groaned again, and, squinting, looked around.

He was lying on his back on a bed, in a bedroom. Both the room and the bed were so familiar that he denied the reality of what he was seeing.

It can't be. I can't be here.

His mouth was dry, an awful flavor lying on his swollen tongue. It tasted as if he had ingested bitter medicine.

Snatches of words surfaced in his memory.

I feel like . . . I've . . . been . . . drugged . . .

That's 'cause you have been, son.

Heart beating faster, Austin sat up. The movement brought a hiss of pain to his lips. His shoulders and lower back throbbed, as if he had spent hours sleeping while contorted in an awkward position.

He peeled aside the bedsheet tangled around his body. He wore a pair of boxer shorts, but nothing else.

His groin ached. Pieces of another memory flickered in his mind: a hand on him, stroking and fondling.

In my arms . . .

He trembled.

The room was simply furnished. It contained the double-bed on which he lay, a nightstand bearing a lamp, a dresser with an oval-shaped mirror, and an upholstered forest-green chair that stood near the foot of the bed. A blue Nike jogging suit was draped across the arm of the chair. His sneakers and socks lay beside the chair.

The door was shut. He was alone in the room.

Nausea tugged at him. This had to be either the most vivid nightmare he'd ever experienced in his life—or something much worse.

Sounds came to him. The clatter of dishes. A ripple of distant laughter; a woman's laughter.

He smelled something, too. The familiar aroma of bacon cooking. It made his stomach churn with hunger.

How long had he been asleep? He didn't see a clock on the nightstand.

He didn't see his phone, either—or any phone, for that matter.

Just a bad, bad dream, he thought. That was how he would handle this situation, as if it were a terrible dream. Because it could not be anything else. It could not be real.

He swung his legs to the side of the bed and put his bare feet on the cold hardwood floor, pushed into a standing position. Dizziness quivered through him, the headache twisting like a stiletto through his brain. He waited, drew deep breaths.

Where is Brooke? Khari?

His memory of where they had been before he had awakened into this dream was slippery. There was a dinner party at his house with the Xaviers, but Naomi hadn't been included. He remembered laughter, good food, a fine bourbon, a stunning child custody proposal . . .

Then, blackness slammed down like a steel gate in his memory.

He dressed in the jogging suit and slid on the socks and sneakers. They were his own clothes and fit perfectly. What did that mean?

It means you're still dreaming, he reminded himself.

The bedroom featured two windows. The blinds on one window were shut; on the other, half-open. He resisted the temptation to peer outside. Doing so might reinforce the reality of this nightmare.

He opened the door. A shadowed hallway lay ahead of him. Photographs hung on the walls, mostly of a wedding that had occurred many years ago, a day he wanted to forget.

Tremors shook him so badly that he contemplated returning to the bed, yanking the covers over his head, and praying that he went back to sleep and would later awake outside of this dream.

But another voice reached him, drew him forward like a hook. A boy.

"Thanks, Mom," the boy said.

It can't be.

Austin shuffled along the hallway, his feet feeling as if they were cast in lead. He resisted looking at the framed photographs that flanked him on either side. They were reinforcements of a reality that he could not swallow.

The kitchen was on the left: the source of the smells and sounds. It was an eat-in kitchen where he had prepared and consumed many, many meals, but not in seven years.

"Good morning, sleepyhead," Naomi said. She stood near the gas range. She wore low-rise jeans, a yellow halter top, flip-flops. A small handheld device that looked like a walkie-talkie was clipped to her waistband.

Holding a pair of tongs, Naomi removed strips of bacon from a cast-iron skillet. She smiled at him. "You need to eat, Austie. You'll feel better once you do."

"Dad!" Khari said. He sat at the dinette table with a tall glass of orange juice in front of him and a plate piled with pancakes dripping with melted butter and syrup. His son wore his Black Panther pajama set. He grinned at Austin. "This is great, isn't it?"

Austin staggered forward. His stomach buckled. He thought he was going to vomit. The impact of everything crashing over him was too much to bear, a tsunami of unthinkable circumstances.

"Hang on there, Austie." Naomi set down the tongs and rushed toward him. "Son, help me get your dad into a chair. He needs our help."

Khari got up to help, too, but Austin swung away from them and stumbled back into the main corridor that cut through the house. He saw the door ahead.

That door that would lead to the end of this nightmare if only he could reach it and leap through it.

"Austie, wait," Naomi said, behind him.

Like a drunk, Austin lurched down the hallway. He grabbed the knob. Twisted. Flung the door open.

The brightness of the day washed over him.

He moaned. "No, no, no, no, no."

He wobbled across the veranda steps, stumbled onto the paved walkway. He spun around and around. Vertigo struck him like a club, and he collapsed to his knees with a sob of such force it seemed it would tear his chest in half.

He was on the Xavier family farm, and he had stumbled out of the house that he had once shared with Naomi.

Hot tears seared his eyes. How? *How?*

Naomi was suddenly kneeling next to him. She put her hand on his shoulder.

"Our family is reunited, Austie," she said. "Me and you and our baby. Isn't that wonderful?"

Her beautiful eyes glittered with what could be only madness. He had long known Naomi was dangerous, a sociopath. But her engineering a situation like this was beyond anything he had ever contemplated.

"Brooke," he said in a ragged voice. He swallowed. "Where's . . . where's Brooke?"

"Listen to me." Naomi lifted his chin so that they were eye to eye. "She's safe. Your baby is safe. But if you run away from me, you'll never see her again. Be a good husband to me, a good daddy to our son, and you just might. Are we clear, Austie?"

He opened his mouth to speak again, but no sounds came out. A cool wind gusted, the trees around them shaking, leaves flapping with a sound like a massive flock of birds suddenly taking flight.

. . . if you run away from me, you'll never see her again . . .

"Austie, did you hear me?" she asked.

Austin screamed.

38

Brooke dreamed that she floated in a dark, warm sea. The only sound was a slowly pulsating beat, throbbing in the water and sending echoes deep into her brain. She was not blind, she could see, but there was nothing *to* see. She waved her arms, and her hand brushed against something attached to her stomach, an organic tube, like an umbilical cord . . .

She awoke with a gasp. Darkness enveloped her on all sides. Something was attached to her face, covering her eyes. She reached for it, and realized her hands were bound together with something cold and heavy.

Panic rose in her, blasting away the fuzziness in her thoughts.

My baby, she thought. *Is my baby safe?*

She lowered her bound hands to her belly. She felt her child twitch, as if in response to her question. A measure of relief washed over her, but it was short-lived. The truth of her situation pressed on her.

She was in serious trouble.

Her memory was spotty. There was a dinner with Austin's ex in-laws, good food and engaging conversation. But she couldn't recall anything else, couldn't pinpoint how the evening had concluded. It was as if her brain suddenly had been unplugged.

She grasped for the thing covering her eyes. She felt a soft velvety material, like an eye mask; it was covered with something smooth and sticky at the edges. Duct tape?

Who had wrapped duct tape over her head and bound her hands? When? Why?

Naomi, she thought, and when the woman's name formed like a mushroom cloud in her mind, she knew it explained everything. Somehow, the woman had schemed to trap Brooke, no doubt with her family's assistance. Probably it had happened at dinner—that was why she couldn't remember anything. They must have drugged her.

What about Austin? Khari? She feared to contemplate what had happened to them.

She tried to peel away the duct tape on her head. Strands of her hair came loose as she tugged, and she bit her tongue against the tearing pain. With the duct tape free, she tore off the eye mask, and, blinking, took stock of her surroundings.

"Sweet Jesus," she breathed.

She lay on a thin mattress on a dusty floor, a sagging pillow lying beside her. Sturdy silver handcuffs bound her wrists. A heavy steel chain wrapped around the links that connected her cuffs; that chain stretched for about five feet and then looped around a thick concrete pillar that extended from the floor to the ceiling. An industrial-grade padlock secured the chain to the support post.

Several bands of duct tape secured her ankles together, and her feet were bare. She was dressed in the same clothing she'd worn at dinner, a green maternity dress. It was covered in grime and damp with perspiration.

She shuddered. How long had she been here? Her mouth was dry, and her stomach growled with hunger. Her back ached as if she'd been poked with multiple hot irons.

Her prison looked like a rarely used, unfinished basement. A naked, low-wattage light bulb hanging overhead cast pale light. There were concrete walls on all sides. Wooden rafters and steel pipes on the ceiling, festooned with dusty cobwebs. Bric-a-brac and sagging boxes and crates scattered along the walls and floor in no discernible order. A white door stood on one side of the room, hanging ajar; it looked like it led into a small bathroom.

An exposed staircase lay across from her, leading upward into the main level of whoever's house she had been brought into for confinement.

The basement didn't have any windows. She had no idea of the time of day, couldn't decipher where this place was located.

It was eerily quiet, too. There was the faint hum of a water heater, perhaps, and the whisper of the wind, the creaking and settling noises of the house, but nothing else. The chamber smelled of her own sour sweat and something rotten.

What if she was alone in this place? What if they had left her in here to starve to death?

My baby.

Panic tugged at her again. Bile surged up her throat. She tried to choke it down, but she couldn't. It spilled out of her, hot and raw. She gasped, wiped her mouth with the back of her hand.

"Help!" she cried. Her voice was raspy, as if her throat had been scrubbed with a Brillo pad. "Someone, please. Help!"

Even as she pleaded for help, she realized the futility of her cries. The people who had brought her there had no interest in helping her. If they had, they would not have chained a pregnant woman to a concrete pole in a dirty basement.

But the raw thirst for survival override logic.

She tugged at the handcuffs, rattling the thick chain.

"Help!" she yelled. "Help me! My baby!"

As if they didn't know she was carrying a baby.

"Please, help!"

After what felt like an interminable delay, she heard something new: footsteps creaking across the floor above. Hope leaped in her heart.

She would say anything, anything at all, to get out of this situation. And she would do anything.

All that mattered was keeping her baby alive and unharmed.

Above, the door opened.

39

Naomi had left Austin at the house, with a stern warning: *Don't you get any ideas about leaving the farm, Austie. Remember what I said. You leave, you ain't never gonna see your baby mama again. Be a good boy while I'm gone, make yourself comfortable. This is your home again. Go on in your house and eat, all right? I'll be back in a bit.*

After conferring with someone on the walkie-talkie she carried on her hip, Naomi zoomed away in a Gator UV that had been parked beside the house. The Gator was like the utility vehicles the family had used to travel around the farm when Austin had lived there previously. Painted lime-green, with yellow highlights, it reminded Austin of a rugged golf cart.

Sitting on the porch steps, Austin watched Naomi drive along the gravel lane that led away from the house and disappear in the dense woodlands that surrounded the property. Khari sat beside him. He had hugged his mother before she departed.

"We're going to find a way to get out of here, Son," Austin said. "Trust me. I'm getting us out of here as quickly as I can: me, you, Brooke. That's a promise."

"Why?" Khari asked.

Austin stared at him. "Why?"

"I mean, I kind of like it here." Khari picked up a small stone and tossed it across the yard. "It's nice and quiet. And it's *our* land, right? I don't remember it, but we used to live here."

"They abducted us, Khari. Do you understand? They took us out of our home against our will."

"I wanted to visit." He shrugged.

He's in shock, Austin thought. *He's in shock, and he's confused. Naomi and her family have completely twisted his thoughts.*

He felt like yelling at his son, shaking him and trying to talk some sense into him, but he stopped himself. He couldn't blame the boy. Khari was only twelve, immature and innocent and trusting. He was his son's protector, and he had failed him and Brooke with one grave mistake: he never should have agreed to the dinner. That was his fault. He hadn't realized the depth of Naomi's cunning, hadn't imagined that her family was following her orders. She had outmaneuvered him with a move so brazen that he had never seen it coming.

The Naomi he had known prior to her incarceration never would have done something like this. Attack him with a knife in a jealous rage? Sure. Plan and execute the abduction of an entire family? Never. But hard prison time had sharpened her predatory instincts. He had thought he could deal with her like a reasonable person, try to resolve their problems via attorneys and judges, court orders and custody agreements. He realized now that his approach was like trying to tame a pit viper with a pat on the head. The entire time since she had busted back into their lives, she was playing an entirely different game.

She was playing for keeps.

Austin told himself that this situation couldn't last for long. He was a business owner with clients, friends. People would wonder why he had vanished, make inquiries. Brooke had a big, close-knit family—no doubt, they would report her missing within a day or two. Khari's school would note his absence. Missing persons reports would be filed; their faces would be on the news. Police would break down the front door of his house and search for clues. There was a paper trail documenting their issues with Naomi, and those breadcrumbs would lead to the Xavier family farm.

But how long would it take for those levers to be pulled and that machinery to grind into action? A couple of days? A week? Two weeks?

Worse: Even if authorities suspected the Xaviers of foul play, what if Naomi and her family managed to hide them? Their orchard was immense, included several residences and a vast number of buildings connected to their pecan business. They could lock away Khari, Brooke, and Austin wherever they wanted, keep them hidden until the heat cooled. A savvy detective might uncover the truth, eventually, but how long might that take? Austin remembered the news story about the psycho guy in Ohio who had kept several women imprisoned in his basement for *years*, and he pulled off that wickedness while living in a normal suburban neighborhood—not on a massive farm with countless hiding places and no neighbors for miles.

As the terrifying depths of their predicament settled over him, Austin started to shake so badly that he had to get up, move around. He went back inside the house, not waiting for his son to follow him.

The aroma of bacon drew him to the kitchen. He was ravenous. Naomi had cooked an entire one-pound package of the thick-cut, hickory-smoked bacon that he loved and left the pieces to drain on paper towels sitting on the counter beside the range. He stood there at the counter and ate every slice, licking his fingers, eating the crumbs, too.

Afterward, he opened the refrigerator and found a jug of water. He chugged half of it directly out of the bottle, savoring the coldness coursing down his gullet.

"Hungry, Dad?" Khari watched him from the kitchen doorway. "Wow, you ate all of the bacon? I didn't get any."

Austin wiped his mouth, burped. "Have you seen my phone? Or any phone?"

"Mom says I don't need a phone here."

"Don't believe everything your mother says. Do you think her taking away my phone is okay?"

"You took *my* phone, Dad."

If Austin's hair were longer, he might have pulled out a few plugs of it right then. "This is a completely different situation. I need to know: Have you seen my phone?"

Khari shook his head, his eyes without guile. Austin believed him. Naomi would not have entrusted their son with any vital information at this stage. She was much too savvy to make such a mistake.

But Naomi obviously had taken possession of his belongings: his phone, his wallet. She would not have missed confiscating those vital items. But what had she done with them?

"Help me look for a phone," Austin said. "Can you do that?"

Doubt pinched Khari's face. "Who do you wanna call?"

"Brooke is pregnant, Khari. Remember? We need to get help to make sure she's safe, need to know that our baby she's carrying is healthy. Your little bro on the way."

"Mom said they'll take good care of her. She says my grandma used to be a nurse."

He had an answer for everything, didn't he? It was like talking to a replicant of his son that spouted only answers that Naomi had installed in him.

Shaking his head, Austin proceeded to search the kitchen.

When he had lived in this house with Naomi seven years ago, they had kept a landline telephone on the wall, next to the refrigerator. Predictably, that phone had been removed, an unpainted rectangle remaining where the phone used to be.

Austin searched the drawers. He found culinary tools, but no phone.

He moved on to other rooms, starting with the bedroom in which he had slept, which he knew from prior experience served as the guest room. No phone in the nightstand drawer. He opened the closet. It was bare.

Next, he moved to the master bedroom suite he had once shared with Naomi. Every detail of the room looked exactly as he last remembered it, down to the colors of the duvet and the arrangement of the decorative pillows.

Emotion pierced his chest like an arrow. This room held so many vivid memories, a mixture of high and low points from their roller coaster of a marriage. In there, he'd enjoyed some of the most amazing lovemaking he'd ever experienced in his life. But terrible fights, too. Naomi had once grabbed that wedding photo on the dresser and chucked it at his head.

He went to the walk-in closet. In there, he discovered items she had brought from his house: shoes, jeans, shirts, suits.

But no phone. The nightstand drawers and the dresser didn't conceal one, either.

He moved on to search the rest of the rooms. He didn't find a phone of any kind, landline or mobile. He didn't find any computers, either, didn't see any keys. The house didn't contain a single device or tool that would facilitate contact with the outside world.

He might as well have been marooned on an iceberg at the North Pole.

He found Khari in the family room watching an anime show on the large flat-screen television.

"Find it?" Khari asked.

"No."

Khari looked pleased, as if Austin locating a phone would have cut short a fun-filled vacation.

"Do you have any idea where they put Brooke?" Austin asked him. "Did you overhear anything? Think hard. It's important."

"Nah." Khari shrugged and directed his attention back to the TV screen. "Mom said she's safe. She said I shouldn't worry about anything, that we'll all be fine."

"Of course she did."

"Oh, and she says I can do school online, too. Like I did during the pandemic."

"You didn't enjoy that very much, Son. You missed seeing your friends."

"I missed my mom and her family more."

Austin winced. "If you stay here, you'll never see your friends again. Is that what you want?"

Khari shrugged, focused his attention on the screen. Feeling powerless, Austin circled back to the front porch.

He could make a run for it. This residence, though located deep within the farm, was about half a mile from the nearest road. He could get to the road and flag down a vehicle and beg a Good Samaritan to call the police.

You leave, you ain't never gonna see your baby mama again.

But if he summoned the police, what would Naomi and her family do to Brooke? He didn't know where the family was keeping Brooke, and he doubted they would peacefully hand her over to anyone. If he'd learned nothing else thus far, he had learned that Naomi was willing to do anything to get her way. Did it make sense to doubt a sociopath who was willing to abduct his family?

His choice was clear: he couldn't involve the police, not at this stage, and risk Brooke's life and the life of their unborn child. Somehow, he needed to find a way to get the upper hand on Naomi.

And then he needed to find Brooke himself.

40

As Brooke heard the door at the top of the staircase creak open, she braced herself for anything.

Keep my baby safe, she thought, over and over, in a mantra. *That's all that matters. Keep my baby safe.*

Although moving was painful, she tugged herself into a sitting position. The handcuffs chained to the post gave her a measure of leverage. She angled the pillow behind her for the meager support it could provide.

She expected to see Naomi, and she was not disappointed. Austin's sociopathic ex-wife took her time coming down the steps. She wore shorts, a yellow shirt, and flip-flops, and her braids were pulled back into a ponytail. As if she were just bumming around the house on a weekend, not coming to visit a pregnant woman that she was holding captive.

Naomi stepped off the last stair and strutted toward Brooke with that flirty, hip-swinging walk of hers. Brooke noticed that she had a small black radio clipped to her waist. A walkie-talkie?

Naomi smiled a shark's grin at her. Brooke's blood went as cold as an icy river.

"I always win, honey," Naomi said. "Didn't Austie tell you that? Sooner or later, I always get what I want."

"You crazy bitch!" Brooke screamed, her voice breaking because her throat was so dry. The words exploded out of her, unplanned, fueled by pure rage. "Get me out of here!"

Naomi clucked her tongue. "Take a chill pill, sweetheart. I don't wanna see your water breaking right here in this smelly-ass basement."

Brooke swung her bound legs toward Naomi, trying lamely to kick the woman. Naomi danced out of the way.

"You're going to prison for the rest of your life for this," Brooke said. "They're gonna put your crazy ass *under* the goddamn jail!"

"Look at you. You're doing a lot of big talk for a skank with no leverage." Naomi put her hands on her waist and snickered. "Hell, I could keep you locked up down here as long as I want. Meantime, Austie's in my bed—yeah, hoe, he's at *our* house—and I'm laying down this soft and wet brown sugar pussy on him every night." She rubbed her hand across her crotch and giggled. "You think he'll be pining for you while he's busting nuts deep in me?"

Brooke was sweating, shuddering. She was losing control of herself. *Keep my baby safe.*

"I need." Brooke swallowed, her tongue clicking in her too-dry mouth. "I need . . . to keep my baby safe. Please."

"Now that's something we can agree on, girlfriend." Naomi reached into her pocket and slipped out a shiny object.

It looked like a knife. Brooke's heart slammed.

Naomi unlatched the blade. It was the butterfly-style knife that Austin had warned Brooke about. Probably the same knife she had used to slice him up like Jack the Ripper seven years ago.

Naomi performed a series of dexterity tricks with the blade, the steel glinting in the light as she flicked it around expertly, tossed it from one hand to the other like a circus performer. Brooke watched, willing her heart rate to slow.

With the blade still unsheathed, Naomi knelt on the floor next to Brooke. Brooke tried to scoot away, but Naomi raised the knife and said, "Be still, skank. Or I do cosmetic surgery on that pretty face."

Brooke obeyed. "Please. I only want to keep my baby safe."

Naomi laid the knife against Brooke's cheek. Trembling, Brooke closed her eyes.

"Look at me, girlfriend," Naomi said.

Brooke opened her eyes. Scalding tears crawled down her cheeks.

"My, my, I really do see why he picked you," Naomi said in a soft, contemplative tone. "I told you before, you and me, we could be sisters. I kinda like that. You know why?"

Brooke didn't answer. She didn't trust herself to speak.

Naomi continued, "'Cause when you have this baby, it might look like a baby Austie and I would make."

Brooke gulped. "Don't hurt us."

"Hmm." Naomi traced the tip of the knife down Brooke's throat, along her chest, and stopped at the large swell of Brooke's stomach.

Brooke held her breath. *Please, Jesus.*

"I love me some babies, girl," Naomi said. She traced a circle around Brooke's stomach with the blade's sharp tip. "Your little bun in the oven is all right. We drugged you good, but we checked on you while you were sleeping. His little heart was just beating away, kinda like a baby bird."

"Please," Brooke said. "What do you want from me? I'll . . . I'll do anything, just don't hurt my baby."

"Why would I hurt a baby?" Naomi's face puckered. "Do you think I'm a psycho or something? I told you, I love babies, and I think yours is gonna look like one of mine."

Salty perspiration seeped into Brooke's eyes, but she was afraid to move. Naomi still balanced the edge of the knife on her stomach.

"What . . . what do you want from me?" Brooke asked.

"We got plans for you. Mama said you keep a clean house, and when I was there last night, I can testify to that. You got skills, girl. We happen to need a housekeeper."

"A housekeeper?"

"Do you wanna be called a maid? It doesn't matter to me."

"You want me to . . . to clean your house?" Brooke felt as if she had lost the thread of the conversation, as if she had blacked out for a beat and snapped awake into some bizarre dialogue exchange.

"Mama and Daddy's house, girl," Naomi said. "I clean my own damn house. Did Austie ever tell you how domesticated I am? Shit, I cook, I clean, I do laundry, all of that. I take care of my family."

Brooke didn't respond; she didn't know what to say. Naomi lifted the knife from her belly, finally, and Brooke sighed.

"You'll be their maid," Naomi said. "After you have the baby, of course. We ain't crazy. We wouldn't have someone pregnant as you doing housework."

"You'll take me to the hospital to have my baby?"

"What do you think?" Naomi tilted her head and smirked. "Yeah, doc, she's gonna have this baby here and then we're gonna put her shackles back on and take her home to be our maid. Don't worry, it's all good."

"A home birth," Brooke said, the words flat on her tongue.

Her OB-GYN had scheduled a C-section for her. Due to her previous miscarriages, and then a myomectomy to remove several uterine fibroids (the bane of so many Black women) her doctor had advised that a cesarean birth was safest for her and the baby.

But did she dare to share that information with a wicked woman who had just pressed a knife to her belly?

"Mama used to be a nurse. You'll be fine. Somewhere in the world, right now, a woman just like you is giving birth in a little mud hut or something. The baby'll be all right. It ain't no big deal. It's only biology."

How did I get here? Brooke asked herself. *What did I do to deserve this?*

She wanted to cry and scream, but her eyes were barren of tears. Besides, crying would not bring any mercy from this madwoman.

"But you know the best part?" Naomi asked. She tapped the edge of the blade against her lips as if it were a pencil. "I'm gonna raise your baby as my own."

"You're going to raise my baby?" Brooke asked. *Over my dead body.*

"I can't have any more kids. This all worked out so perfectly it gives me chills." Naomi shivered with apparent delight. "You do your housework, and maybe, if I'm in a good mood, I'll let you see the little one sometimes. Maybe."

"I was planning to breastfeed him," Brooke said.

"And? You'll pump some of that liquid gold for me and I'll give him a bottle. I did it with my son. Why you getting all caught up in details?" Naomi sneered. "We're gonna do what *I* want, you hear?"

"You're a wicked, crazy bitch," Brooke said. "I'll never let you have my baby. Ever."

Naomi snickered. "Mama bear protecting the baby cub. I get it. I'm the same way. Why you think I fought so hard to get back to my boy? But you forget, I'm running the show here, Miss Thang."

"I need to pee," Brooke said.

"Later." Naomi unclipped the little walkie-talkie she had on her hip. She spoke into it. "She's good. Come on in, y'all."

"Copy that," a woman answered.

The door at the top of the staircase creaked open. Noisy as a herd of cows, the Xavier family tromped down the steps: Edward, Karen, Charlotte. The women wore shapeless, drab blue housedresses. Edward wore a wide brim straw hat, denim overalls, a plaid shirt, and scuffed work boots edged with mud.

Last night—she believed it was last night; she couldn't be sure—these same people had sat around the dinner table in her and Austin's home, bowed their heads, prayed to God, and then broke bread with them and engaged in pleasant conversation. Now, they gathered around Brooke like members of some crazy doomsday cult, their eyes shining with madness, their lips peeled back into wolfish grins.

"Ain't she pretty?" Karen said.

"Ready to pop, she is," Charlotte said.

"Gonna give us a beautiful baby, that's for sure," Edward said.

"All of you, you're going to jail!" Brooke said. "People will be looking for me, understand? They'll find me; they'll find you!"

"Ain't nobody gonna find you," Naomi said.

Naomi laid her hand on Brooke's stomach. Brooke twisted away from her touch, but then Charlotte knelt and clutched Brooke's belly. Brooke squirmed, the chains tinkling, and she lost her balance and flopped back onto the mattress with a cry. Karen pressed her hand against her stomach. Brooke tried to roll away. Edward reached down and put his big, callused hands on her abdomen. All of them were smiling and touching and rubbing, sweat shining on their faces and their eyes bright with savage glee.

Brooke screamed.

41

Austin was searching through the house again, fruitlessly so far, when he heard a vehicle approach. He looked out the front window and saw a gigantic John Deere tractor rumble into the front yard, Edward Xavier sitting at the controls.

Austin's hands clenched into fists, fingernails digging into his palms deeply enough to leave behind pale half-moons. Edward was as much to blame for their predicament as Naomi. As the patriarch of the family, he could have stopped Naomi's plan, talked some sense into her, for once. Austin vowed that when he eventually escaped with Brooke and Khari—and he was *going* to safely get them out of there, somehow—Edward would pay a high price for his actions, old man or not.

Slowly, Edward climbed down from the cab, reached back up, and retrieved something from the tractor.

It looked like a rifle. Edward angled it across his shoulder as casually as a boy toting a fishing pole on a lazy stroll to the lake. He approached the house, knocked, and then opened the door without waiting for Austin to answer.

"Morning," Edward said. Dressed in a big straw hat, Dickies bib overalls, a plaid shirt, and worn boots, he smelled of tobacco and freshly trimmed grass. "Y'all settled in now, son?"

Like Naomi, Edward wore a walkie-talkie clipped to his waistband. Austin figured the radio was their means of keeping in touch with one another, eliminating the need for them to carry cell phones.

"You tricked me." Austin glowered at him.

"Tricked you?" Edward squinted. "Talk plain, boy."

"That custody proposal you gave me last night. It was bullshit."

"It's called *bait*." Edward's eyes twinkled with amusement. "Was actually my idea. Worked, didn't it? You snapped on it like a flathead catfish on a nightcrawler."

"You're the head of a multimillion-dollar company. You're gonna lose it all over this? I don't get it."

"Get older, get sicker," Edward said with a shrug. "Your priorities might change a bit."

"Do you want to spend your golden years rotting away in a prison?" Austin asked. "Because that's what's waiting for you at the end of the road, *Eddie*."

The web of crow's feet around Edward's eyes tightened. Austin knew the man hated to be called "Eddie," or "Ed"—anything but "Edward." Austin had once seen Edward toss a salesguy out of his office over the man's use of the wrong Christian name.

"For all anybody knows, you left 'lanta on your own," Edward said. "You know Peach. She's a slick one, my girl is."

"What the hell are you talking about?"

"Talk to your wife. Y'all gonna have plenty of time to get friendly again."

"Brooke's my wife, and you know it. Where are you keeping her?"

But Edward only nodded toward the back of the house and stepped past Austin. "We kept up the place for y'all. It's like you never left. Peach thought you'd appreciate that."

"Edward, please." Austin touched the man's shoulder as he moved past him. "Brooke doesn't have anything to do with this, and she's pregnant. Let her go. Please."

"Girl is doing all right," Edward said. "Saw her 'fore I came over here."

So that's where Naomi went.

"Is Brooke in your house?" Austin asked.

Edward chuckled. "You know I ain't telling you that."

"Please, Edward. Let her go. You know it's the right thing to do."

"You gonna lecture me 'bout the right thing to do? You kept our grandson away from us for seven years." Sneering, Edward shrugged off Austin's hand. "Ran off without a word and we couldn't call the boy or even send him a goddamn birthday card. Now, you gotta sleep in that bed you made."

"Maybe you're right," Austin said. "But Brooke is innocent in all of this. We've been married for only a couple of years."

"The two shall become one flesh," Edward said. "Know where that comes from? Look it up."

"I never realized it until now, but you're as crazy as your daughter."

"Crazy like a fox." Edward grinned, showing his ultra-white dentures. "Gonna go fetch my grandson now."

As Edward shuffled along the hallway, Austin looked at the gun the older man carried on his shoulder, the muzzle pointed toward the ceiling. Edward was bigger than Austin, both in height and girth, but Austin knew he was physically stronger than the slump-shouldered man. What were his chances of wrestling the firearm away from Edward and, at gunpoint, forcing him to give up Brooke's location?

Austin stepped forward. Edward swung back around with startling agility. His hazel eyes glinted, as if he were aware of Austin's mutinous thoughts.

"Better be a good boy." Edward winked. He slipped his finger around the trigger guard. "I'm always two steps ahead of you."

42

Khari left the house with his grandfather, who wanted to take him on a tour of the orchard. Naturally, Khari was thrilled at the opportunity, and Austin didn't argue against it. What would have been the point? He had no authority over Khari in this place. All Naomi had to do was whisper a threat in his ear about harming Brooke, and he would give in. Here on the Xavier farm, he was Khari's dad in title only.

Standing on the porch, he watched the grandfather and grandson rumble away into the woods on the tractor. Khari waved at Austin as they trundled out of sight, and Austin returned a reluctant wave. His son seemed delirious with delight.

If only we could have done this the right way, Austin thought. *With a real custody agreement, like reasonable, sane people.*

But the Xaviers weren't reasonable people, and their sanity was questionable. He used to like and respect his in-laws. They were protective of Naomi and always took her side, but that was to be expected. What he hadn't expected was that they would go all in with her on a felonious plan that would send all of them to prison for a long time.

For all anybody knows, you left 'lanta on your own . . .

What had Edward meant by that remark?

Austin looked around. His gaze settled on the attached two-car garage. He realized he hadn't yet searched it. You wouldn't expect to find a cell phone hidden in such a place, and from what he recalled, they had never had a landline installed in there. He hadn't bothered to look.

Now, he approached the garage. A pair of decorative, wrought-iron handles were set flush in the center of the sectional door. He gripped them and tried to raise the door, but it didn't raise an inch.

Returning inside the house, he approached the interior door at the edge of the hallway. When he had lived here previously, access through that door had been controlled via a basic turn button, on the inside knob.

Now, opening that door from the inside required a key. He hadn't noticed that detail before.

What's Naomi hiding in there?

He hurried into the kitchen. In the junk drawer—it hadn't been emptied despite Austin's long absence—he found Naomi's old, laminated member ID card for the local YMCA.

It was time to attempt a trick he hadn't used since his bachelor days of renting a crappy apartment in downtown Albany.

He jiggled the card into the narrow juncture between the door and the frame, slid it down next to the knob. Leaning hard against the door, he wiggled the card back and forth.

After a few tries, the latch clicked.

Finally, I get something right.

He pulled the door open. The windowless garage was dense with shadows and smelled faintly of motor oil and exhaust fumes. He reached inside the doorway and flipped the light switch.

Brightness poured from the overhead fluorescent tubes.

He saw Naomi's white Mercedes-Benz SL550 convertible coupe parked nearest the interior door, chrome wheels sparkling. It was the same vehicle she had owned when they were married. Edward had given Naomi the car on her thirtieth birthday, triggering a sour memory for Austin. He had bought Naomi a gold herringbone chain for that occasion, spending over a thousand dollars, but his gift had looked cheap in comparison to her father's extravagant present. Back then, he had sometimes felt as if he were locked in a silent competition with Edward to win Naomi's affection.

He looked past the Mercedes. He did a double take. His own Dodge Durango was parked in the other spot.

For all anybody knows, you left 'lanta on your own . . .

"Shit," Austin muttered.

The audacity of Naomi's plan hit him like a slap to the face. He understood what happened: one of them had driven his SUV to Albany, while the rest of them had traveled there in another vehicle, probably the Winnebago.

For anyone investigating their disappearances, the SUV missing from his Marietta home would give the impression that Austin had left of his own will and taken Khari and Brooke with him, on a journey to parts unknown. He could imagine the headline attached to a story on a Facebook news feed: *Marietta man takes his wife and son and disappears in the night.*

A methodical police detective might probe deeper, but the missing vehicle would create multiple possibilities that had to be considered and researched, wasting time and taxpayer dollars, and depending on the department's caseload and the public's interest in the case, the police might look no further. *The family vanished—who knows why? We've got other, more important matters to handle.*

The urgency of their situation pressed on him, a tangible weight on his shoulders. He rounded the front of the Mercedes and opened the driver's-side door of the Durango. The interior light clicked on.

He searched the vehicle for the key fob. He looked inside the cupholder and checked the various storage compartments, including the glove box. He turned down the sun visors.

No key fob. No cell phone, either.

He popped open the rear cargo door. His roadside emergency kit was stored in a collapsible trunk container, but the kit didn't contain a phone.

He closed the trunk and slid back behind the wheel. Hoping that the key might be nearby and merely hidden from view, he pressed the "Start" button. If the fob were in range, the engine would kick on.

A message flashed on the dashboard's digital display: *Key fob not detected.*

"Dammit." He punched the steering wheel.

There had to be a way to hot-wire the SUV. Unfortunately, he had no idea how to do it. He was an accountant, not a car thief.

Besides, he wasn't going anywhere without Brooke. Leaving without her was out of the question.

Sitting behind the wheel, he scanned the dashboard, thinking. On impulse, he dug the owner's manual out of the glove box and skimmed it.

The manual featured several chapters about the "UConnect" system, which came standard on all vehicles. UConnect enabled Bluetooth access to his phone, SiriusXM, and other technology features.

It also provided GPS tracking, he read. In theory, law enforcement could use the GPS unit embedded in the SUV to track its location, if the vehicle was reported stolen.

But who was going to report the SUV stolen if Austin were missing, too?

He was right back to the annoyingly plausible story of him having left home willingly with his family.

Worse: without the key fob, and without a mobile signal paired to the UConnect system, he couldn't activate any of the SUV's other capabilities—including those that might allow him to summon help.

Finding his Durango was a meaningful discovery, but it hadn't moved them any closer to freedom.

43

Khari couldn't remember the last time he had been so excited.

He sat beside Grandpa—it felt weird to call someone "Grandpa" again and for it to be his *real* grandfather—as they rode the tractor around their family property. Grandpa drove him deep into their vast pecan orchard. The orderly rows of pecan trees seemed to stretch to the ends of the earth, lined up like an army of giant, attentive soldiers.

Grandpa had a gun propped up beside him, the muzzle pointed to the overcast sky. Khari didn't understand why he had brought the firearm. Were there wild animals wandering the farm that he needed to scare away? Was he planning on hunting later?

He wanted to ask about Miss Brooke, too. He really liked her; she had always treated him well, and no one had told him where she was and what was going on, and Dad was so upset about it.

Khari was conflicted about how all of this had happened. He knew Mom could go to prison again for what she had done, and that his grandparents and aunt could get into serious trouble, too. The prospect scared him. He was only starting to get to know his family again and couldn't bear the thought of them getting taken away.

He felt guilty about it. Like somehow, everything was his fault. Would Mom have abducted (he hated using that word, but it was the truth) Miss Brooke and Dad if he wasn't her son? Nope. His very existence had triggered her to do these things. It bugged him.

All the questions and worries bubbling inside him made his head hurt. He wanted to just enjoy being out there in the fresh air with Grandpa.

I'm only a kid, he thought. *What can I do about any of it? Grown-ups are going to do whatever they want anyway.*

"Someday, all of this is gonna be yours." Grandpa gestured toward the columns of trees. "Did you know that?"

"Wow," Khari said. "All of it?"

"All eighteen hundred and thirteen acres." Grandpa brought the tractor to a stop underneath the biggest pecan tree Khari had ever seen in his life. It was at least a hundred feet tall, with a massive span of branches.

The two of them were alone out there. Nature was their only companion: chirping birds and the sighing wind. During their tour, Grandpa had told him that they employed dozens of people during the harvest season, which began in October and ran through December. Since it was April, he required a much smaller crew to maintain the orchard, and those people had the weekend off.

"The orchard's been in our family for three generations now," Grandpa said. "We're gonna keep it in the family, too. That's a big reason why we wanted you here. You've gotta learn the Xavier family business."

The enormity of it all blew Khari's mind. He'd heard they had a farm, had seen it before, but he was too young to remember; to see it now as an older boy was awe-inspiring. To think that he would one day be responsible for such a place was incredible. Dad had worried that he would miss his friends, but usually all they did was play video games anyway. Playing video games seemed silly in comparison to the real-world obligations that awaited him on his family's empire.

"I want to learn everything," Khari said. He loved the idea that he would be entrusted with something of value, instead of being reminded that as a child—not even a teenager yet—he was too young to contribute anything worthwhile. Why did grown-ups always assume kids were ignorant? "This is more important than school, so please teach me everything."

"My Lord." Choking up, Grandpa fished a red handkerchief out of his front pocket and used it to blot his suddenly wet, glistening eyes. "Son, it's such a blessing to have you here at home with us, where you belong. You ain't got no idea how much we missed you."

Khari felt a knot of emotion tighten in his chest. To keep himself from crying, too, he pointed at the gun next to Grandpa.

"What's the gun for?" Khari asked. "Are there bears or something out here?"

"Bears?" Grandpa laughed—hearty, belly-shaking laughter that felt good to hear. "Naw, son. Ain't got no bears out here. What we mainly got are pests that can damage our crop, like tree squirrels."

"I hate squirrels. One got into our house once when I forgot and left the back door open. Dad had to chase it out with a broom."

"Yep, they're rambunctious for sure. Those little suckers climb up in the trees, chew the branches, and tear through damn near fifty pounds of nuts if you don't watch 'em. We spray a pesticide to keep 'em away, but every now and then I like to plink 'em with my rifle here." He placed the gun across his lap and laid his hands on it as if it were a valued treasure.

"Oh," Khari said. "You kill them?"

"It ain't a squirt gun." Grandpa studied Khari closely. "You ever fired a rifle?"

"In *Call of Duty*," Khari said.

"Huh?" Grandpa squinted.

"It's a video game," Khari added. "You play as a special-ops soldier, and you use different weapons."

"Don't know about that, but this here's the real thing." Grandpa patted the stock of the rifle. "Your daddy's a city boy, so I ain't surprised you haven't learned. I shot my first rifle when I was eight years old. You're twelve. We gotta get you caught up on a lot of things, boy, if you're gonna run this farm."

Khari nodded. "It'd be fun to learn."

"How about right now?" Grandpa asked.

Khari hadn't expected this, but before he could say anything, Grandpa set the rifle aside and climbed out of the tractor, then reached back and pulled the gun down with him.

"You coming?" he asked Khari.

Khari swallowed and hopped out of the cab. Grandpa waited for him several feet away from the tractor, the rifle lying across his shoulder like a baseball bat, his lips slanted in a crooked grin.

"You're one of us through and through," Grandpa said. "Goddamn, when I see you it's like I'm looking in a magic mirror and seeing myself sixty years ago."

"Genetics," Khari said.

"That's right, genetics." Grandpa seemed about to say something else, then looked away toward the trees, and for a beat he seemed to forget that Khari was there.

"Grandpa?" Khari asked.

Grandpa gave a start, swung back toward him. He lowered the gun from his shoulder, keeping the muzzle pointed away from Khari.

"All right, this here is a Ruger 10/22," Grandpa said. "Perfect for small-game hunting and for folks new to shooting. I can't think of a better way to get you started."

"It's only for shooting little animals?" Khari asked.

"It's still a gun, boy. You point this at a man and pull the trigger, he ain't gonna react like it's a love tap." Grandpa offered the rifle to him. "Here you go. Don't point it at nothing unless you intend to shoot it, always assume it's loaded—and keep your finger off the trigger 'til you're ready to fire."

Khari accepted the gun. It was heavier than he expected, as if its lethal potential imbued it with extra weight.

But it felt good in his hands. He caressed the fine wood grain running along the stock. What would his friends think if they could see him now? *Shove* Call of Duty *up your ass,* he thought. *I'm out here in the real world.*

He had been thinking he would ask Grandpa about Miss Brooke, but once Grandpa put the gun in his hands, the subject slipped out of Khari's mind like a penny out of a torn pocket.

"It seems brand new," Khari said.

"That's 'cause it is," Grandpa said. "Bought it just for you."

"It's mine?" Khari thought he missed what his grandfather had said.

"All yours." Grandpa grinned his lopsided smile. "Ready to learn how to use it?"

Khari thought he might explode from excitement. "Yeah!"

44

Brooke needed to pee so urgently it felt as if her bladder might rupture like a balloon if she didn't get release soon. After the family had surrounded her, pawing at her stomach as if she were the featured exhibit in a roadside circus freak show, they had abandoned her in the basement again, despite Brooke's pleas.

Before, all she had wanted was to keep her baby safe. Now, all she wanted was to urinate in a toilet. The six-pound fetus in her uterus pressed like a basketball against her bladder.

Her evolving hierarchy of needs was almost comical.

She screamed for help until her throat was raw. She didn't know how much time passed before she heard footsteps again: quick, feathery taps across the floor above her, reminding Brooke of a fleet-footed ballerina. It was a woman for sure, but which of them was it? Did it matter? All of them were dangerously unhinged.

The door creaked open. It was Karen, the mother. Perhaps an improvement over Naomi, but Brooke suspected the family matron had drugged her last night when she'd served the food.

"I need to pee, ma'am," Brooke said. "*Please*."

"Oh, don't I know it, Mama." Karen giggled and hurried down the steps. Underneath her right arm, she carried a blue plastic dish: a bedpan. In her left hand, she toted a roll of toilet paper.

Brooke had to go so badly she didn't care what the woman brought, so long as she didn't suffer the indignity of pissing on herself.

"Relax, dear." Karen approached. "Lie back on the bed there. I've done this a thousand times in my day. I was a nurse in the maternity ward at Albany Memorial Hospital."

Nodding, Brooke drew in a deep breath and lay back on the mattress, grabbed the sagging pillow to support her back. With the familiar manner of the nurse she said she was, Karen shifted Brooke's body, peeled down her panties, and put the bedpan in position.

"Ready when you are," Karen said.

Brooke let her bladder go. It felt so good to gain relief she thought she might cry with gratitude.

"Thank you," Brooke breathed.

Afterward, Karen thoroughly cleaned her with the tissue and pulled up Brooke's undergarments.

"I'm sorry this is happening," Karen said in a hushed tone, as if she worried a member of her family might overhear. "In my opinion, this ain't no way to treat an expectant mother."

As Brooke hauled herself upright, Karen went into the small bathroom on the other side of the cellar. She emptied the bedpan and the used tissues into the toilet; when she flushed it, Brooke heard water rushing through the plumbing with a thunderous clamor that made the concrete post in front of her vibrate.

When Karen ambled back into the main area, Brooke carefully regarded the woman as if seeing her for the first time, since her memories of last night's events were foggy at best. Karen was in her mid-sixties and quite attractive; she was an older version of Naomi. Her auburn hair was so long and thick that Brooke guessed it was a wig. The way that her breasts filled out her housedress, the plumpness of her lips, and her oddly synthetic smile made Brooke suspect Karen had gotten her share of cosmetic surgery.

Vanity runs in the family, Brooke thought.

But Karen might be reasonable. Unlike Naomi, she didn't have an axe to grind against Brooke in some delusional competition for Austin's heart.

"Let's go get you something to eat," Karen said. "And to drink, too. You ain't had no water in a while."

"Thank you, ma'am," Brooke said. "Where am I? No one's told me anything."

Karen hesitated. Then she shrugged, as if deciding no harm could come from sharing some information.

"You're at our farm in Albany," she said. "In one of our houses."

From her discussions with Austin, Brooke knew the Xavier family held a large amount of property in the Albany area, that they were people of means due to their pecan distribution business. She didn't understand why they would put their fortune at risk by holding a woman hostage.

Simply because people are rich doesn't make them law-abiding citizens, she reminded herself. In fact, the opposite might be true. Because they were rich, they might think they could get away with anything.

"Is Austin here, too?" Brooke asked. "And Khari?"

"The whole family is here," Karen said. "They're doing fine, uh-huh. Getting settled in with Peach."

Getting settled in. As if they had come here of their own will for a spring break adventure.

Karen headed for the staircase.

"Can you get my socks and shoes, please, ma'am?" Brooke asked. She nodded toward her bare feet. "My toes feel like icicles."

"Of course, dear." She grinned, and her smile had never looked more plastic. "Gotta keep Mama bear nice and comfy. Be right back."

Karen hurried up the staircase, went through the door, and closed it behind her.

I've got to find a way out of this, Brooke thought. Could she use Karen's apparent kindness to her advantage? Karen had indicated that she didn't agree with Brooke's current confinement. Would she be willing to take Brooke into another section of the house?

It struck Brooke what being thrown into a desperate situation could teach you about yourself. She had long believed herself to be without guile, a plain, honest person. But she was willing to tell one lie after another to

Karen if doing so would give her an edge.

The thirst to survive trumped all.

About ten minutes later, Karen returned carrying a plastic shopping bag with the Target logo printed on it, and a folding TV tray table, like the one Brooke's father used when he hunkered in front of the tube watching football while he ate dinner. She set up the table nearby, dropped the bag onto it, and retrieved several items from the bag: a turkey sandwich wrapped in plastic, a water bottle, Brooke's sneakers, and a pair of athletic socks. She'd also brought a fresh pair of undergarments and a clean maternity dress. Brooke recognized the items of clothing; they came from her own collection.

They searched through my things at the house, Brooke thought. The realization compounded her sense of violation.

It wasn't until then that she remembered that, last night, she had been wearing her wedding set, too. Now, her ring finger was naked. No doubt, Naomi had seen to stripping away that piece of jewelry.

"Here you go, honey," Karen passed her the food and the water bottle.

"Thank you." Brooke tore into the sandwich, took greedy slurps of water. "You're so kind, ma'am. I appreciate this."

"Certainly." Karen beamed at her.

"Is there any chance you can take me to another bedroom, upstairs?" Brooke asked. "This mattress is murdering my back."

"If it was up to me . . ." Karen blushed, shook her head. "Sorry, but it ain't. That's for Peach to decide."

Damn.

"But I can bring you some more pillows," Karen said.

"That would be great." Brooke finished off the sandwich, literally ate every crumb. She took another long chug of water. "I need to put on these shoes, get up, move around a little, change clothes. And I think I need to use that bathroom over there, please. Would that be okay, ma'am?"

"I guess so." Karen's eyes narrowed to slits. "In your condition, it ain't like you gonna run off, is it?"

"Slow as a turtle," Brooke agreed.

45

Brooke won private time in the bathroom, without the restraints.

You try anything sneaky and you won't be getting any more special privileges, Karen warned as she used a small key to unlatch the handcuffs. She dropped them onto the mattress. *Don't make me regret this, you hear?*

I promise on my new baby's heart, Brooke said, which she thought sounded appropriately sincere.

Karen had peeled the duct tape off Brooke's ankles, too. Brooke had spent a couple of minutes shuffling around the cellar, stretching her aching joints and sore muscles before she wandered into the bathroom.

Karen allowed her to shut the door behind her. The bathroom had a toilet bearing rusty water stains; a single vanity with an oval-shaped mirror in a tarnished silver frame, a hand towel hanging on a rack; a dingy shower curtain concealing a tub ringed with dust. It looked as if it hadn't been cleaned in years.

We happen to need a housekeeper . . .

The absurdity of Naomi's remark nearly made Brooke laugh.

Not on your life, girlfriend, Brooke thought.

Brooke changed clothes, put on socks and shoes, and washed her face and arms with warm water and the wafer of soap lying on the edge of the sink. Afterward, she felt almost human again.

There was a cabinet underneath the sink. Brooke opened it—the small door creaked—and peered inside.

It was a dank space draped in dusty cobwebs. She found a bottle of rubbing alcohol, half-full. A block of Ivory soap that looked as if it had sat in there for a decade. Nothing useful like, say, a fully charged cell phone.

Karen rapped on the door. "You all right in there, honey?"

"I'm fine." Brooke straightened, nudged the cabinet shut. "I'll be out in a few minutes."

Karen muttered something that Brooke couldn't hear. Brooke turned her attention to the tub.

A narrow, rectangular window was installed in the wall above the bathtub, the glass filmed with dust. Brooke twisted on the sink faucet to help mask any noises, carefully climbed into the tub, and stepped onto the rim of the basin, to get a better view of whatever lay beyond the window.

She cleared away grime with the palm of her hand and peered through the glass.

Probably only ten feet away, Naomi buzzed past Brooke's field of view driving a vehicle that looked like a souped-up golf cart. Brooke froze. If Naomi spotted her, her new privileges would promptly be canceled.

Naomi zoomed out of sight. Brooke's vantage point didn't offer any clue as to where Naomi was headed. The small window provided only a limited view of gray sky, grass, and trees.

Karen knocked on the door again. "I'm coming in. You decent?"

"One second, please."

Carefully, Brooke stepped off the tub and onto the tile floor. As she was turning off the running water in the sink, Karen opened the door. Her brows were furrowed.

"What the heck are you doing in here?" Karen asked.

"I took a whore bath," Brooke lied.

"A what?"

"Washed my pits, tits, and naughty bits with this towel here." Brooke indicated the towel draped on the edge of the sink. "I think I'll need a fresh one, ma'am."

"Oh." Karen laughed. "I never heard anyone say that before."

"I'm full of surprises," Brooke said.

Karen ushered her out of the bathroom. Brooke pointed to an upholstered chair heaped with junk that sat in a corner of the cellar.

"Can I sit on that chair, please, instead of lying on the floor?" Brooke touched her aching back. "I think it would feel so much better."

"Peach might not like it." Karen sucked in her bottom lip. "But heck, I gotta do what's right. We gotta look out for that baby, don't we?"

She touched Brooke's stomach. Brooke hated for strangers to touch her belly without asking permission, but she bit her tongue. She seemed to be earning this woman's trust and needed to stay on her good side, keep gaining concessions, keep loosening their hold over her.

And once Brooke found her opportunity, she was going to take full advantage.

46

Austin decided to leave the house and search for Brooke.

Naomi had warned him against leaving the farm, and he wasn't going to take that risk. But she hadn't said anything against him exploring the property.

Khari was still out with his grandfather. Edward hadn't said when he would bring the boy back.

There was a magnetic notepad affixed to the front of the refrigerator, where, during their marriage, they used to add items for their weekly grocery list. Austin used the attached black marker to scribble a message: *Went out for walk. Khari with your dad. Be back soon, Austin.* He left the note not out of thoughtfulness, but because he didn't need Naomi flipping out and harming Brooke because she assumed he had left to contact the police.

He stepped out the front door and into the overcast afternoon. He heard cawing birds, a gentle wind ruffling the shrubbery, a carpenter bee buzzing around the eaves. What he didn't hear: cars, sirens, airplanes, and other signs of civilization. Under ordinary circumstances, the sounds of nature would have calmed his spirit, but now, the rural soundscape reminded him of how far away they were from help, and triggered fears of him ever escaping this place with Brooke and Khari and resuming their old lives.

He approached the gravel roadway and started jogging.

The expansive farm was home to multiple single-family residences. Austin wagered that they were keeping Brooke at her parents' house. It was the largest of all the houses and included a basement.

As he jogged at a brisk pace, he didn't see anyone else at all. He might have been the only surviving human traveling across a planet struck by an apocalyptic event. When he and Naomi were married, he would go on runs around the farm every day, usually early in the mornings, and had loved getting out into the fresh air with only his thoughts to keep him company. Those runs had been therapeutic, a means to find peace in his otherwise chaotic life.

Now there he was, running again, and he was hoping to find a measure of peace, again: he would not rest until he confirmed Brooke was alive and unharmed.

He had run these paths so many times that he could have traveled them blindfolded. But when he followed a bend in the road and saw the big house standing in the distance, he thought he had made a wrong turn somewhere.

The big Colonial-style farmhouse stood on a plot of land shaded by mature pines and maples, but the home looked as if it had fallen into neglect. Shingles were missing from the roof, like plucked feathers. Unchecked kudzu crawled like a cancerous tumor along the white clapboard exterior. The rooster weathervane atop the house had been snapped in half and wobbled in the wind.

Had hard times finally reached the Xaviers, too?

As he neared, he saw the Winnebago parked in the driveway in front of the three-car garage, alongside a Ford F-150 and a Cadillac sedan. The luxurious motor home was in better condition than their house.

The gravel road diverged into three paths, with one of the branches leading toward the residence. Austin left the gravel to cut through the thick, knee-high grass. As he got closer, it seemed prudent to stay off the road in case one of the Xaviers wandered outdoors.

A six-foot-high, white wooden fence that badly needed to be repainted enclosed the large backyard. Austin peered between the long planks.

The yard was trimmed, but empty. A wicker patio set stood on the spacious wooden deck, the seat cushions bleeding stuffing, as if squirrels had chewed into them. An extra-large Big Green Egg grill that used to be Edward's pride and joy sat at the edge of the deck, the trademark green paint dulled from exposure to the elements.

Skirting the fence, he reached the eastward side of the house. On that side, he located two basement windows. Kneeling, he looked closer.

Heavy curtains had been drawn across the windowpanes, concealing the cellar.

Straightening, Austin cursed under his breath.

He would have to go inside.

47

The long, wide veranda wrapped around the front of the farmhouse. Several balusters in the decorative iron railing were either missing or spotted with rust, yet four fresh pots of ferns hung from the awning. Austin suspected the plants were Naomi's handiwork; she had hung the same greenery outside their house.

No, not their *house,* Austin corrected himself. He didn't dare to slip back into the old mindset of someone who lived here. Doing so would be fatal to summoning the strength to get the hell out of there.

The trio of Adirondack chairs standing on the veranda were empty.

Austin climbed the short staircase and reached the exterior storm door. An elegantly designed decal with family initial, the letter *X*, was attached to the center of the frosted glass, the letter framed by an intricate weave of wrought iron.

It looked as if the interior door beyond was open.

He wasn't surprised to find the open door. The Xaviers regarded the farm as their personal kingdom where they were safe from the threats that existed in the outside world.

The storm door opened quietly. He crossed the threshold.

Shadows draped the interior. The house smelled of a recently applied disinfectant, a lemony fragrance. Although the exterior of the residence needed work, as he crept along the entry hall, he found the interior was organized and clean. He didn't see any clutter; the hardwood floor glistened; family photographs, of which many hung on the walls, were as neatly positioned as if they had been aligned with a level.

He didn't hear anyone inside. But he didn't risk assuming the Xaviers were gone, either. The two-story house featured five bedrooms, a den, a study, a living room, a dining area, a basement. To get to the basement, he had to enter the kitchen.

The kitchen was ahead, on his right. Moving slowly, he entered.

The room was full of shadow, but he saw nothing out of the ordinary. It looked much like he remembered. How many meals had he eaten in here? His memories of this house, of which most were pleasant, pressed upon the cold reality of his present circumstances.

The cellar door was on the other side, next to the refrigerator. Stepping toward the door, he happened to glance at the pegboard hanging on the wall near the telephone. The family kept their keys hanging on hooks attached to that board.

He saw the key fob to his Dodge SUV.

Without hesitation, Austin pocketed the fob. Would they realize he had taken it? He didn't know, or care. It belonged to him, and he had no intention of hanging around here any longer. He was going to find Brooke and get the hell out of there.

Taking Khari away presented a different challenge, but he didn't have time to think about that.

The cellar door opened without resistance.

A narrow flight of wooden steps dropped into darkness. He found the light switch and flicked it on. Fluorescent light poured into the stairwell.

He didn't hear anyone make a sound in response to the lights turning on. It concerned him. If Brooke was kept down there, she would have made a noise in response.

Unless they've gagged her.

After pulling the door shut behind him, he descended the staircase. It was an unfinished basement, mostly, that the family used for storage. He saw a water heater, the furnace. Shelving stocked with items. Assorted odds and ends.

But no Brooke. They had to be keeping her elsewhere, in either another section of the house, or a different house entirely.

Dammit.

Somewhere upstairs, a door slammed. He heard shuffling footsteps.

Austin's heart lurched. He doubled back to the staircase and hurried up as quietly as he could.

When he emerged in the kitchen, he saw Charlotte standing on the other side of the kitchen, near the pantry. She had a gigantic bag of fried pork skins tucked underneath her arm.

She gawped at him, redness flushing her light brown complexion. "Austin, you ain't supposed to be here."

"I need to find my wife. Where is she?"

"I'm telling Peach." Charlotte reached for the walkie-talkie she wore clipped to her waist.

"Wait!" Austin stepped forward, hand raised in supplication. "Please. I only want to make sure Brooke is okay. I haven't seen her or talked to her."

"I've seen her." Charlotte nodded. "She's doing fine."

"Where is she?" He took another step forward. "You're not like your sister. I know that. You're a reasonable person. Tell me where I can find my wife. Please."

Charlotte's lips quivered; unshed tears glistened in her large brown eyes. She put the bag of pork skins on the counter and pulled her fingers through her hair.

She's going to break, he thought. *She's the weak link in the family, and always has been.*

Austin heard another door open. It sounded like the front storm door. Then, he heard fast-moving footsteps coming down the hallway.

Sighing, Austin turned, knowing who he would find.

"There you are, love," Naomi said. She looked from Austin to Charlotte and back to Austin. A grin creased her face, the smile of a wise mother who had caught a child making mischief. "What did I miss?"

48

Hours later, as dusk settled over the farm, and rain began falling, Austin sat on the sofa in the living room of the house he had formerly shared with Naomi. A glass of cabernet sauvignon stood on the coffee table in front of him, the wine untouched. Freshly showered and shaved, Austin wore khakis, a polo shirt, and a pair of loafers, all items taken from his home in Marietta.

Austin sat so stiffly on the couch cushions, back straight as a board, that he might have been a model posing for a portrait artist. But his pulse raced.

From the kitchen came the sounds of dishes clattering and culinary tools clinking. The aromas of cooking onions and melting butter traveled through the cool air. An old-school Panasonic turntable in the hallway spun a Miles Davis album, *Kind of Blue,* the trumpet's plaintive cries warbling through the rooms.

Naomi was busy preparing a "date night" dinner: a savory, home-cooked meal for the two of them. Khari was spending the evening at his grandparents' house.

Austin still didn't know what had happened to Brooke: he hadn't seen her, spoken to her, or laid eyes on any evidence that she was even alive. But when Naomi discovered him at her parents' house, she had offered him a deal.

Spend the night with me, Austie. Let's be together like we were before. Then we'll let you spend some private time with your baby mama.

Without any leverage to counter her offer, Austin accepted her proposal.

I've got to only get through the night, he thought, as he checked the clock on the wall for perhaps the tenth time in the past five minutes. *One night with my ex-wife, a woman I used to love and crave like food. I can do this. Go through the motions. Smile, eat, compliment her cooking, laugh at her jokes. I can do this. Think about Brooke.*

But Naomi was expecting much more than an appreciative dinner guest. Every path she laid before him that evening was leading to the master bedroom, like the yellow brick road routing to Oz. What was he going to do then?

He didn't want to dwell on it.

He still had the key fob to his SUV. Naomi hadn't realized he had stolen it from her parents' kitchen. He had placed the fob in a hidey-hole that he had used during their marriage, when he wanted to keep small gifts hidden from her. He was confident that she wouldn't find it—but he wasn't sure when he would get to use it. He couldn't cut and run without Brooke.

One stride at a time, he told himself. Back when he competed in track, that was the mindset required to win a race. *Make every stride count. Don't look too far ahead. Nail the next stride.*

After a final trumpet warble, the hallway turntable rotated into silence. Austin might not have noticed the cessation of the music if Naomi hadn't called out: "Put on another record, Austie! Something romantic!"

Something romantic. Jesus. Is this really happening?

Like a man in a fever dream, Austin rose from the sofa and shuffled into the hallway. The turntable's tonearm had slid back into its rest position. He looked at the record player as if studying an ancient artifact, but he suddenly remembered: this used to belong to his aunt Valerie. When Aunt Val had died, it had been one of the valuables he had salvaged from her house, including a collection of vinyl albums, many of which now occupied the glass-fronted oak cabinet underneath the record player.

He had left behind these things when he had moved out seven years ago, and he couldn't remember why. But he remembered rushing out of the house as if fleeing an imminent hurricane, packing only what felt essential, tossing everything into a U-Haul and getting the hell out of there.

He got on his knees so he could scrutinize the album collection. As he knelt,

Naomi strutted into the hallway. She wore house shoes, and a white apron over a plain blouse and shorts. She'd promised to "throw on something sexy" before they sat down to dinner.

She edged into his personal space. She put her hand on the back of his head, trailed her fingers from his crown to the base of his neck in a single feathery stroke.

It was a touch that used to make him shiver with desire, but now, all he wanted was to shove her away. Gritting his teeth, he tolerated her touching. *Get through the night. Think about Brooke.*

"How about some Sade?" she said.

He found Sade's *Love Deluxe* album and fished it out of the cabinet.

"Good boy." She gently tugged his right earlobe, another of those keys she had often used to unlock his body. "All of this is adding up to a night you won't forget, baby. Believe that."

She sashayed back into the kitchen. Austin switched out the records and put the tonearm on the edge of the new selection. The first track, "No Ordinary Love," began to play. Naomi parroted the vocals in a husky contralto that Austin wanted to hate, but grudgingly accepted was impressive for an amateur singer.

Arms crossed over his chest, he leaned against the kitchen doorway and watched his ex-wife. She twirled from one cabinet to another as she crooned. Her braids, pulled into a ponytail, swayed along her slender back and shoulders.

She noticed him watching and crooked her finger at him in a come-hither gesture. "Come dance with me."

"What?"

"Get over here and *groove* with me. You still got moves. I know it. You've always had that natural rhythm."

"I'm not in the mood for dancing, Naomi."

"Remember our deal." She rocked her hips, but cunning flickered in her eyes. "Gimme the night you promised."

Austin felt like a man walking a plank suspended above a shark-infested sea as he went toward her. *Think about Brooke.*

Naomi put her hands on his shoulders and kissed him lightly on the lips. Then she whirled around and ground her hips against his groin in a sinuous twirl.

"You know you want this." She took his hands, placed them on her waist, and thrust her behind deep into him.

Despite every element of his mind and heart rebelling against this violation, Austin's body had its own, baser intentions. A shiver washed over him as the telltale bulge in his khakis grew.

Dammit, think about Brooke.

A timer on the oven chimed. Naomi whirled, stepped away from him with a knowing smile.

"To be continued," she said. "I've gotta go get dressed. Dinner will be served in a few minutes, love."

49

Naomi ushered Austin into the dining room. The room was spotless, the cherrywood table and matching chairs looking brand new—they practically were, Austin recalled, so rarely had they been used during their marriage. They typically would eat in there only on special occasions.

The table was set with white candles standing in candelabra, two fine bone china place settings with chargers, and cloth napkins bound in silver rings. Naomi lit the candles with a lighter and insisted on Austin sitting at the head of the table. He had forgotten his wineglass in the living room, and she brought it to him.

"Don't worry about a thing." She touched his shoulder. "I'm gonna take care of you tonight. This is a celebration, baby."

"A celebration of what?"

"Your homecoming, obviously. Our reunion."

She's insane, Austin thought. *Completely.*

But visually, Naomi was transformed. She had changed into an alluringly cut black maxi dress. She had replaced her house shoes with stylish black pumps, freshened her makeup, added some jewelry (including her wedding set), let down her braids, and put on perfume, a familiar fragrance he recalled she would wear on date nights.

Austin had given up asking himself if he were dreaming, or if he were suffering through a hyper-realistic, drug-induced hallucination. Those would have been pat answers.

The truth was that Naomi was unhinged. When had she gone full lunatic? Lost her grip on reality?

As he sat there with his clammy palms in his lap, Naomi brought serving dishes from the kitchen to the dining room. She had prepared a full spread: buttered corn bread muffins, pan-seared lamb chops, scalloped potatoes, roasted brussels sprouts, glazed carrots. A dizzying amount of food, none of which he had any interest in eating, but despite his thoughts on the matter, his stomach rumbled loudly enough to elicit a smirk from Naomi.

"This home cookin's got you salivating, hmm?" she asked. "You know I'm a woman of God, honey. Let's bless the meal and then you can dig in."

He stared at her. "I can't."

"We'll do it together." She stepped behind his chair. Her perfume enveloped him. She put her hands on his shoulders and slid her fingers down his arms, until she finally grasped his limp hands in hers and gripped them tightly.

"Bless this reunion, bless this meal, dear Lord," she said in a solemn tone. "In Jesus' name we pray, amen."

Out of reflex, Austin muttered an *amen*.

"That wasn't so hard now, was it?" She squeezed his hands again, kissed the back of his neck, and took the seat on his right. "Now, let's eat!"

Dinner was better than it had any right to be. Every item was perfectly seasoned, expertly cooked. Austin mechanically shoveled food into his mouth and sipped wine, while Naomi chattered endlessly, like an actress performing a monologue. She had always been capable of holding a conversation with little input from him except for the occasional nod, grunt, or mumbled *uh-huh*.

He barely registered a word she spoke; she might well have been babbling in a foreign tongue for all he knew or cared. He was thinking about Brooke. Was she okay? Had she eaten? Was she in pain? How was the baby? What would he tell her whenever these lunatics allowed him to see her?

How was he going to get her out of there?

He was using a steak knife to slice through the lamb chop. What if he took that blade and pressed it against Naomi's neck and said he'd kill her if she didn't order her family to free Brooke at that very minute? Could he do that? Would the Xaviers believe his threat? Was he capable of such violence?

They didn't believe he had it in him, did they? Weak, compliant Austin, the boring accountant. Why else was Naomi sitting there twittering like a goddamn bird without a concern in the world for her safety? They thought he was weak. Impotent. Gutless.

Weak ass, a voice said in his mind. It was Naomi's voice, full of mocking. *Weak ass, you ain't gonna do a damn thing. I own you. You do what I say.*

He tightened his grip on the knife handle.

Naomi didn't notice the tension that coursed through him. When she fell into one of her manic states, she literally seemed incapable of shutting up. She gestured wildly, bracelets jangling, hazel eyes glittering like shiny coins.

He could envision the murder happening, clear as a picture on a flat-screen TV: he could swipe the blade right across her soft, pretty neck, severing the carotid artery. She would gush crimson like a busted fire hydrant. Then he would leave, drive to her parents' house, and take care of them, too, if they didn't hand over his wife. *I'll kill you all.*

Naomi was talking, talking, talking, a gushing storm of brain-numbing words. As he clutched the knife tighter, his knuckles brightened as white as ivory.

Can I do it?

Then his gaze fell across the framed photo standing inside the glass-fronted china cabinet next to the table. A family portrait from nine or ten years ago. Austin, Naomi, and Khari. Khari was only a toddler and sat on his mother's lap, grinning, as if there were nowhere else in the world he would rather be.

Could he kill his son's mother and ever face his son again?

The answer to the question was so obvious that he immediately let the knife clatter onto the plate.

"It looks like you're ready for dessert!" Naomi chirped.

Heart thumping, Austin blinked as if emerging from a nap. "Huh?"

"Be right back, hon." She squeezed his knee, rose from her chair, left the room.

He wasn't a killer. He wasn't a man of violence. He was a go-along-to-get-along kind of guy.

A lamb, trapped in a den of wolves.

He put his hands in his lap and lowered his head.

After a few minutes, Naomi returned with dessert.

50

Charlotte, not Karen, brought Brooke's dinner.

Brooke was circling the cellar when the woman opened the basement door and came downstairs bearing a Tupperware container and a bottle of water. Pacing helped Brooke to think, kept the gears of her mind churning. Also, her back ached from when she'd been chained to that concrete pillar and allowed only to lie on the lumpy mattress. Alternating between walking, stretching, and sitting for brief periods on the upholstered chair helped to dull some of the pain.

Until Charlotte's arrival, Brooke estimated she had been alone for four or more hours. Naturally, when Karen left her shackle-free and had departed the basement, Brooke had carefully and as stealthily as possible (*true* stealth didn't seem possible when you were as pregnant as she) climbed the stairs and pressed her ear against the door.

She hadn't heard anything on the other side. After several beats of silence passed, she believed she might be alone in this hell house, wherever it was.

She tested the doorknob. It was locked, of course; the keyhole was on the other side of the door. If her captors were careful, they probably had a deadbolt lock on there and perhaps a security chain, too.

She pressed against it with her shoulder, to little effect. Doing so nearly caused her to lose her balance, and that scared her. She didn't dare fall down the steps, and promptly gave up on that flimsy plan.

There was a lot of junk in the basement, but no tools, and nothing that could be improvised as a device that would jimmy a door open.

Which left her with only one viable option: she would have to take advantage of an opportunity when Karen visited her again.

She was so tired, her entire body sore. She missed her bed; she missed their house. Had anyone back at home called the police yet? Surely, her mom would have tried to call her by then, would have been alarmed at the lack of response, would have tried to call Austin, and that failing, too, would be on the hunt for answers. This situation could not last.

But she couldn't shuffle around waiting on a rescue, not from the police, not from Austin, not from *anyone*. She had to take matters into her own hands.

The safety of her child depended on it.

When Charlotte arrived with the food, not Karen, Brooke wasn't sure whether that would be a good thing for her or not. She'd had limited interaction with the older sister at dinner the prior night. She seemed nice enough at the time, but then she was participating in this wicked scheme of theirs, too, wasn't she?

So she wasn't that nice. She had to be considered an enemy.

"Hello there!" Charlotte rounded the bottom of the staircase. She wore a frumpy housedress and flats. Her bushy hair was pulled back from her broad, but unremarkable face. She hadn't inherited the good looks that the other Xavier women possessed in abundance, and Brooke wondered how that had affected her, as both Naomi and Karen had enough vanity about themselves for a whole tribe. Had Charlotte been overlooked in the family? And if so, how could Brooke use that to her own benefit?

"Hi." Brooke stopped pacing. "Your mother was sweet enough to let me walk around. It's not as though I went full Hulk and broke free."

"Oh, I know that." Charlotte giggled. "Mama told me, but we didn't tell Peach." Charlotte lowered her voice to a conspiratorial whisper. "It's our little secret."

"It's safe with me." Brooke mimed zipping her lips shut and tossing away the key, as if she were in on the plan, a co-conspirator in her own captivity. "You brought me dinner? How sweet of you."

"Yup." Charlotte placed the plastic container and bottled water on the TV tray that her mother had brought earlier. She dragged the tray closer to the upholstered chair. "We got fried catfish, grits, and collards. All homemade. I threw in some of my famous peach cobbler, too."

"Sounds delish. I take it you really are the baker in the family."

Charlotte beamed. "I hope you like it. I woulda brought some ice cream but I worried it would melt on the drive over here, sorry."

"Not a problem." Brooke shuffled to the chair, peeled off the container's lid. Wonderful aromas issued from within, and her mouth literally watered. She licked her dry lips. "You came from your parents' house?"

"It's a hop, skip, and a jump from this old dump. My uncle Charlie used to live here but he passed on, oh, like five years ago, I think?"

Brooke made mental notes: she was alone there. But it wasn't far from her captors' residence.

"Do you mind if I eat while you're here?" Brooke asked. "And *please* stay. I'm dying for company."

"Sure." Charlotte grinned. She looked around for somewhere to sit, didn't see a spot, and leaned against the thick pillar that Brooke had been chained to earlier, the post creaking as she rested her weight against it.

Brooke sat and studied the container. Generous portions occupied the various compartments. They also had included packets of Texas Pete hot sauce, napkins, and utensils. Alas, the fork and knife were plastic and would not amount to suitable weapons.

"You included hot sauce," Brooke said. "That was considerate."

"My idea, honey. You can't eat catfish without the hot sauce."

Brooke was ravenous and could have shoveled the food in her mouth like a machine, but she forced herself to slow down and speak to Charlotte between bites. She had heard the jingle of keys when Charlotte came down the staircase, and she heard them when Charlotte shifted around as she leaned against the post. Those keys undoubtedly rested in the side pocket of her housedress.

Charlotte had a walkie-talkie clipped to her pocket, too. Brooke didn't see a cell phone; Karen hadn't carried a phone, either.

As Brooke ate, she lobbed questions at Charlotte. The woman appeared to be in her early forties and lived with her parents, and she worked a low-level admin job in their pecan farming business. She had no significant other, no children, and either no prospects or interest in acquiring one or the other. She was a simple woman who enjoyed baking for family and friends, reading cozy mysteries, and watching TV soap operas.

"I know I sound like an old maid," Charlotte said with a self-deprecating chuckle and a shrug. "Especially to a lady like you. I saw them pictures of you in your house. You and Peach are in that same glam class. Betcha had fellas swooning over you your whole life."

"You've got me beat in the baking department." Brooke indicated her dish. "I sure could go for another helping of that cobbler—I've got out of control, pregnant lady cravings. Is there more?"

That made Charlotte grin. "I could run back to the house and get you some. It ain't no trouble at all."

"With vanilla ice cream on top this time?" Brooke asked. She turned on her best smile. "Pretty please?"

"You got it, honey. Gimme fifteen minutes."

Charlotte pushed away from the support post and ambled to the staircase. She climbed the steps, opened the door. Shut it and locked it.

Brooke drained the bottle of water, and then set aside both the bottle and the container.

She had fifteen minutes to plot her escape.

51

Driving through the evening rain, Charlotte parked the Gator XUV in front of her dead uncle Charlie's old house. She shut off the engine and the headlights, but left the key in the ignition, as she always did.

In a Tupperware dish sitting inside the insulated bag on the passenger seat, she had packed a huge portion of peach cobbler: plenty more for Brooke, and plenty for herself. She'd included a half-gallon tub of vanilla ice cream she grabbed out of their deep freezer, too, the tub solid as a brick. Additionally, she'd brought a scoop, bowls, spoons, and more napkins.

Mama had asked her where she was going. *Me and Brooke are getting acquainted,* Charlotte had said. *I think she and I are gonna be good friends.*

Mama had rolled her eyes and waved Charlotte away, but the truth was, Charlotte wanted Brooke to like her. Probably, that wasn't what Peach wanted, but Charlotte couldn't help it. Brooke was pregnant for God's sake, and most of all, she seemed like a genuinely good person. If it were up to Charlotte, Brooke wouldn't even be there.

But it ain't up to me, Charlotte thought as she shuffled to the front door, the insulated bag swinging from her shoulder. *I never get to decide anything.*

She loved her little sister dearly and was glad she was out of prison and all, but Charlotte missed the quiet times her family had been enjoying before Peach came home. Wherever Peach went, drama followed, like a shadow. She had been like that since she was a child when she would start fights in school with other children. *Oh, you're Naomi's sister,* teachers would say and shake their head whenever they met Charlotte, and you just knew what they were thinking. *Your sister's a hellion and I feel bad for you.*

Look at this mess they were in now. Kidnapping the whole family! It was all Peach's doing. She'd been in prison for so long she had picked up true criminal tendencies and now she had dragged the whole family down into her sordid underworld. Daddy went along with it 'cause he was dying and felt guilty for Peach going to prison. Mama did whatever Daddy wanted. And Charlotte . . .

Well, she only wanted to get along with folks, that was all. A family had to stick together through thick and thin. If you weren't loyal to your closest family members, what did you have?

That was why Charlotte, as bad as she felt about it, would never let Brooke go free. She'd give her food and desserts and let her be comfortable, but no way was she going against her family's wishes and letting her walk out of that basement, pregnant or not.

Once inside the dimly lit, junk-filled house, Charlotte ambled to the cellar door. She unlocked it, pulled it open.

"I'm back!" Charlotte started down the steps, twirling the keys on her index finger. "Brought you more cobbler and ice cream, like I promised!"

Brooke didn't respond, and once Charlotte got halfway down the steps, she could see why. The woman was kneeling on the mattress next to the support column in the middle of the basement. She had one hand on her stomach and another on the pillar. Her face was pinched with distress.

"Oh God." Charlotte's stomach dropped. "Is it something with the baby?"

Brooke nodded, her lips quivering. She reached toward Charlotte, as if she desperately needed support. Without thinking, knowing only that she needed to help this poor woman, Charlotte dropped the bag and keys on the TV tray, and hurried to Brooke.

Then things happened rapidly. Brooke seized Charlotte's wrist and yanked it toward her, and Charlotte didn't resist. She didn't know what was happening, but she thought the woman was panicking 'cause she was about to have her baby or something. Brooke snapped something cold onto her wrist, and Charlotte looked down and realized it was a handcuff.

Charlotte stammered. "What the—"

Brooke had both her hands on Charlotte by then, and she seized Charlotte's index finger and bent it back. Pain roared through Charlotte in a white-hot sheet. Screaming, she staggered and toppled face-first onto the mattress like a boxer dropped by an uppercut.

Why . . . I only wanted to be nice . . .

Her finger hurt so badly it took her several seconds to summon the energy to look up. Through a veil of tears, Charlotte saw Brooke had scooted away from her. She clutched Charlotte's walkie-talkie in her hand. She had taken advantage of Charlotte's temporary weakness and relieved her of the radio as smoothly as a pickpocket on a Brooklyn subway.

Charlotte tried to get up, but the handcuff, and its accompanying chain looped around the concrete pillar, held her back like a mutt tied to a steel post.

"You bitch!" Charlotte shrieked. "I was bringing you cobbler and ice cream!"

Grim-faced, Brooke struggled to her feet. She shuffled to the other side of the basement and plucked the keys off the TV tray; then she opened the insulated bag, checked its contents, shrugged, and tossed it over to Charlotte.

"Thank you for trying to be nice," Brooke said. "But you're still on their side, and I care only about keeping my baby safe."

Charlotte shoved her free hand deep into her pocket. She had her butterfly knife—she always had the blade. Brooke had fooled her, but she hadn't taken the weapon.

"I got a cell phone in my pocket, too," Charlotte said. "I'll give it to you if you give me back the keys. Come here."

Brooke's gaze narrowed. "You're lying."

Charlotte flicked out the blade and flung it toward Brooke. Brooke turned to dodge the flying stiletto, but she was too slow. It clipped her thigh good enough to rip a scream out of her.

"Goddamn you!" Brooke clutched her leg.

"Peach is gonna kill you." Charlotte grinned through her tears. "We're all gonna kill you now, bitch."

52

Her wounded right leg singing an aria of agony, Brooke dragged herself up the stairs. Despite the pain, she reminded herself that if she hadn't moved when the crazy sister had tossed the pocketknife, the blade would have punctured her stomach. Perhaps maternal instinct had compelled her to spin at that crucial moment.

Keep my baby alive and unharmed.

Desperation had inspired Brooke to hatch her escape plan: she absolutely could *not* spend a night locked in that basement, rolling around on that dirty mattress, her back on fire. Karen had left behind those handcuffs and Brooke knew she had to use them. Charlotte had lowered her guard by going back to fetch more cobbler, and Brooke was determined to seize the opportunity, whether by guile or by force. She had never fought anyone in her life, but she would have scratched out Charlotte's eyes with her bare hands if that had been necessary to get free.

When Brooke finally reached the top of the steps, she stumbled across the threshold. She had the blood-smeared knife the woman had hurled at her, the walkie-talkie, the keys.

Now all she needed was a helicopter to take her to a hospital, she thought with a grim smile.

Below, Charlotte screamed a litany of blood-chilling threats that belied her formerly genial nature. Did a tendency for pathological violence run in this family's DNA?

Brooke slammed the door, muffling the woman's voice. She locked it, too.

How much time would pass before the other members of Charlotte's family reached out to check on their daughter's whereabouts? It might be an hour. It might be ten minutes. Brooke had to assume that time wasn't on her side.

Charlotte had confided that the house in which she was held captive had belonged to a deceased uncle. Dull light issued from dusty ceiling fixtures, and as Brooke scanned the narrow hallway and rooms beyond, she assumed no one had bothered to sort through the place since the man's death; and it was clear that during his life, he had been a hoarder. Junk was everywhere, in a chaotic profusion.

Her leg burned. She navigated to the kitchen, winding through mildewing piles of assorted items: books, newspapers, overflowing boxes and crates bearing thousands of miscellaneous items that looked as if they'd been salvaged from flea markets and garage sales and dumped onto the floor.

On a wobbly table in the kitchen, she found a dust-filmed, unopened roll of paper towels. She tore it open.

Leaning against the kitchen counter, Brooke lifted the hem of her maternity dress and used the towels to soak up the blood on her right leg, wincing as she touched the cut. She assessed her injury. The knife had barely missed the femoral artery.

Luck, again, was on her side. But for how long?

Across the kitchen, a telephone was attached to the wall, almost hidden by a pile of moldy phone books that leaned like the Tower of Pisa. Brooke dragged herself to it, the handset coming away from the receiver with a strand of spiderwebs.

The line was dead. Rescue would not be that easy.

She tucked the paper towels under her arm and found a half-bath off the hallway. She had to nudge aside a pile of crates to squeeze through the doorway. When she flipped the light switch, a fat, furry spider leaped out of the dirty sink like a jack-in-the-box. Brooke bit back a scream.

When she turned the faucet handle, cold, rusty water trickled from the spout. She didn't dare use it to cleanse her wound and risk an infection. Digging in the medicine cabinet behind the mirror, she found a bottle of rubbing alcohol and an expired tube of antibacterial ointment.

Rubbing alcohol, wonderful. This was going to hurt like hell. But beggars can't be choosers, she reminded herself.

She dampened a wad of the paper towels with a few drops of the antiseptic and dabbed the towels against the cut. She gasped. The searing pain was every bit as bad as she thought it was going to be, tears trickling from her eyes.

Next, she applied a generous glob of the salve and rubbed it across the wound. She wrapped up by tearing open a package containing an adhesive bandage and taping it to her leg.

Time to get out of here.

Downstairs, Charlotte continued screaming, her voice ragged. Brooke tamped down any concern she might have felt for the woman. Her crazy family could rescue her.

Moving cautiously, Brooke opened the house's front door.

It was raining, water plinking onto the eaves and gurgling through gutters. A weak light illuminated the narrow porch. Beyond the circle of light, darkness reigned—the kind of deep night that you found only when you departed the city for the country. The house stood in a small clearing amid a thicket of elms and maples. A gravel road wound away from the house and led deep into the trees.

Now that she was finally out of the confines of the claustrophobia-inducing cellar, the outside world felt huge.

She was glad she wore her sneakers, but the very idea of walking, perhaps for miles, made her feet ache. And it *would* be a walk, not a run; her wounded leg and her general discomfort and fatigue canceled any thoughts of a speedy escape.

Then she noticed the green and yellow utility vehicle parked on the other side of the bushes, and for the first time since this nightmare had begun, she smiled.

53

When it was all over, Austin showered.

Water that was one degree short of too scalding to endure rained over him. Head lowered, hands braced against the ceramic tile wall, feet spread, Austin let the purifying heat scourge him, as if by doing so, he could also cleanse his soul, and his memories, of what he had done.

He had given Naomi exactly what she demanded. All the while, he had thought of Brooke, keeping her face in his mind like a lighthouse beacon on a dark horizon. Although he would never speak of this night to his wife, thoughts of her had given him the strength to endure the evening.

If he were another kind of guy, he would have had an entirely different take on things. Naomi was gorgeous, obviously; more than that, she was an eager, imaginative lover. Handcuffs, honey, whipped cream, strawberries, chocolate syrup, black leather, masks—she had dug deep into her bag of bedroom tricks, and another kind of man would have raced back into that bedroom for round two like a meth addict reaching for the pipe again.

But he wasn't that kind of guy. Maybe he was old-fashioned, but he took his marriage vows seriously. Breaking his vow of fidelity was as agonizing as snapping a bone in his leg, regardless of his justification for his actions.

But it was over. It was Naomi's turn to hold up her end of their agreement. She had promised him an audience with Brooke, and he needed her to keep her word.

Austin shut off the shower. Outside the enclosure, he toweled dry. He dressed in the clean clothes he had brought into the master bath: jeans, short-sleeve shirt, sneakers.

The clock hanging on the bathroom wall read half-past nine in the evening. He didn't care if it was midnight. He needed to see Brooke immediately.

He opened the door and entered the candlelit bedroom. Naomi had strategically placed a circle of candles around the bed, using an assortment of tables and stands to support them, giving the room a ceremonial atmosphere. Another Sade album, *Lovers Rock*, had played on the turntable in the hallway, providing a background track to their bedroom activities. Austin used to love Sade, but he would never feel the same way about those songs again.

When Austin had left the bed to take his cleansing shower, Naomi had been lying amid the tangled sheets. Now, the bed was empty.

"Naomi?" he asked.

No answer. He left to look for her.

He found her in the dining room. She was wrapped in a silky green kimono robe, the front partially peeled open, exposing her nakedness. An open bottle of Moet champagne stood on the table in front of her, alongside the walkie-talkie.

She looked up as he entered. Her eyes smoldered like charcoal briquettes.

A bolt shot through Austin's chest. What was wrong now?

"Hello, Austie." Naomi took a swig of champagne from the bottle. She belched. Then she took another sloppy swig of bubbly.

She was in that dangerous state that he recognized all too well. As carefully as a game warden approaching an alligator, he stepped toward her.

"Are you okay?" he asked.

"I *should* be okay." She stared at him, evil twin glare in full effect. "After spending seven long-ass years apart, I fucked my husband again. Laid it on him hard. Reminded him that I've got the best pussy he's ever had in his life. But what did he do?"

"I gave you what you wanted." Austin's jaws clenched. "You need to give me what you promised."

"He called out the woman's name!" Naomi slammed the bottle onto the table, the candelabra clattering. She catapulted out of her chair, robe fluttering open. A wild profusion of hives had spread across her chest. She stalked toward him like a lioness on the prowl. "Oh, he whispered it. Just a soft whisper. But I heard it. I heard it." She pointed at him, her finger shaking. "The whole time you were fucking *me*, you were thinking about *her*!"

"So what?" He spread his arms. "We had sex like you wanted to, all right? Now, you damn well better do what you promised."

She slapped him hard enough to almost fracture his jaw—which was still healing from the last time she had hit him. His head snapped sideways. His vision whirled, blackness popping at the edges of his eyes.

"I ain't giving you shit! No deal!"

She slapped him again, on the other side of his face. He staggered.

"You cheated on me!" she shrieked.

She swung her arm to strike him again. Austin trapped her wrist.

"Don't you ever touch me again," he said.

She glared at him—and pistoned her knee into his groin. Pain burst through him in a nauseating wave. He sagged to his knees, tears welling in his eyes and hot bile rising in his throat.

"Learned that in the joint," she said, "fighting off those damn COs. Who you think you are, huh? *I own you*, boy. Till death do us part. I will kill you before I let you go."

Roaring, drunk on fury and pain, Austin lunged at her. He grabbed her arms and drove her up, up, up, and back. With a startled scream, she hurtled toward the dining room table and slammed against it, her head snapping hard against the edge, the champagne bottle tipping over, chairs tumbling as her legs flailed. She collapsed on the carpet.

When Austin steadied himself and looked down at her, he noticed she wasn't moving. She lay like a broken Barbie doll on the floor, head twisted sideways, eyes shut, mouth gaping, robe still open.

Was she dead?

He stared, disbelieving, and an old memory surfaced: finding his mother lying on the kitchen floor after his father had punched her and she'd struck her head against the oven. Had he followed in his father's footsteps despite doing everything in his power to escape his dad's legacy?

That was when he noticed Naomi's chest rising and falling slowly.

No, not dead. Only knocked out.

But it was all he needed.

54

With Naomi unconscious, Austin worked quickly.

She had beaten the hell out of him, and he couldn't imagine how his battered face looked, but as he worked, he was numb to the pain, despite also taking a knee to the family jewels. Probably he was tweaked with adrenaline and wouldn't feel the full brunt of his injuries until later.

He took the pair of handcuffs she had placed on him during their bedroom romp and used them to restrain both her hands, looping the cuff's short chain around one of the dining room table's sturdy legs.

The table was constructed of solid wood and weighed over a hundred pounds. When she awoke, her attempts to get free would eat up some time.

He clipped her walkie-talkie to his waistband. He doubled back to the bedroom and fished his key fob out of his hiding place in the back of the walk-in closet: a niche underneath a loose floorboard in the corner that he had discovered purely by chance, years ago.

As he was pocketing the fob, he heard Naomi howl. She sounded like an animal caught in a bear trap.

Here we go, he thought.

He returned to the dining room. She writhed on the carpet, arms stretched above her as she tugged at the cuffs. As her braids swished across her face, he saw the crimson bruise on her right temple where she had struck her head against the table.

When she spotted him, her face transformed into a visage of malice that rivaled Medusa's killing gaze.

"Goddamn you!" She tried to kick him, but he was well out of her reach.

"You should have kept your word," Austin said. "We had an agreement. Do you really think I wanted to be with you?"

She spat at him. The saliva missed his shoes by an inch.

"Now, I've got the walkie-talkie." He tapped the radio on his side. "And I've got the key to my SUV—yeah, I snatched it when you found me at your parents' house. You didn't notice that."

He saw the realization settle over her face. She snarled. "Let me go!"

She kicked at him again, a useless gesture. Her robe was completely open, exposing her nakedness, her skin glistening with perspiration. But he didn't feel any desire as he regarded her, no tickle in his loins or stirring in his spine. All he felt was sadness lying like a stone on his heart. He had broken his vow of fidelity to Brooke and gained nothing in return except regret.

"I've got one question for you," he said. "Where's my wife? I know she's not at your parents' place."

"She's dead." Naomi smirked. "Yeah, Austie. We killed the bitch. Carved her up like a glazed ham. Dead!"

"You're lying." Austin clenched his hands into fists.

"What do you care, when you got me?" She spread her legs wide and flicked her tongue at him. "We can make this another game, baby." She wriggled her toes and gyrated her hips. "I *love* it when we fight. Did you know that about me? Seeing you mad makes me wet, 'cause I know it means you love me."

"Where is Brooke, dammit!"

Naomi laughed and wagged her tongue.

"I'm done with this," he said.

His head pounding, Austin backed into the hallway. He opened the garage door; when he had jimmied the lock earlier, he hadn't bothered to lock it again.

"Hey!" Naomi shouted. "Get your ass back in here!"

The button for the garage door opener was in the same location he remembered. As the door lumbered open, he hustled behind the SUV's steering wheel.

When he slammed the door, it muffled Naomi's shouts. The Durango's engine awoke with a hearty rumble.

He pulled out of the garage, into the depths of the rainy night.

55

Naomi thrashed on the carpet underneath the dining room table, her chained hands braced between her legs. Heart racing, she listened to the SUV's engine growling, the vehicle pulling out of the garage.

Her head throbbed. It felt as though she had a bruise the size of a lemon forming on her temple. Her sweet, predictable Austie had finally surprised her.

She giggled.

In all their years together, the ups and the downs, he had never truly fought back. What he didn't realize was that she always had *wanted* him to fight back. To respond to her violence with violence of his own. It had long been a fantasy of hers to make him angry enough for him to knock the shit out of her. She considered it the ultimate proof of love.

She had learned that lesson from watching Mama and Daddy. Daddy was slow to anger, but if you pissed him off—whoa, look out below! Mama's face had kissed Daddy's fists on more than one occasion. But afterward, their make-up sex made the walls tremble as if an earthquake were passing through.

Austie really loves me, she thought as the bruise on her temple pulsed like a tumor. *No matter what he says about his baby mama, deep down, he wants me.*

Lying on her back, Naomi positioned her bare feet against the underside of the table, about shoulder-width apart. Her butt was scooted right up against the table leg the handcuffs were wrapped around, her hands resting between her thighs.

Like lifting weights, she thought. *It's a leg press.*

She snatched in a deep breath. On the exhale, she pushed her legs up.

Seven years in prison, working out with weights pretty much daily, had made her strong. She lifted the table off the floor a few inches and dragged the chain away from the table leg. Then she relaxed her legs and set the table back on the floor.

Did you think something that easy would slow me down, Austie?

She rolled across the carpet and bounced to her feet.

In the bedroom, the candles were still aglow, flames casting quivering shadows on the walls. She found the keys for the handcuffs in a tray standing on the nightstand, right where she had left them.

She had nimble fingers; in ten seconds, she was free. Dressing took another minute. One more minute to dig her iPhone out of the small lockbox stored underneath the bed, in which she also had hidden Austin's phone and wallet.

Daddy answered on the third ring.

"What's up, Peach?" He yawned. It was almost ten o'clock. She probably had caught him drifting off to sleep.

"You better wake up, Daddy," she said. "We got a situation."

56

Not long after Naomi had called him, Daddy arrived on his big tractor. Despite her murderous mood, Naomi grinned when she saw him pull up outside her house. No matter what was going on, he loved tooling around their farm on that tractor, sitting high in the cockpit. She would have expected nothing less from her father.

What she didn't expect was to find her son sitting next to him. The boy wore a hoodie pulled over his head to ward off the night's chilly rains, and he smiled when he saw her, his teeth shiny in the glow of the tractor's dashboard lights.

"What're you doing here, honey?" She hoisted herself up into the roomy cab and kissed his forehead. "We're out here handling grown folks' business tonight."

"Grandpa said I could come."

Naomi glanced at Daddy. Her father shrugged, his straw hat tilted on his head at a rakish angle.

"Boy's got a knack for computers, Peach." Daddy indicated the iPad nestled in Khari's lap. "He's been fooling 'round with that thing all night. He's a natural, as they say."

"But did you tell him *why* I dragged you over here tonight, Daddy?"

"Figured you could run down all that." Daddy grinned in that cocksure way of his, and Naomi found it impossible to be angry at him for too long.

"Lemme see what you're doing there." Naomi huddled next to her child, their knees pressed together side by side. Khari slid the tablet over so she could get a clearer view of the display.

The tablet was one of the pieces of tech equipment that her family had implemented prior to Naomi's prison stay. They were running a multimillion-dollar agriculture business, and keeping their land and their product secure was key to the health of the enterprise. One of the pillars of security was 24/7 surveillance monitoring.

On every acre of the farm, they had mounted cameras enabled with motion-detection sensors. Those cameras fed data to custom-designed security system software. They kept a security terminal at company headquarters, and in an office in her parents' house. They'd also installed the software on several iPads with cellular data connections, so they could tap open the app and view the network of cameras no matter where they happened to be on the property.

"I've seen people driving around our farm," Khari said. "It's weird."

Naomi liked how he said *our farm*. He had begun to see himself as part of her family. She rubbed his back.

"Show me," she said.

Khari tapped the screen and enlarged the view of one of the hundreds of cameras running around the clock.

"Also, did you really mean people—plural?" Naomi asked.

"Yeah, people."

Her heartbeat boomed. She would have expected him to say he saw a *person*—namely, hapless Austin—not *people*.

"Two cars," he said. "I can't zoom in close enough to see everything, but someone is driving what looks like my dad's Durango, and another person is driving one of those ATV things you were riding earlier."

"Probably your sister," Daddy said, glancing at Naomi over her son's shoulder. "She went to take some food to the pregnant lady."

"I want to see that first," Naomi said.

"I've got it here." Khari tapped the display.

From the camera's vantage point about twelve feet above the ground, Naomi watched one of their XUVs crawling along the gravel lane. It moved at a slow pace.

Naomi read the caption underneath the live feed. The text indicated the camera's location.

"Why would Charlotte be driving around in the East Orchard?" Naomi asked, scowling. "That's nowhere near Uncle Charlie's house."

"Kinda strange, but you know your sister." Daddy shrugged. "Might've went out for a drive. We gonna get going now?"

"One minute." Naomi took the handheld radio that was clipped to a holder in the tractor's dashboard.

She tried to raise her sister on the walkie-talkie. Charlotte didn't respond. Could she have left the radio behind somewhere? Naomi's intuition warned her otherwise. Events had turned against her as of late. She was going to assume the worst.

"Mama, you there?" Naomi said into the speaker.

"I'm on, Peach. Sounds like Char ain't got her radio with her?"

"Go to Uncle Charlie's and check on things," Naomi said. "To be sure, all right?"

"Copy that," Mama said.

Naomi set the radio between her legs and nudged her son.

"Now, lemme see where Austin is headed," Naomi said.

57

Brooke was lost.

The John Deere farm utility vehicle fortunately had the key in its ignition. She squeezed behind the wheel and buzzed away from the house, the XUV's headlamps slicing through the rain-edged darkness as she bumped along the gravel road.

She was looking for an exit sign. Or traffic passing by on a nearby road. Some clear indication of the world beyond the orchard's boundaries.

But she was finding only an immense, intricate web of gravel roads and trees. Acres and acres of pecan trees standing like silent guardians in the night.

The simple directional signs that she spotted meant nothing to her. The markers were black paint on rectangular white planks, standing on wooden poles: North Orchard; South Orchard.

How about a sign that said: *Get the hell out*?

Charlotte had said that her parents' house wasn't far from the home in which they had held her captive. Brooke realized she must have taken a wrong turn somewhere, because she didn't see any other houses.

Maybe I should have asked her for directions after I chained her up, Brooke thought, and the idea brought an unforced laugh.

Laughter was the only alternative to crying. It was already raining, and the night was getting colder, too; a chilly wind gusted through the trees, making the wet leaves shiver. Brooke trembled. She had found the heater switch on the

XUV's dashboard and turned it on full blast, and while that helped, she was wearing only her perspiration-soaked maternity dress. She hadn't thought to look for a jacket or a blanket before she escaped the house. Dumb oversight.

Next time I'm abducted and escape, I'll remember to look for a coat.

She laughed again, but she felt warm tears on her cheeks. Despite herself, she was crying now, and she ordered herself to stop.

Suddenly, the walkie-talkie she had stolen from Charlotte crackled into life. Brooke swung to the passenger seat where she had placed the radio.

"Char, this is Peach. You there, Sis? Pick up."

Shit, Brooke thought. She had known someone would reach out to the sister. Maybe only fifteen or twenty minutes had slipped by since Brooke had escaped the house.

"Char, pick up the damned radio if you're there. I ain't playing. We got a situation."

A situation? Brooke wondered. There had to be something else going on, but what?

"Mama, you there?"

The mother answered: "I'm on, Peach. Sounds like Char ain't got her radio with her?"

"Go to Uncle Charlie's and check on things. To be sure, all right?"

"Copy that."

Fresh, cold sweat beaded Brooke's forehead. They were onto her now. How long before they began actively searching for her?

She steered around a fallen tree that partially blocked the road. Just past it, at an intersection of three gravel lanes, she brought the vehicle to a halt. There were more directional signs at this juncture.

Production. HQ. West Orchard.

Did she want to go to any of those places? Which one? All she needed was a working phone to call for help.

HQ must have meant "headquarters." It would be an administrative building; such a place surely would contain a functional landline telephone.

As soon as she had resolved to head in that direction, she heard an engine.

She froze, hands clutching the steering wheel, and looked behind her.

A pair of headlights swung toward her.

Did they find me already?

Heart banging, Brooke raised her hand to her eyes to block the glare. She balanced her foot on the gas pedal, ready to floor it.

The vehicle stopped. She recognized the emblem on the hood, and she couldn't believe it.

A man climbed out. "Brooke?"

She started crying again, and she couldn't stop.

58

Based on the live camera feed they watched on the iPad from the warmth of the tractor's cockpit, it was clear to Naomi: Austin had found Brooke. The baby mama had somehow gotten the drop on Charlotte and escaped, and now the two of them were reunited, hugging each other in the middle of the road as if they hadn't seen each other in years.

Naomi wanted to put her sneaker so far up Char's wide ass that her sister would taste shoe leather. How had she allowed a pregnant woman to get the better of her? The baby mama was the only leverage Naomi had over Austin, and now, things were going to get messy.

Real messy.

Without a word, Daddy had put the tractor in motion, his lips set in a resolute line. Naomi noticed that he had brought his rifle with him, like she'd asked. In fact, she saw two guns racked beside him.

"Is that Miss Brooke?" her son asked, innocent as can be as he gazed at the tablet screen.

"Yeah, that's her." Naomi turned on the seat so she could look him deep in the eyes, and she gripped his chin.

His eyes were dark hollows, waiting to be filled with her guidance.

"Listen close, honey," she said. "They're trying to break up our family. Now that they found each other, they're gonna come for you. They wanna take you away from us."

"But I don't wanna go home, Mom. I want to stay here."

"Of course you do. You belong here with us, the Xaviers. We gotta make up for all that time we were separated, right?"

"Uh-huh." He sucked on his bottom lip.

"We need to keep everyone here," Naomi said. "We need to all learn to get along. That means Austin and Miss Brooke, too. We can all be happy together."

"That's all I want." Khari swallowed. "I'm so sick of everybody fighting!"

"With that tablet there." She tapped the iPad. "We can put this whole orchard on lockdown. Did you see that part yet?"

"I saw something about gate access." He squinted at the screen.

"I want you to figure that out fast," she said. "Do it for our family."

"Okay, Mom. I will."

Naomi glanced from Daddy to her son, then back to Daddy.

"Might be time to talk about the skeleton in the closet, Daddy," she said. "The boy needs to know. He's old enough."

"If you think that's best, Peach." Daddy inclined his head slightly.

"Listen up." She touched her son's shoulder, and he looked at her, quiet. "You do that gate thing. And after you take care of that, honey, I'm gonna let you in on a real big secret."

59

Austin couldn't believe he had found Brooke.

He had been driving around with a half-formed plan to search every property on Gold Crest Farms, but as soon as he had pulled out of the garage, he could barely remember the orchard's layout. It was as if the impact of all that had happened had blacked out his memory of the place.

But his mind remained tied to other thoughts. Such as: Had he actually subdued Naomi and chained her to the dining room table? It was something so far removed from his prior experience that it might have been a story someone else had told him about what they'd done to her.

And: How long before Naomi got free? What if she got loose before he found Brooke? He had taken the walkie-talkie, but Naomi surely had another channel to contact her family.

Spurred on by a multitude of fears, he had kept driving, relying on instinct to take him where he needed to go. After a period of wandering, he had spotted a light in the distant darkness, crawling through the woods at a deliberate pace: a vehicle. He had followed it, unsure what he would find.

It had led him, incredibly, to his wife.

He buried his face in Brooke's damp hair, tears streaming down his cheeks. They held each other in the middle of the road, spotlighted by the headlamps of the idling SUV, rain drizzling onto their heads.

"Oh God." Brooke sobbed against his chest. "God . . . so thankful . . ."

"I know." He kissed her cheeks, her forehead. "Are you hurt? Is the baby . . ."

"We're alive." There was iron in her voice; her tone made it clear that she had endured abuses and performed acts that she might never share with him. Her eyes glinted like honed blades. "You look like you've taken a beating."

"Like you said, I'm alive."

"We need to get out of here, far away from these lunatics."

Arm around her shoulder, he escorted her to the vehicle's passenger side, opened the door. She glanced inside and swung to him.

"Where's Khari?" she asked.

"He's with his grandparents."

"Are we going to get him?"

"We need to get moving," he said, avoiding her question.

She climbed in, and he hurried to get behind the wheel.

"Where were you all this time?" she asked.

"Stuck at the house with Naomi. She blackmailed me, said I'd never see you again if I didn't go along with her game. We had a big fight and I got away."

His battered face throbbed dully. He saw nothing to be gained from revealing the devil's bargain he'd struck with his ex-wife, and how it had turned sour. If they survived this ordeal—not *if*, he told himself, *when*—he doubted either of them would ever speak again of this experience. It would be one of those boxes buried deep in a back closet of their marriage, never to be reopened.

"So that's the situation I heard Naomi talking about on the radio," Brooke said.

"I wish I had gotten away sooner. I had no idea what they'd done with you."

"They were holding me in a basement. At Uncle Charlie's house."

"Over the radio, I heard them talking about Charlotte being at Uncle Charlie's." It was one of the residential properties Austin would have approached, given enough time. "Uncle Charlie helped me out of a tight spot once. Was he there?"

"He died five years ago. I was alone there." She cranked up the heater a couple of notches, hugged herself. "God, I've never been so exhausted in my life. All I want is to be home in our bed. A pregnant lady isn't meant to be this active."

"I'm getting us out of here," he said.

"Do you have your phone?"

"She hid my phone and wallet, and I haven't found them." He indicated the walkie-talkie standing in the cupholder. "But like I said, I've got one of these, and apparently so do you."

"And I have this." She showed him a butterfly knife with pearl handles.

"I can't imagine what you had to do to get that." He shifted gears and pressed the gas pedal. "Keep it close."

"Do you know how to get out of here? I think I was lost."

"It's starting to come back to me." He made a right turn at an intersection of gravel paths.

"We need to call the police."

"I don't want to spend another minute here. We need to get you off the farm. Get you to safety. Then we call the cops."

"Are we leaving without Khari? You didn't answer me the first time I asked."

Austin squeezed the steering wheel. "Finding you was my top priority."

"Are you seriously going to leave your son behind with these people?" Her glare seared him like a heat lamp.

"He's not in any immediate danger. He's confused, doesn't understand what's happening."

"He doesn't understand that they abducted us from our home?"

"He *wants* to be here, Brooke. It's like he thinks we're on vacation or something."

"In the lion's den," she said. "It's too dangerous. They're insane."

"We get you out first. I can come back later for Khari."

She didn't press it further. What he didn't tell her: he didn't know how he could persuade his son to willingly come with him. Ever since Naomi had reentered their lives like a bloodsucking parasite, the bond he had forged with Khari had weakened. He could try to force Khari to come, maybe, but the kid would resent him, maybe hate him.

I've gotta do what's best for him, Austin thought. *Whether he likes it or not. That's what parenting is all about: doing what's best for your child. It's not a popularity contest.*

But that would come later. First, he had to consider Brooke and their unborn child. It was a miracle that Brooke had suffered through so much already without serious injury, and he could not put her in further jeopardy.

He increased his pressure on the gas pedal. Since he'd found Brooke, the fogginess in his memory about the orchard's layout had evaporated. He took a series of turns with growing confidence.

"Seems like you know where to go," Brooke said.

"We need to keep away from the main house, for obvious reasons. They're going to be looking for us. We need to find the access road that the delivery trucks use. It's not far ahead. Back in the day, I ran these roads daily."

He cut to the left. Trees crowded the lane on both sides, the headlamps peeling apart the darkness. A possum crouched on the muddy shoulder and turned its pale face toward them as they drove past.

Austin navigated a slight bend in the road. He slowed, staring, his chest tightening with tension.

"It's closed?" Brooke snapped up straighter in her seat.

A chain-link gate blocked the exit. The barrier was about eight feet tall and topped with nasty looking wire coils.

"I'm going to check this out." Austin pulled closer. "Wait in here."

He climbed out and approached the gate. Something with leathery wings—a bat, most likely—streaked above his head, its tiny body silhouetted in the headlamp's glare.

He examined the juncture of where the gate intersected with the perimeter fence. He didn't see a padlock or a simple manual release for the latch, but he found a hooded keypad mounted on a steel pillar next to the barrier.

He had no idea what the PIN would be. He tried numerous combinations, to no avail.

"Dammit!" He kicked the gate. It rattled, only barely.

The fence was too tall for Brooke to climb, and the barbed wire along the edges presented an additional hazard. Scaling the perimeter was out of the question.

Sucking his teeth, he got back inside the SUV.

"Well?" Brooke asked.

"We've got to find another way."

"Drive through it."

"Drive through it? It's a steel fence."

"Back up as far as we can go." She swung around in the seat and gazed through the rear windshield. "A couple of hundred yards, looks like." She turned back to him. "Get as much speed as you can. Bust right through it."

"I don't know."

"What do we have to lose? Can we damage the gate enough to get past it?"

"Maybe. Or maybe a steel shaft crashes through the windshield and impales one of us."

"Then what else are we going to do? Drive around looking for another exit? These maniacs know we're on the loose. What if they've closed *all* the exits?"

Austin's lungs felt like balloons about to pop. Brooke had voiced the same endgame scenario that had crossed his mind. He dimly recalled from his days working at Gold Crest Farms that the Xaviers had installed a high-end security system that covered the entire property, as was fitting for a commercial operation on that scale. He didn't recall the particulars—he worked in accounting, not security—but he remembered something about remotely controlled access points. Didn't it include cameras, too?

He licked his dry lips, studying the gate.

Screw it.

He shifted into drive and nosed the SUV forward.

"Go back," Brooke said.

"Hang on."

The front bumper kissed the gate. The chain link shivered. He pressed the accelerator, continuing to urge the Durango forward. The tires whirred, the gate trembling. The steel wire and the thick horizontal steel support buckled, but only slightly, not enough to force it open.

"We need more speed," Brooke said. "Hit it at forty miles an hour and I bet it snaps in half like a breadstick."

"All right," he said. "Buckle up."

60

Keeping his attention on the backup camera, Austin reversed all the way back to the bend in the road, roughly two hundred yards. They were so far away from the gate that it had vanished in the darkness beyond the arc of the headlamps like a figment from a dream.

"This is a terrible idea," he said to Brooke. "Dangerous as hell. What about the baby?"

"We need to do this *because* of the baby."

He swallowed thickly. His heart knocked so hard it felt it might leapfrog out of his chest. He double-checked his seat belt, and Brooke's, too.

"The air bags are going to pop out," Austin said. "You should move the seat all the way back. I don't want them hitting your stomach."

"Got it." Brooke used the button to inch the passenger seat as far backward as it would allow. "Ready."

With a burst of static, a voice crackled over the radios they had stolen from Naomi and her sister.

"Peach!" It was Karen; she sounded out of breath. "I found Char . . . at . . .Uncle Charlie's. She says that bitch tricked her and . . . and chained her up in the basement!"

Austin glanced at Brooke. She flashed a hard grin at him and flipped her middle finger at the handheld radio.

"Y'll can head on back to the house," Naomi responded, her voice eerily calm. "We're out here taking care of business. Ain't none of them going nowhere."

"We'll see about that," Brooke muttered, and turned to Austin. "Go!"

Austin tapped the accelerator. The vehicle leaped forward like a whipped stallion. He watched the speedometer climb: ten miles per hour . . . fifteen . . . twenty . . . twenty-five . . .

The gate floated into view. They were closing in fast. His natural reflex was to pump the brake pedal. He had been driving since he was fifteen and trained to never, ever deliberately crash into anything, and here he was, purposely planning to smash into a steel gate, and every ounce of common sense in him screamed: *Stop, you idiot! Stop right now!*

The collision warning system was flashing, too.

When the speedometer shuddered past thirty, his survival instinct took over. He tapped the brakes. They struck the gate at maybe twenty miles an hour.

Nevertheless, the air bags deployed with a loud *pop*. He had been bracing for the moment, but the sensation of the material snapping against his face was like being hit hard with a pillow. Brooke cried out.

Primal fear shot through him. *I knew this was a bad idea, and now the baby is hurt, Brooke is hurt . . .*

A foul, chemical odor suffused the air. Austin coughed, and, shaking, pushed the inflated bag away from him. Brooke was wiping her hands down her face, the puffy material sagging in front of her.

"Are you okay?" he asked.

"Yes!" she cried and pointed ahead of them. "Look!"

The gate had caved inward significantly like a soda can crushed under a heavy boot, but it held. Barely.

"Do it again!" she said. "One more hit should knock it free."

He shifted into reverse and backed up to the bend in the road.

Bright light washed over the interior of the vehicle, momentarily blinding him.

What the hell?

With one hand up to his face to shield his eyes, he turned in his seat, tried to see what was going on.

The light came from Edward's big tractor bearing down on them on Austin's side of the SUV, its headlamps glowing like a pair of demonic eyes.

As his gut seized with fear, he saw three silhouettes riding in the cab, and thought, *I'll be damned—doesn't one of them look like my son?*

The tractor smashed into them. Brooke screamed. Austin shouted, too, stomped the accelerator and twisted the wheel, but the tractor was a far more powerful vehicle and drove them off the road, into the bushes, and slammed them against a tree like a schoolyard bully. Austin felt the jarring collision in his bones. Branches and leaves rained down on the windshield like confetti. Light from the tractor's headlamps poured into the vehicle, blinding him.

"Go, go, go!" Brooke shrieked. She was wild-eyed, nostrils flaring.

"I can't! We're pinned!"

He mashed the gas pedal. The screeching tires coughed up divots of earth, but the SUV lurched forward only a couple of inches.

"Get out of the goddamn car!" Naomi said, over the walkie-talkie. "You can't go anywhere! We've closed all the gates!"

Austin grabbed the walkie-talkie and squeezed the comm button. "I'm coming! Back off so I can open the fucking door!"

He looked at Brooke. She was shaking her head.

"Don't you dare get out," she said.

"I'm getting out." He pressed the button to slide the seat backward. "You stay in and get behind the wheel. When they back up that tractor, you haul ass out of here, got it?"

"Got it." Her eyes were steel.

"Get away, get somewhere safe, get the cops. And keep the radio."

"I love you, Austin."

He touched her tear-streaked face. The rumbling tractor edged backward. Austin holstered the radio and opened the door—it took a few tries, as the crash had smashed it out of shape, but he finally popped it open. His legs felt like soft clay when he stepped out into the tamped-down weeds and shrubbery, and the foul odors of oil and exhaust fumes nearly made him gag.

He didn't dare look behind him at Brooke. He was afraid he would try to go with her. He needed her to live, more than anything.

As nimble as an acrobat, Naomi maneuvered out of the tractor's cab. Edward lumbered out, too. He had a rifle slung over his shoulder like a war-weary general climbing out of a tank.

But one figure remained seated in the cab: his boy. It didn't look as if he were even moving, and Austin knew, instructively, that something was wrong.

Naomi stomped toward him, mud splashing around her shoes.

"Goddamn you for dragging me out here!" she screeched.

She went to smack him, but he raised his arm, blunting her swing. He shoved her away. She staggered and fell hard to the grass on her butt.

"I told you, I'm not taking any shit from you anymore," he said.

She looked up at him, a stunned expression on her face.

Behind him, the SUV roared.

61

I can make it, Brooke thought.

As tempting as it was to watch the drama unfurling between Austin and his lunatic ex-wife, Brooke didn't risk delaying. It took her a frantic minute to hoist and twist herself over the console between the seats and get behind the steering wheel; if Austin hadn't put back the driver's seat as far as he had, she wouldn't have been able to fit at all. Strapping the safety harness across her belly took another precious few seconds.

Outside, Naomi wailed like a harpy at Austin.

She didn't know what would become of Austin if she left him there, but they both knew that her survival, and most of all, the survival of their child, was all that mattered. Sometimes in life you had to make difficult decisions.

She was crying again, and her hands shook, but she kept moving. Got all strapped in and slammed into drive and stomped the gas pedal.

The engine hollered like a wild thing, the tires grinding. She worried for a beat that the SUV was mired in the mud, but the tires found traction on gravel, and she bolted forward and navigated onto the lane.

I can make it.

The headlamps were damaged from the collision with the fence. They cast stuttering, broken arcs of light as she rumbled ahead. If she hadn't already known the road ahead was a straightaway to the gate, she might have lost her way in the gloom, slammed into a tree.

Suddenly, she heard what sounded like a gunshot. Glass exploded behind her. She screamed. Wind whistled into the SUV, and she risked a quick look over her shoulder and saw a ragged hole in the rear windshield.

Fresh fear seized her heart.

Someone was shooting at her.

62

When Brooke took off in the SUV, grinding out of the weeds and back onto the road, Austin wanted to cheer.

She's going to make it, he thought.

In the corner of his eye, he saw Edward raise the rifle. Austin spun, fear washing over him in a cold wave.

Smoothly, as if he did such things every day, Edward squeezed off a shot. The Durango's rear windshield shattered, and it veered crazily on the gravel path.

"No!" Austin shouted.

He lunged at the older man, but not before Edward fired yet another shot at the Durango. Perhaps it was a suicide move to attack a man who wielded a semiautomatic rifle, but concern for his own safety was the last thought on his mind. Brooke had to get away safely—*she had to.* They hadn't come this far only for her to die.

Edward swung toward Austin, but Austin was quicker. He slugged Edward in the jaw with a right hook. Edward's straw hat spun like a Frisbee off his head, and his mouth went slack. But throwing the punch sent Austin spinning off balance. As Edward crumpled to the ground, Austin fell on top of him.

Somewhere behind him, Naomi was screaming, her voice coming to Austin distantly, as if from the far end of a long pipe.

He and Edward wrestled like teenage boys in the dirt, grunting and scrambling. Edward tried to knee Austin in the kidney. Austin got a fistful of the man's shirt. He pounded Edward with another punch to the face, and Edward's eyes rolled back like marbles.

A rifle cracked, divots of mud flying nearby.

"Get off him!" Khari screamed.

Austin looked up. Khari had gotten out of the tractor's cockpit. He had a rifle of his own.

He aimed it at Austin.

Blinking, Austin raised his hands. "Son?"

"*I'm not your son!*" Tears and snot smeared Khari's cheeks. "I never was. Get off my father!"

Austin couldn't process Khari's words. "What?"

"Mom . . . told me . . . everything," Khari said, voice trembling. He kept the muzzle pointed at Austin. "Get off him! Get back!"

Feeling as if the nightmare he was living had just taken another awful turn, Austin rose on unsteady legs.

63

At first, Brooke had been confident she was going to make it. But when gunshots hit the SUV, she was confident she was going to die.

The first shot had blown out the rear windshield, and such panic had overtaken her that she struggled to keep control of the SUV. She half-veered off the road, the front bumper clipping a series of bushes that scraped like claws along the vehicle's side.

When the second shot echoed, she thought it was going to take off her head, but then she heard something burst, and a shudder rippled through the Dodge. The vehicle jerked so wickedly that this time she *did* lose control, the steering wheel tearing through her fingers. She pumped the brakes, but couldn't avoid plunging off the road and plowing into a large shrub.

Someone was screaming. She realized that the screams were coming from her.

On the dashboard, the tire pressure gauge flashed.

Someone shot a tire, rear left tire.

Through the jagged branches, Brooke saw the damaged gate lay about a hundred yards ahead.

She couldn't go back. Someone with a gun was back there and would keep shooting until they either killed her or rendered the vehicle useless.

She twisted the steering wheel and shifted into reverse. She prayed the ruined tire wouldn't immobilize the SUV.

She rocked backward. Shifting to drive again, she tapped the gas, and dug out of the thicket of shrubs, back onto the road.

No one shot at her again, and she didn't wait around to see what had happened. She stomped the accelerator.

With a damaged tire and the vehicle threatening to tear away from her like an unruly bronco, she couldn't gain the speed she wanted. She slammed into the fence at about twenty miles an hour. Metal creaked and popped, chain link shrieking. She backed up, and then slammed forward again. At last, the gate crumpled, and she squeezed through.

She shouted in triumph.

But the instant she burst through the exit, it started raining harder, a sudden and torrential downpour. The rain, the darkness, and the unfamiliar environment disoriented her. She brought the SUV to a halt on the road's shoulder. Rain hammered the windshield.

"Thank you, Jesus, thank you, Jesus." She laughed. If she could have, she would have gotten out of the SUV and danced.

I made it.

She ran her fingers across her stomach and felt her baby kick, as if he were celebrating, too.

"We made it, baby," she whispered.

But how far could she get on a ruined tire? How far would she have to drive before she found help?

What if those lunatics came after her? Would they? In the movies, the crazies never stopped coming.

Maybe it was too early to celebrate her freedom.

Shivering, she switched on the windshield wipers to the fastest setting and started driving again.

64

I'm not your son. I never was . . .

As those impossible words echoed in Austin's mind, he rose to his feet. The world seemed to tilt and sway underneath him. It took all his strength to keep from buckling over from the impact of the boy's revelation.

He looked to Naomi. Naomi smirked, as if she had played an epic prank on him. She sashayed past Austin and knelt next to Edward, who was struggling to sit up and slowly working his jaw.

Khari kept the rifle aimed at Austin's chest. His son's hands shook. Austin gazed into the boy's eyes and saw so much turmoil that his heart ached, but he didn't dare make a quick move.

"Listen, Khari," Austin said. "Lower the gun, please. Lower the gun, and we'll talk about this. We'll have a calm chat about this crazy new *lie* your mother told you."

Austin saw conflicting emotions twisting Khari's face, but Khari didn't take the gun off him.

"Mom?" Khari said. "Grandpa? Tell him what you told me!"

But Naomi only grinned at Austin. She helped Edward to stand, and Austin realized Edward had never been at risk of losing possession of the rifle; it was strapped securely across his chest.

Blood dribbled from Edward's lip. Naomi wiped away the blood with her thumb, and then she slipped her thumb into her mouth and sucked with evident pleasure.

Disgust knotted Austin's stomach.

It can't be true. Can it?

Edward slid on his hat, and lifted the rifle to his shoulder. Austin backpedaled several paces.

"It doesn't have to be this way," Austin said. "Let me go."

"Oh, I'm gonna," Edward said. "I'll give you 'til the count of ten. You ain't running to that gate to join up with your woman, either, or I'll cut you down 'fore you get five feet out. Go on another way."

"You're coming after me, regardless," Austin said.

Edward winked and slid his finger to the trigger.

"One . . . two . . . three . . ."

Austin turned and fled.

65

Heavy rain burst from the night sky as if a dam had collapsed in the firmament, but as Austin sprinted through the woods, he barely registered the cold raindrops snapping through the trees and dampening his skin and clothes. He was worried about Brooke, wanted to know if she had managed to escape after Edward had damaged the SUV, needed to try to raise her on the walkie-talkie.

Yet, a single, all-consuming question raced through his mind, overriding everything else: Could it be true?

Memories cascaded through his thoughts, starting with Edward and Karen, perhaps ten years ago. During a family dinner at his in-laws' house, after several rounds of drinks, hadn't Edward joked that he and his wife were second cousins? Karen had laughed, and Charlotte had giggled, and Naomi had looked across the table and smirked at Austin in that way that she did that made him wonder if she were pranking him. No one had brought it up again, and Austin became convinced that it had been only a strange, off-color joke. He rarely saw other members of the Xavier family outside of their circle—the reclusive Uncle Charlie rarely came around, preferring to stay in his own house—so it wasn't as though Austin could have easily asked someone else to confirm the veracity of Edward's statement.

Only a joke, he concluded, as disturbing as it had been to hear.

Could it be true?

But the interactions he'd observed between his ex-wife and her father had always unsettled him. Like her habit of casually sitting on her father's lap. Or how Edward seemed to relish running his fingers through her hair. And their unusual—and uncomfortable to watch—tendency to kiss each other on the lips.

Could it be true?

There were the gifts, too. Edward had long seemed to be in an unofficial competition with Austin for his daughter's affections, presenting her with outrageously expensive presents that Austin couldn't hope to match, or items that were inappropriate. A Mercedes-Benz coupe for her thirtieth birthday. A diamond-studded tennis bracelet for Christmas. Red roses and chocolates for Valentine's Day. Once, when Naomi had revealed a new lingerie set on one of their anniversaries, she casually dropped that her dad had bought the clothing for her, to "help them set it off."

Could it be true?

Hadn't he sometimes glanced at Khari and wondered when the boy would begin to look more like him? Khari already was on track to be taller than Austin: he stood nearly six feet, and Austin was six-one, while Edward was six-four. Austin realized that children didn't always share the same physical traits as their parents . . . yet the other differences in their appearance were stark. Khari's skin was several shades lighter than Austin's rich oak complexion, which Austin had always attributed to Naomi, as she had golden beige skin like her father. Austin had black, kinky hair; Khari's auburn hair was soft, wavy. Austin had eyes the color of tarnished pennies. Khari had striking hazel eyes, like his mother.

Like Edward, too.

The thoughts were so agonizing that Austin felt cramps shooting throughout his body. He halted and leaned against a tree slick with rain. Bending over, he dry-retched, his stomach convulsing. Raindrops coursed down the back of his neck and the channel of his spine.

Naomi had known the truth all along, hadn't she? Edward had known, and surely the rest of her family was in on the secret, too. What kind of people condoned such depravity?

The kind of people who abduct you and your family from your house, that's what kind of people do this shit, man. Are you surprised anymore by anything these people have done?

The truth about the Xaviers had been staring him in the face for years. He had been willfully blind, seduced by their wealth, entranced by Naomi's beauty, rendered complacent by his conventional ideas of human behavior. Those factors had obscured the obvious truth of who they really were.

I'm not your son. I never was.

Now, his own son had pointed a gun at him. Regardless of their genetic bond—or lack of one—it was unfathomable for Austin to think of Khari as anything except his own son. The day of Khari's birth, Austin had changed his first diaper. Khari's first word had been "Dada," and he said that word while grinning at Austin. Austin had dedicated his life to raising the boy to the absolute best of his ability. The absence of a genetic bond would never change that in Austin's mind.

But he pointed a gun at me.

Khari was confused—that was what Austin chose to believe. He was young and couldn't understand what was happening, couldn't comprehend the significance of the abominable revelation that had been shared with him. If the two of them ever got out of this situation, they would need intensive therapy to sort through these issues, to salvage the ruins of their relationship, to move forward.

But at this stage, Austin wasn't sure he would live to see the dawn.

66

Austin found shelter at Uncle Charlie's old house.

He hadn't planned to go there. His only intention had been to stay out of the Xaviers' immediate orbit. Brooke had shared that they had held her captive there, and he'd overheard the chat between Karen and Naomi about Charlotte and figured that everyone had vacated the place by then. When he approached at a jog, the windows were dark, and he didn't see any vehicles parked nearby.

Seeing the dilapidated, ranch-style home brought a tide of memories charging back into his thoughts. The night Naomi had attacked him with the knife, he'd run here and used Uncle Charlie's phone to call the police.

"What happened to you, boy?" Uncle Charlie squinted at him, his eyes owlish behind his bifocals. A lumbering bear of a man like his older brother, Edward, he stooped in the doorway, studied Austin up and down, and let out a low whistle. "Uh-oh. Somebody cut you?"

"Naomi," Austin whispered. He was nearly dead on his feet.

"Oh, yeah," Uncle Charlie muttered. "That girl crazy like her daddy."

He ushered Austin inside and led him to the phone.

"Go on and call the police," Uncle Charlie said. He grunted. "She ain't right for this."

And Uncle Charlie stepped out of the kitchen to get bandages . . .

The front door creaked open when Austin tried the knob. On the farm, no one ever locked their doors.

Inside, the place looked as if it had been spun in a giant blender. Austin didn't find this surprising. The word in the family was that Uncle Charlie was a disorganized pack rat, and when Austin had finally entered the man's house those years ago, he had witnessed the contained chaos for himself.

What surprised him was that no one had bothered to clear out the place since the man's death. The air smelled of rot and mildew. Random junk was heaped everywhere, mantled in a layer of dust, and spiderwebs were strewn across various items like grotesque connective tissue.

"I don't know what I'm doing here," Austin muttered. His wet shoes squished across the floor as he tramped around switching on dust-filmed lights.

He believed the Xaviers had security cameras installed throughout the farm. They could likely find out where he had gone to ground. Was he going to run somewhere else before they closed in on him? He was like a rat in a boxed maze, with no escape, fated to run in circles until someone decided the game was over.

In the kitchen, Austin found a telephone. It was the same phone he had used those years ago to call the police.

The line was dead.

He laughed at this finding; of course, there was no telephone service. Brooke would have used the phone when she was there if it were functional, and all of this would have been over hours ago.

He shoved a stack of moldering phone books off a kitchen chair and collapsed onto it. Leaning forward, he cradled his head in his rain-drenched hands.

He needed to raise Brooke on the radio. Find out if she had made it out. While he'd been running through the woods, his radio had crackled a couple of times, but he hadn't heard any clear voices, and he was in such a state of mind that he had wondered if he had imagined the noises.

He slid the radio off his hip and clasped it in his hands. A channel button enabled him to scan different frequencies. Why hadn't he considered that before? He could reach someone who might be listening and ask them to send help.

He activated the scanner. Static squawked from the speaker as the radio spun through various channels. He heard only fuzzy snatches of conversation, like ghostly whispers from beyond.

He squeezed the push-to-talk button. "Is anyone there? Can anyone hear me?"

Indistinct words threaded with static answered him. He wasn't sure anyone heard him at all. If the Xaviers had acquired these radios for their own private use, they might have programmed them to broadcast only on their family's channel.

He returned to the original frequency. "Brooke, are you there?"

Silence answered him again.

Was she out of range? Or was she . . .

He couldn't think about it. Wouldn't. If he refused to dwell on it, perhaps it would not come true.

"Brooke," he said. "Please, answer if you're there."

Another voice answered: "Baby mama didn't make it."

At the sound of Naomi's voice, Austin squeezed the radio so tightly that if it had been an egg, it would have cracked.

"We found your SUV smashed at the gate," Naomi said. "Big-ass hunk of metal buried in baby mama's belly. Mama and baby bled out. So sorry about that."

She snickered. Austin was shaking his head. *She's lying again, she's always lying!*

"Is Khari there?" he asked, and he didn't wait for Naomi to say anything. He rose from the chair and started talking, words rushing out of him like pent-up air: "Son, hey, it's your dad. Yeah, I'm calling myself your dad, and you know why? It's 'cause all I ever wanted to do right, all I ever cared about, was being your father. The perfect father." He laughed, ran his fingers through his damp hair, and kept pacing around the kitchen, weaving around piles of junk. "I know I haven't been perfect. Far from it. Especially lately. But I've tried to be there for you, Khari, from day one. I wanted to be the father for you that I never had. I'm sorry for whatever mistakes I've made—there's too many for me to count them all. But I want to let you know that no matter what anyone says, I'm always gonna be here for you, Son. Always. I love you. Brooke loves you. We'll always have a place for you in our home. In my mind, you'll always be my son, I'll always be your dad. Lord help me, I hope that's enough."

He stopped talking, heart whamming, lips dry. The radio felt heavy as a kettlebell. He set it on the counter next to the sink.

"That was so sweet," Naomi said, but her words couldn't mask her anger. "Too bad the boy wasn't around to hear it. Bye now."

Closing his eyes, legs weak again, Austin eased back onto the dusty chair. For what felt like a long time, he sat there. He ought to get moving again, try to find a way off the farm, perhaps return to the gate he and Brooke had been attempting to clear, but he couldn't summon the energy to move.

The walkie-talkie crackled once more. Austin raised his head.

Ever so faintly, a voice said, "Austin?"

It was Brooke.

67

Brooke hadn't gotten far.

Only a few hundred yards away from the mangled gate, she encountered a massive oak tree blocking the road. It looked like a giant had ripped it out of the ground and tossed it aside.

"Perfect," she muttered as the wipers ticked back and forth across the glass.

The fallen tree was too big for her to simply drive over it. To continue, she had to drive around it, crawling into the ditch skirting the road's shoulder, and back onto the gravel.

She got bogged down while arcing around the oak's tangled roots. The soil was softened from the day's rainfall. Ever try to drive an SUV with a blown rear tire through a mud-caked ditch? The more she ground the wheels, the worse her predicament. She tried to reverse, shift into other gears, go back and forth, and none of it helped.

She was stuck.

She slapped the steering wheel. "Dammit, dammit, dammit!"

Rain pounded the SUV, leaked inside through the ruptured rear windshield. She would have to walk. She glimpsed an intersecting road perhaps a quarter mile ahead, where this access lane finally entered civilization. She could walk and flag down someone and then this terrifying adventure might end.

She grabbed the walkie-talkie and tried to raise Austin. He didn't respond. She wasn't sure her words were reaching him, or if he still had the radio.

Or if he was still alive.

Of course he's alive. That crazy bitch is in love with him.

She took the umbrella from the storage pocket on the door. Opening the door required a few hard shoves. She bounded outside into the mud.

The mushy earth sucked at her sneakers as if it wanted to swallow her. Cold rain slanted into her face. She opened the umbrella to blunt the rain, but she didn't have a solution for treading through mud. Rain boots weren't part of her post-abduction ensemble.

She slogged to the back of the vehicle. The road behind her was dark, empty. Did the lunatics know she was stuck? Were they coming after her? She'd heard snatches of voices on the radio, but they were too garbled for her to understand what they were saying, or who was speaking. For all she knew, they were coming from a different channel.

She opened the rear cargo door. Water dripped from the edges as she lifted it, and the interior light blazed. Austin, bless him, kept an emergency cache stored back there in a canvas bin. She dug inside and found a first aid kit, jumper cables, a can of Fix-a-Flat, bottles of water, a rain parka, a blanket, a flashlight, and a six-pack of LED road flares.

There was a spare tire in the cargo area, too. Although she knew how to change a tire—her parents had made sure of that when she was sixteen and got her first car—she saw no point in trying to swap out a tire while mired in the mud.

She twisted open one of the water bottles and chugged half of it in a few gulps; then she found Tylenol in the first aid kit and washed down two tablets. Her wounded leg throbbed and her back ached. Any relief from pain would help her continue.

The parka was sunflower yellow. It was big on her, but she welcomed the protection from the elements and the multiple pockets it offered. She stashed the other water bottle in a side pocket, took the flashlight (after confirming it was operable), and grabbed the pack of flares. After scanning the directions a couple of times, she stuffed the lights in another pocket.

Her plan? Walk to the intersecting road ahead, activate one of those flares, and flag down someone driving past. Who could ignore a pregnant woman standing next to an emergency beacon? Surely, some Good Samaritan would stop for her, take her to the police or a hospital.

With that plan settled, she slammed the cargo door, edged back to the driver's side, and retrieved the key fob. They could return for Austin's SUV when this was done.

Clutching the umbrella, Brooke carefully maneuvered around the fallen tree. Her foot got snared in a root as she was maneuvering, and she almost—almost—lost her balance and fell face forward on the ground.

Girl, be more careful, she admonished herself. *Falling out here, so close to escape, is the last thing you need.*

Her baby kicked, as if in agreement.

Once past the tree, she trudged onto the road. Rain snapped against the umbrella. She tried to take swift, measured strides, and she kept a good pace despite her aching leg—she was thankful for the many hours she had spent at the YMCA during her pregnancy power walking around that indoor track. She was in better shape than she had any reason to be considering what she had suffered through.

As she neared the adjacent road, she noted traffic grumbling past. Mostly semitrucks. She had not seen many vehicles. They were out in a rural area, and at that late hour, in the blinding rain, only people who had good reason to be out driving would be found on these roads.

All she needed was one kindhearted person to brake for her.

She took the walkie-talkie out of her pocket and mashed the push-to-talk button.

"Austin," she said. "Babe, are you there? It's Brooke."

Static in response.

"Austin," she said again. "Please, if you can hear this, let me know. Let me know you're there."

A garbled voice said, "Brooke?"

She was so grateful to hear him that she almost stopped right there and sank to her knees on the pavement.

"You're alive," he said.

Or that's what she thought he said. It was tough to decipher his words. They had a bad connection, perhaps because of the storm and the distance between them.

"Damn right, I'm alive," she said. "I'm going to get help. You hang on, okay? I'm going to get help for us. We're going home soon."

He said something in response, but she couldn't make it out. Only hearing his voice was enough. If he were alive and responding via the radio, that meant he had some measure of freedom from the crazies at the farm.

Hang on, baby, she thought. *Hang on a little bit longer.*

The crazies would have heard their exchange if they were monitoring the channel, but that couldn't be helped. She wasn't going to let them stop her.

She reached the intersection. She looked both ways, but there was no traffic; only trees framing the winding, two-lane road on either side. Beside her, a sign said: "*Gold Crest Farms—Commercial Traffic Only.*"

Setting up there, so close to the farm, felt risky. She was convinced the crazies would try to find her. Why make it easy for them?

She crossed to the other side of the road and plodded farther along the shoulder. She didn't see any signs of a residence, or another commercial property. The Xavier family farm was the only established location in sight.

About a hundred yards ahead, she found shelter underneath the broad span of a sugar maple. She propped the umbrella against the tree and dug the flares and flashlight out of her pocket.

She used the flashlight to review the instructions again. Finally certain of what she was doing, she tore open the six-pack, removed a single beacon, and pressed the button to switch it on.

The LED light burned like a supernova in the night, temporarily blinding her. She bent and positioned the device on the ground, keeping it under the shelter of the tree.

She stepped back a few feet, scanned back and forth along the road. Flashing light strobed over her and the surrounding trees.

All right, come on. Someone must see this!

She kept the flashlight in her hand, too. Between the flare, and the flashlight, her rescue ought to be assured.

But the road was empty. When she had gotten out of the SUV, she noticed the clock had ticked close to eleven o'clock. She had seen the last truck grumble past maybe ten minutes ago.

The beacon continued to glow and pulse. She would wait all night if she had to. Eventually, someone had to show up.

At least ten minutes had passed when she heard the grumble of an approaching vehicle. It came from her left—the south, she believed. A pair of headlights crested an incline, the vehicle rising into view.

Her heart stuttered.

It was a motor home bearing the Winnebago emblem.

No, no, no.

Brooke spun around, frantic. She couldn't stand there like an idiot and wait for them to catch her.

The RV thundered toward her, headlamps glowering. A horn sounded.

They had spotted her.

Without thinking, Brooke plunged into the trees that lined the road.

She found herself in thick foliage that fought her at every step, like some enchanted, malevolent woods in a fairy tale. She used the flashlight to try to clear a path, yet leaves with blade-like edges scraped at her face. Vines groped for her legs. Gnarled branches wrestled with her arms as she battled to advance.

She heard the camper's idling engine and looked behind her. A slender figure—it had to be Naomi—picked up the beacon and heaved it like a softball to the other side of the road.

Bitch, Brooke thought.

Anger powered her forward. She would not lie down and quit. She would press on. She would find help.

She still had the knife, too. If she were cornered, she would fight back.

She fought her way forward for several minutes when she looked over her shoulder again and saw the RV grumbling away down the road. That made her uneasy. Where were they going? She *knew* they had spotted her, recognized her—they had honked, and in the sunflower-yellow parka, she was about as visible as a bumblebee on a birthday cake.

Keep going.

She wiped perspiration out of her eyes and swung around the flashlight. Was there a house up ahead, in a clearing? She thought she saw a shack-like structure and some sort of vehicle, perhaps a pickup?

Hope rose in her chest.

With renewed vigor, she plowed on, hacking aside the undergrowth. When she finally reached the edge of the forest, she staggered forward and gasped with relief.

Her arms felt like melted rubber. Her legs wobbled. Her feet ached. She had never been so exhausted.

But she couldn't rest yet.

She scanned the clearing with the flashlight. The residence was a tar paper shack that looked as if it had been built by someone unfamiliar with basic carpentry. Mismatching wood planks formed the exterior walls, and the roof was missing several shingles. A single window set in the back wall was boarded up with slats of wood, and no light escaped between the narrow gaps.

The rust-spotted, blue Chevy pickup parked alongside the shack dated from at least thirty years ago.

Brooke didn't care. All she needed was a working telephone, or, failing that, someone who could drive her to the police.

She approached the residence, slogging through mud. She shone the flashlight inside the truck. A red bandana dangled from the rearview mirror. She tested the door handle; the door was locked. She panned beyond the pickup, the light revealing a muddy driveway riddled with potholes that led to a gravel path.

The front of the shack resembled the rear: dark and vacant looking. A rocking chair that looked one hard wind away from collapsing stood on a sagging front porch.

The floorboards groaned beneath her sneakers as she approached the door.

A dingy curtain hung in the front window, obstructing her view of the shack's interior.

She didn't see a doorbell. She knocked three times on the tarnished red door.

"Hello!" she said. "I need help! I need to call the police!"

She heard a soft, creaking noise sound from inside. Behind the tattered curtain, a dim light winked on.

She suddenly heard a sound that instilled terror in her heart: a rumbling engine that she recognized all too well. She glanced over her shoulder and saw headlights puncture the darkness.

She banged her fist against the door. "If anyone's inside, please help! Help!"

She twisted the doorknob, but it was locked. She heard shuffling footsteps. The click of a disengaging lock.

"Please, hurry!" Brooke cried.

She checked over her shoulder. The motor home rumbled into view, invading the rural oasis like a sentient machine from a dystopian future, leaving shattered branches in its wake.

The door opened. A petite woman wrapped in a white shawl stood on the threshold, her wizened face leathery as a prune. But her deep-set, aqua-blue eyes shone with fierce light—and suspicion.

She held a shotgun in her grip, the muzzle directed at Brooke.

"Who're you?" the woman asked. "What you banging on my door for?"

"I'm pregnant." Brooke raised her hands, but she stepped aside, away from the shotgun's black muzzle. "Please, I need help. The people in that RV want to hurt me."

The Winnebago ground to a stop in the driveway. The old woman squinted as the camper's headlamps found her lined face. Her jaws worked, but she didn't speak.

"Please, ma'am," Brooke said. She was barely aware of the tears flooding her eyes, dripping down her cheeks.

The motor home's passenger door opened. Naomi climbed out, followed by her father. Both bore guns.

"This is family business, ma'am," Edward said. "Don't let this woman fool you. She tried to rob us. We tracked her down here. Probably she's gonna rob you, too."

"That's a lie!" Brooke said.

The old woman's sharp gaze alternated between Brooke and the new visitors. She seemed to be weighing the situation, and then something in her eyes resolved.

"Step aside, miss," she said to Brooke in a hushed voice. "Get on behind me and go inside."

"Thank you," Brooke breathed.

The woman raised the shotgun to her shoulder and stepped forward. Brooke heard the sudden discharge of a rifle, and it made her heart plummet. Her would-be Good Samaritan fell to the porch like a puppet whose strings had been severed.

Brooke screamed. The older woman's head rolled so that her face was angled at Brooke. She had a perfectly placed crimson hole right between her eyes. Her dead gaze seemed accusatory.

The gag reflex seized Brooke's stomach, but the survival instinct surpassed it. She lunged for the shotgun lying on the porch. Edward issued a sharp whistle, and she froze like a trained canine.

"Don't do it, girl," he said. "Get on back in the RV and we'll forget about this. We'll treat you right, won't we, Peach?"

"You had a good run." Naomi strutted forward through puddles, the gun slung across her chest. She gave only a casual glance toward the dead woman. "But Daddy can hit a gnat on a horse's tail from damn near a thousand yards. You put up a good fight, but it's over now."

Brooke's hands were less than a foot away from the shotgun. So close. But Naomi levered her gun against Brooke's head. The metal felt like an ice block against her skull.

"Think about your baby," Naomi said.

Sighing, Brooke closed her eyes and raised her hands.

68

As Naomi directed their captive baby mama toward their camper, keeping the rifle jabbed against her spine, Daddy approached the front porch of the run-down home.

"Come back out here after you get her squared away, Peach," he said.

Her father's pensive tone concerned her, but she could deal with him shortly. She was going to relish every moment of her victory over Brooke.

"You led us on a hell of a chase, huh?" Naomi said to Brooke and poked the woman's back with the muzzle. Brooke stumbled as she sloshed through a puddle. "Getting Mama and Char to trust you, getting the drop on Char back at the house. Hooked up with Austie and busted out of the damn gate! You're something else. It was a good plan, kind of, but we know these woods back here like we know our own faces in the mirror. Now you got that poor lady back there killed. Her blood's on your hands, girlfriend."

Brooke didn't answer, but she bowed her head. Naomi liked to see that; maybe they had broken this woman's spirit, at last.

Brooke shuffled up the steps into the RV. Naomi bopped her on the back of the head with the muzzle, and Brooke winced.

"Get your fat ass up in there," Naomi said.

Mama and Charlotte waited inside. Khari was in there, too, but her son had seemed almost comatose since the confrontation with Austin. Her boy huddled in the corner playing his Nintendo and barely glanced up when Naomi brought Brooke inside. Naomi knew he was struggling to accept the truth that she had walloped him with earlier that evening, and Austin's rambling, sappy monologue over the radio hadn't helped matters. Her son was going to need time to get his mind right.

But he would be okay. He was a Xavier, after all.

"Look who's back," Mama said to Brooke. She grinned. "You got spunk, honey, I'll tell you that."

Char wasn't so appreciative. She backhanded Brooke across the face, a blow that sent the woman reeling like a drunk against Naomi. Naomi shoved her away, back into her sister's arms.

"*I was nice to you!*" Charlotte shrieked.

She smacked Brooke again. Brooke yelped and sank to the floor. She sobbed, thoroughly broken. She reminded Naomi of her formerly problematic cellmate after Naomi had hooked up with a gang and they had crowded the woman in the cell and beaten her down one night. After that night, she'd never had another issue with her bunkmate.

"Y'all put the cuffs on her," Naomi said. "*Keep* them on her this time, hear? I gotta go back outside and chat business with Daddy."

Naomi returned to the shack. Daddy hadn't moved. He stood on the porch, rifle hanging from his shoulder, hat clasped in his hands as he stared at the dead old woman lying at his feet.

"What is it?" she asked.

He didn't look at Naomi. He kept staring at the body.

"We can't come back from this, Peach," he said. "We dug us a deep hole and there ain't no climbing out of it now."

"Did you know this woman?" Naomi nudged the woman's leg with her sneaker.

He nodded. "Name's Sara Brighton. Brighton family's had this little shack here for years. They're simple folk, kept to themselves, never bothered nobody."

"I didn't tell you to shoot her," Naomi said.

Daddy turned to her, his gaze hotter than the camper's headlamps.

"*You* dragged me into this mess, Peach. You dragged *all* of us into it."

"Hey." Naomi swallowed. "That ain't fair, Daddy. *You* promised to help me set things right with my husband. We're all in this together."

"Does this look like we're setting things right, Peach?" He gestured to the dead woman. "She's living alone out here, but somebody's gonna come check on her. Police'll investigate."

"We'll burn it all down, then." Naomi swept her gaze over the ramshackle home. "I bet she's got something inside we can use to light it up."

"Burn it all down?" Daddy gawked at her.

"Drag the body in there and set the place on fire. Cover our tracks. Problem solved."

"Christ in heaven." Daddy put his hand to his mouth as if holding back words, closed his eyes for a beat.

Naomi touched his arm, squeezed. "It'll be all right, Daddy. I'll do it."

"Sometimes, Peach . . ." He glanced at her, and she couldn't read the emotion in his eyes. Was it fear? Horror? Disgust? "I worry about what that place did to you."

She knew what he meant. He meant prison. Seven years of watching her back, making allies and enemies and doing whatever it took to stay alive, to stay on top. It had changed her; she knew that. Hard time changed everyone, and don't let anyone tell you otherwise.

But she believed it had changed her for the better.

"I'm a survivor," she said. "Go on back to the RV, Daddy. I got this."

Suddenly looking every minute of his age and weakened condition, Daddy trudged back to the motor home. Naomi waited until he got inside, and then she headed into the tar paper shack.

It didn't take long to find a match.

69

Back at Uncle Charlie's house, when Austin first heard Brooke over the radio, he felt hope swell in his heart. But as their spotty connection faltered and her voice faded in a flurry of static, his hope stalled, too.

What if she didn't make it? What if something went wrong? The entire day had been nothing *but* events turning against them. Naomi wouldn't hang back and allow Brooke to get away clean.

Austin searched the house for something useful—a rifle stored in a case would have been a prize finding—and discovered only a Louisville Slugger wooden baseball bat sticking out of a dusty cardboard box. He pulled it out, tested its heft.

For now, the bat would have to suffice. It was time to get moving.

Outdoors, the night sky continued to shed icy rain, albeit at a slower, monotonous drizzle.

He tried to reach Brooke on the radio again and got no response. With the bat balanced across his shoulder, he started jogging.

It had been an exhausting day in literally every way, but his brief break at Uncle Charlie's had helped him find a new gear. Fresh endorphins surged through his blood. He didn't know what would happen with Khari, but he had said what was on his heart, and he only hoped that the boy heard him.

He was ready to lay it all on the line for Brooke, too.

It took about ten minutes for him to close in on the Xaviers' principal residence. The motor home's headlamps burned. They were pulling out of the driveway.

"Shit," he muttered.

Were they going on the run because they worried Brooke would contact the police? Or were they going after Brooke?

The motor home swung around through the horseshoe-shaped driveway and rumbled to the entry gate, taillights glowing in the gloom. The remotely controlled gate opened; the camper turned left onto the adjacent road.

"Brooke!" he shouted into the walkie-talkie. "They're coming in the RV!"

She didn't respond. He wasn't sure whether she had received his warning.

He raced to the house, clutching the bat in one hand like a relay baton. A Ford F-150 stood in front of the garage. Edward's vehicle.

He tried the truck's door. Locked.

They had locked the house's front door, too. Thinking, probably, that they would keep Austin out while they were gone on their errand.

He used the baseball bat to smash a front window, and in short order, he climbed inside.

70

Inside the house, his heart thudding like a metronome, Austin switched on lights as he scrambled from one room to the next. He still carried the bat but doubted anyone was there to challenge him. His former in-laws' house was quiet and felt empty.

He sought three items: a phone, a better weapon, and the key to the Ford pickup parked outside.

Earlier that day (which felt like years ago, so much had happened since then) he had found the key fob to his SUV hanging on a pegboard in the kitchen. He went there first. The truck's fob hung in the middle of the board.

He grabbed it and headed to the staircase leading down into Edward's den. A safe room at the edge of the den housed a large gun cabinet, he remembered. Edward never passed up an opportunity to show off his firearms collection.

He glanced around the den for a phone, didn't see one, kept moving to the storage chamber.

The door opened at his touch. Inside, a tall, glass-fronted cabinet held an assortment of weapons.

Austin selected a Mossberg twelve-gauge, pump-action shotgun. Hands shaking, he loaded the gun with buckshot shells.

He knew his way around the twelve-gauge, ironically, thanks to Edward. After he and Naomi wed, Edward had given him a similar gun and taught Austin how to use it, driving Austin out to a remote section of the farm where he had set up a homemade shooting range.

A man's gotta be able to take care of his family, son.

Was he capable of aiming at one of these people and pulling the trigger? Edward, Karen, or Charlotte? Naomi, a woman to whom he had once proposed on bended knee?

Keep moving. You're wasting time.

He hustled out of the house and raced to the pickup.

The truck started immediately, engine rumbling to life, and the fuel tank had plenty of gas. A song blasted from an R&B channel on the radio: "Stairway to Heaven" by the O'Jays.

A weapon rack hung from the interior ceiling. The shotgun fit.

He swung around the driveway and drove to the gate.

A remote gate opener was clipped to the sun visor; he mashed it with his thumb. The gate opened, and he crossed the threshold.

He paused as he neared the adjacent road. Tall trees and dense foliage framed the road on either side.

Which way did they go?

He clutched the steering wheel. His brain felt like a derailed train, and for a moment, panic seized him.

He recalled Brooke's voice over the radio. *We're going to make it,* she had said. At least that's what it had sounded like, and he fastened on to that.

We're going to make it.

He sucked in a deep breath, let his pounding heart slow.

Left, he remembered, the image of the RV flashing in his thoughts. *They went left.*

He turned left, too.

71

Although fear tangled his stomach, Austin avoiding flooring the gas pedal. Instinct warned him to keep his speed on the lower end of the speedometer and to pay attention to everything revealed in the truck's headlamps.

What do you expect to see anyway, Austin? She made it, right? She's free, like a bird.

But if he'd been speeding, he might have missed the road flare.

He was about a quarter of a mile away from where he'd started when he saw the emergency beacon lodged in bushes along the left edge of the road, LED light pulsing in the drizzle.

He slowed, parked on the shoulder beneath a maple tree.

Parking there brought another bracing shock. The umbrella he kept stored in the driver's door of his truck lay against the nearby tree; it was royal blue and gold, the school colors of his alma mater.

What was going on? That road flare, he was sure, came from his own emergency roadside kit, too.

Brooke must have been there. But where is she?

He didn't see any other signs of her. He dragged in a shaky breath, climbed out of the truck.

Rain drizzled into his eyes. He checked both ways, and then trotted across the road, water spraying from his shoe soles. He fished the device out of the shrubbery.

Why did she need to use the beacon? What happened to his Durango?

Edward had fired twice at the SUV. Had he damaged it so badly that Brooke couldn't drive? Had she abandoned the vehicle somewhere nearby and gotten out to walk?

Austin returned to the other side of the road. He retrieved the umbrella, weighed both items in his hands like an investigator considering evidence.

He didn't like the conclusions he reached. Had the Xaviers found her, forced her into their RV, and taken her somewhere?

He was about to get back in the truck when a sharp sound stilled his heart.

Rifle fire. A single, declarative shot.

What the hell?

The gunfire came from the woods beyond the road's shoulder. Weak-kneed, Austin crept to the damp foliage and scanned ahead.

The forest was too dense and dark for him to make out anything. He could wade into the woods, but instinct warned him that he needed to hurry, needed to find a quicker approach.

He got back into the truck and mashed the accelerator, mud churning from the tires as he peeled back onto the asphalt. A short distance ahead, he neared the intersecting road he expected to find on his right.

People lived back there, he remembered. Whenever traveling back and forth to the orchard, he had passed this road thousands of times, had driven back there once out of curiosity, and found old tumbledown homes that looked like relics of a bygone era.

He veered onto the road and powered ahead.

72

Austin found himself on a twisting gravel road enshrouded with dripping foliage. He didn't remember where any of the roads led. At the first branch, he made a right, thinking it would take him to the source of the gunshot.

The truck chewed through the gravel, the headlamps finding overlapping waves of leaves and shrubs. About fifty yards ahead, the road dead-ended at a driveway marked with a rusted mailbox atop a slanted wooden pole. He peered through the windshield as the wipers ticked, straining to see what lay beyond the reach of the headlamps.

"Can't see anything," he muttered.

He got out of the truck and slogged ahead through the mud and gravel. Farther ahead lay a small, ramshackle house floating on an island of darkness. He didn't see any lights, any other vehicles, any people. Whatever had gone down that involved gunfire couldn't have happened there.

His heart pounded. *I'm wasting time.*

He scrambled back into the pickup and executed a U-turn, the truck's back end nearly destroying the old mailbox for good. As he retraced his route, he tried to orient himself, again, to the location of the gunshot.

Another turn took him to yet another dead end. A narrow driveway lay ahead, so choked with weeds and shrubs it was impassable. No one could possibly live back there.

Think, dammit.

On a hunch, he lowered the truck's windows, and the outside world seeped in.

The radio broadcast an old-school R&B song by the Commodores, "Brick House." Annoyed, he twisted the volume knob to zero.

He stuck his head out the driver's-side window, rain snapping against his face. He listened. He heard water plinking against the truck. Felt the blowing of an icy wind. Smelled rich, damp flora and fauna.

Was that the odor of smoke, too? Was something burning?

He also thought he heard a rumbling engine, and it didn't belong to the F-150. Somewhere ahead, to the left.

He drove on, taking a branch he had passed up previously. The road curved, and he bumped over a pothole that tossed him halfway out of his seat, water splashing from the tires.

Come on, come on, come on . . .

At the next branch, he made a left. The road twisted again, and he was unable to see what lay ahead, but surely someone else lived back here. Or else he was going in circles, and he didn't believe that.

The engine sounds grew louder.

Austin increased his speed as much as he dared back there. He was getting closer. Soon, if he reached the Xaviers, he would have to decide his next steps.

Find them first.

As he hung a right around a bend, he saw another vehicle's headlamps washing over the foliage as a vehicle approached from the opposite direction.

He braked.

The Winnebago barreled around the curve. In the dark woods, it looked super-sized, the roof scraping against the tree canopy, leafy branches cascading along its sides.

The road was too narrow to accommodate both vehicles. But Austin didn't back up. Heart smashing against his rib cage, he held his ground.

The RV plowed to a muddy halt about twenty feet away from him. Headlamps seared the truck's interior.

He couldn't see if Brooke were inside or not.

The walkie-talkie squawked.

"Get your ass back to the farm, Austie!" Naomi shouted. "We got your baby mama!"

73

"*We got your baby mama!*" Naomi had warned.

Sweat trickling down his face in fat bullets, Austin gripped the steering wheel as the RV's headlamps speared him. Indecision had glued his hands to the wheel.

If he obeyed Naomi's order and returned to the farm like a chastened runaway, what then? This daring escape that he and Brooke had attempted would have been for nothing—and he would bet his bank account that Naomi would never give them another chance to get away.

But if he kept pushing . . . what then? What would Naomi do to him? To Brooke? To the baby?

The old Austin, prior to this living nightmare, never would have considered such a dangerous, uncertain course of action against his ex-wife. Mr. Docile Accountant, always bending to Naomi's will, would have trotted back to the farm with his head down.

But Austin didn't believe that man existed anymore.

"Move it!" Naomi screamed over the radio.

Austin swallowed, his cotton-dry tongue clicking in his throat.

If you give her what she wants, she won't keep her word. She can't be trusted. Ever.

"Now!" Naomi shrieked.

Never give her what she wants. We've come this far. See it through.

Heart thudding, Austin slid his hands off the wheel.

He reached above him for the shotgun.

74

The Xaviers had left Brooke handcuffed and lying on the queen-size bed in the motor home's sleeping compartment. After fighting so hard to escape, Brooke no longer wanted to move. It felt *good* to lie on the mattress with pillows wedged underneath her head, breathe deeply, let her body go numb, and free her mind to drift like a raft on a vast sea.

Pale light filtered from a lamp on the small nightstand. Partially swathed in shadows, Karen sat on a chair in front of the sliding double doors that separated the area from the rest of the camper. Legs crossed, arms knotted over her chest, Karen kept watch on Brooke like a warden.

Brooke didn't care. Her window of opportunity to escape these crazies had slammed shut.

She was so, so tired. She closed her eyes. If she allowed herself, she could imagine that she was at home in her own bed.

Questions spun through her mind in a disjointed blur. Would she ever lie in her own bed again? What had happened to Austin?

And what was going on with Khari? The boy didn't even look at her when she passed him. His attention was buried in that Nintendo, as if she were a stranger to him.

What would happen to her baby?

It was too much to think about, and she turned her mind away from it all.

But terrible things were happening outside the camper. She overheard Naomi laughing about torching the tar paper shack, incinerating the remains of the kind lady who had agreed to help Brooke. Brooke initially thought Naomi was lying, but the sour odor of smoke tainted the air.

Warm tears trickled down Brooke's cheeks and pooled on the pillowcase.

My fault, she thought. *That lady's blood is on my hands. If I hadn't knocked on her door, she would be alive.*

She had to let go of her guilt. There was nothing she could do about it anymore. She was beaten. Done.

The RV rumbled and jerked.

"We're on the move." Karen smiled, as if some exciting adventure awaited. "We'll get you back home and in bed. Everything will be fine, dear."

Brooke turned her head away and closed her eyes. They passed over a bump that jostled her in the bed. With her bound hands, she pulled the pillow closer and buried her tear-streaked face against it.

They had left her wearing the rain parka and hadn't bothered to pat her down, assuming, apparently, that with handcuffs on her wrists, she was helpless. But she still had the knife in her pocket.

What good would it do now? She had no fight left in her.

The motor home swayed as it wended through twists and turns. It was a comforting feeling, like being a baby in a rocker. Sleep pawed at her, and the random images flickering in her thoughts sank into darkness.

So tired . . .

But after only a couple of minutes, the RV slammed to a stop. Brooke heard something crash to the floor. She opened her eyes, twisted around.

Karen had left her post. The double doors were parted only a few inches, and it was too dark up there for Brooke to see what was going on. But she heard the chatter of agitated voices.

She sat up. Khari poked his head through the gap in the doors and peered at her.

"Hey," Brooke whispered. "What's going on? Why did we stop?"

Khari only stared at her, mouth slack. The kid looked bewildered, as if he had awakened and had no idea of his surroundings. What had happened to him?

Up front, Naomi shrieked. Brooke heard the words *baby mama* and realized Naomi was referring to her.

Was Austin there? Hope lifted her heart, her fatigue sliding away.

She swung her legs to the side of the mattress.

In a hushed tone, she asked Khari: "How do I get out of here?"

The boy sucked in his bottom lip. His glance flicked toward the heavy curtain on her left.

Brooke eased off the bed, balanced her feet on the vinyl floor. She still had her sneakers on, the soles crusted with mud.

Her chained hands in front of her, she stepped toward the curtain and peeled it aside.

A pair of exterior doors lay ahead. She searched for a door handle; the shadows made it difficult to see. The next thing she knew, Khari was at her side. He touched a lever on the side of the panel.

The doors opened with a pneumatic hiss. A soft chime sounded, an LED light glowing above the doorway.

Could Naomi and the others know what they were doing? Did some indicator notify them that the back doors were open?

No matter. The rainy night beckoned.

"Thank you," Brooke said to Khari. "Come with me, sweetheart. We'll find a way to your dad."

Khari looked away from her. But he touched her shoulder, and then he jumped off the edge of the doorway. She followed him and landed on the gravel, and without the use of her arms to balance, she would have tipped over if Khari hadn't grabbed her elbow and prevented her fall. She gave him a grateful smile.

"Don't suppose you have a key to these handcuffs?" she asked.

He shook his head and, turning, softly closed the RV's doors. Brooke crept to the left of the camper, her shoes sloshing through a puddle.

Ahead, what looked like a pickup blocked the road. The headlamps were too bright for her to make up the details of the tableau unfolding up there, but she could only pray that it involved her husband.

I knew he'd come.

Khari grabbed her arm and pulled her with him.

"Wait," she said.

She swept aside the folds of the parka and found the butterfly knife in her pocket. Flicking out the blade, she used both hands to plunge the knife into the RV's left rear tire, tearing open a deep gash.

Payback.

But a heartbeat later, she felt something in her own body rupture, too.

"Oh God," she gasped, feeling warm wetness trickle down her pelvic area.

Her water had broken.

75

Gripping the shotgun, Austin got out of the truck.

No clever plan had come to mind. His only intention was to *resist*. They had Brooke onboard. He couldn't allow them to leave with her.

They would have to drive through him first.

While the RV grumbled, headlights blinding his eyes, Austin came around the pickup's nose. In the backsplash of the lights, he saw Edward at the motor home's steering wheel and Naomi at his side, father and daughter united against him.

Worry about Khari came to mind, and Austin tamped it down. He had laid it on the line for his boy, and whether his son came around or not, it was out of his hands.

Austin flicked off the shotgun's safety and racked the pump action. He lifted the gun to his shoulder and pointed it at the windshield.

Leering, Edward mashed the horn. The sharp sound made Austin's head swell. But he stood his ground.

"Let her go!" Austin's throat was raw.

The RV edged forward, thunderous vibrations from the great engine shaking the ground, a trembling Austin felt in every joint and bone.

He pointed the gun at the tree canopy above the camper and squeezed the trigger. The weapon's kick knocked him backward a step and cleared out his eardrums. Shattered branches and shredded leaves rained onto the motor home's roof and trickled down the windshield.

"Let her go!" Austin said.

Edward laid on the horn again, assaulting Austin with sound. Naomi was screaming something, her face twisted into a visage of fury.

They urged the RV forward. Austin didn't move, but he could feel the pickup behind him, knew he was only a couple of feet away from getting mashed between the vehicles.

He pumped the shotgun and aimed at the windshield.

"Let her go or I'll shoot!" he yelled.

Edward slammed on the horn and pushed the RV closer.

They won't back down.

But neither will I.

Austin pulled the trigger.

Buckshot sprayed the glass, glittering bits clattering to the ground. A web of cracks had spread across the sections of windshield that remained, obscuring Austin's view of the occupants.

But he heard someone screaming. More than one scream. One on his right?

He pivoted.

Brooke emerged in the headlights, Khari at her side, his slender arm around her shoulder. Her hands were bound in restraints.

"The baby's coming!" Brooke cried.

76

Naomi had dropped to the floor a heartbeat before Austin blew out the windshield. In the glare of the headlamps, she had seen the implacable resolve in the man's eyes and realized that he was likely to do anything.

Pushed him too far and now he'll never quit.

Kneeling, she covered her head with her arms. Not a second later, the shotgun boomed. Someone—it sounded like Mama, behind her—screamed. Bits of the shattered windshield peppered Naomi's skin like embers.

"Mow him down!" Naomi ordered Daddy.

But Daddy issued only a feeble groan. Naomi waited a beat to ensure Austin didn't fire again, then rose and squinted at Daddy. Her stomach dropped.

Daddy was sprawled in the seat, limbs hanging loosely, his hat askew. Plugs of bloodied flesh marked his face, neck, and shirt. A lurid mixture of gore and drool slipped from his mouth.

She couldn't believe what she was seeing. Daddy, hurt? Daddy, dead?

No way. He's gonna be okay.

"Daddy? Daddy!"

She grabbed his shoulders and shook him. His head rolled as if it were too heavy for his neck to support it, hat sliding into his lap. Something gurgled deep in his chest, sounding like water rumbling through busted pipes.

She became aware of Mama and Charlotte, clustered around her and wailing. Charlotte tried to shove Naomi out of the way to get closer to Daddy, and Naomi forgot herself and backhanded her older sister across the face so hard that Charlotte tumbled backward as if she had dropped through a chute.

Naomi heard doors slamming shut. She looked out the ruined windshield and saw Brooke and her son getting in the pickup Austin had stolen from their farm. How had they gotten out of the RV? When had that happened? Why was her baby leaving? Naomi felt as if she had fallen asleep and awakened into an unbelievable situation.

Now they were getting away. The truck peeled backward, spitting up gravel.

Naomi shoved her mother aside and seized Daddy again.

"Daddy, go get them! They're driving off! Get them!"

But a fat bubble, pregnant with blood, swelled in Daddy's nostril. His eyes swam, exposing the whites.

"Peach," he whispered.

Naomi heaved him aside. It was like moving a dead horse. He sagged against her. She nudged him into the passenger seat and climbed over his long legs and twisted herself behind the steering wheel.

Austin had executed a U-turn. The red taillights of the pickup glowed as the vehicle pulled ahead and spun around a bend in the road.

"Get back here!" Naomi screamed.

Mama and Charlotte pawed at her shoulders. They were all over her, hovering around Daddy, sobbing. Naomi swung her elbow and smacked Mama in the stomach.

"Get back!" Naomi said.

She floored the gas pedal. The RV rumbled forward like the *Titanic*, so damned big and slow she couldn't hope to catch Austin.

To hell with that—he's not getting away.

Hot tears flooded her eyes. She had sacrificed too much, waited too long, loved too hard. She would never let him go. Ever.

On the dashboard, an orange light flashed, warning her about a damaged tire. She ignored it and pressed forward.

The RV clipped a tree. Branches skidded across the busted windshield, and leaves tumbled inside along with the rain and the cold wind.

Growling and cursing, Naomi wrestled with the big vehicle, keeping it on the gravel road. They banged across a pothole that set Daddy sliding to the floor, drawing another chorus of wails from her mother and sister.

"Sit your asses down!" Naomi shouted.

But her words were in vain. Grief had sent them over the edge.

They barreled like a cannonball onto Burrow Road, the main thoroughfare that ran adjacent to the farm. She hung a right—she spotted the dwindling taillights of the pickup heading in that direction. Where was he going?

She urged the motor home to a higher speed. The speedometer climbed to fifty miles an hour . . . sixty . . . sixty-five. Trees sped past in a dark blur. Wind and rain howled through the ruptured glass, and Naomi's braids whipped around her head.

She was closing in on the truck. The taillights grew larger.

Naomi realized that she was screaming curses, chanting like a shaman intent on bringing down divine destruction from the sky, her hair in her eyes and rain smacking her cheeks.

The truck zipped around a tight curve. Naomi didn't slow as she plunged the RV into the turn. She couldn't afford to slow down; if she did, they would get away, and she wasn't letting them get away. That was her family up there. They *belonged* to her.

But the ruined tire and the rain-slick road were too much for the speeding motor home, and the vehicle hydroplaned as they pitched through the curve. Naomi's stomach flipped, Mama and Charlotte screaming for a different reason now. The steering wheel tore through her fingers. They launched off the road, punched through bushes, and dropped onto a steep embankment, the camper slamming onto its side. Naomi hadn't been wearing her seat belt. As the motor home tumbled end over end, she hit the ceiling, banging her head, air bags deploying, but it was too late.

Blackness swallowed her.

77

When Austin blasted out of a sharp turn and hit a straightaway, he checked in the rearview mirror and found the Xaviers were no longer following him.

He didn't dare celebrate. His exes were like the monsters that would not die from a drive-thru creature feature. He couldn't let his guard down.

Especially then. Brooke sat nestled against him, drawing in deep, measured breaths. Their baby was on the way. Talk about timing.

"Hang on, babe," Austin said. "We're almost there."

"Better hurry." Brooke's cuffed hands were balled into fists, her knuckles milk white.

From the rear seat, Khari peered over Austin's shoulder. Austin still couldn't believe the boy was with them, that he had helped Brooke escape. But Khari hadn't said a single word since he had rejoined them.

Lights twinkled ahead as the woodlands gave way to blessed civilization: fast-food restaurants, hotels, big-box stores.

"Hang on a little longer," Austin said.

He glanced in the rearview mirror again. The road behind them was a ribbon of darkness.

He remembered the location of Albany Memorial Hospital. Naomi had birthed Khari at the same facility, in the middle of a November night twelve years ago.

The irony wasn't lost on him.

Two minutes later, he veered into the hospital's parking lot and screeched toward the emergency entrance. At that late hour, no one else was there. He parked underneath the well-lit portico.

"See?" Austin said. "We're here."

Brooke laughed. "We made it."

"Damned right, we made it."

He kissed her and got out to help her. Khari took her other side, one hand on Brooke's arm.

Inside the hospital, they found a bleary-eyed woman at the front desk.

"My wife's having a baby," Austin said. "Right now!"

The receptionist immediately summoned the medical staff. Someone brought a wheelchair for Brooke.

"I need to have a C-section," Brooke said, easing into the wheelchair. "Call my OB-GYN, in Atlanta. I'll give you their office info—they'll have someone on call who can confirm my status. I don't have my insurance card, but I'll give you my name, SSN, date of birth, whatever you need to verify my identity."

"Why is she handcuffed?" a female nurse asked. Her eyebrows furrowed, her sharp gaze darting from Brooke to Austin. "And you look like you've been in an altercation, sir."

"I was abducted," Brooke said. "All of us were. Can we please talk about that *after* I have this baby?"

"Get some bolt cutters," Austin said.

Although Austin had attended Khari's birth, this experience with Brooke was far more surreal. A maintenance worker found bolt cutters and snapped the chains binding the cuffs, but the cuffs themselves would have to wait until after the medical team delivered the baby. They wheeled Brooke into the emergency operating room, and at the door, they tried to turn away Austin and Khari.

"I need my family with me!" Brooke said, puffing, face reddened. "Do you know how hard we worked to find each other?"

The staff relented and allowed them inside. A nurse gave Austin and Khari masks to wear and requested for them to wash their hands in a nearby sink.

In short order, Brooke's status was verified with her doctor's office, and the anesthesiologist on duty administered an epidural for Brooke. From there, the C-section delivery progressed smoothly. *Everything's gonna work out,* Austin thought, though beads of cold sweat kept rolling down his forehead. *At last, everything's gonna work out for us.*

When Austin saw their new baby emerge with a healthy, full-throated cry, he realized he was crying, too.

78

Perhaps three hours after the child's birth, they were in a private room, the four of them: Austin, Brooke, Khari, and Austin Junior. A short while ago, the sleepy-eyed police officer on duty at the hospital had stopped in to interview them.

"Your ex-wife abducted you guys?" The revelation had prodded the officer awake. He was a man of perhaps twenty-two with a peach-fuzz mustache.

"My ex *and* her family," Austin said. "It's a long story, and we're too exhausted to cover all the details right now. But—they could still be searching for us."

"I saw them kill a woman," Brooke said in a somber tone. She lay in the bed at an elevated angle, clasping the swaddled baby to her bosom; an IV tube trailed from her hand to a bag hanging from a bedside stand. "It was an elderly woman who lived in a little house across the street from their farm. When I got away from the farm, she was going to help me, but they found me there, and they shot her."

"Do you know the lady's name, ma'am?" the officer asked.

"Sorry." Brooke shook her head. "But I think the Xaviers might have set fire to the house, to hide the evidence."

"I'll report this to my captain for sure." The officer lifted his chin and slid his hand to his holstered firearm. "You guys are safe here. We'll get on top of this, I promise. But at this hour, might take some time to round up the cavalry."

"Evil never sleeps," Brooke said. "Can you stay nearby, sir? Please?"

"Yes, ma'am, I'll be right outside." The officer tried to stifle a yawn and shuffled to the door. "Guess I need to get another cup of coffee."

Brooke had used the room's landline telephone to call her parents. As Austin had expected, her family had already sounded the alarm about her whereabouts when they had tried contacting her over the past thirty-plus hours and gotten no response to any of their messages. Brooke was too tired to relate all the details and assured them that they were safe, and their new grandson was doing fine. Her folks declared they would be driving to Albany around eight o'clock in the morning.

"I'm so thankful we're all here," Brooke said. Austin leaned over the bed and kissed her. She smiled, kissed Junior's forehead. "Our little man is one hundred percent healthy, not a scratch on him."

"You wouldn't let it happen." Austin ran his hand along their son's delicate frame. He felt tears tugging at his eyes again. After living on the knife's edge of terror for so many hours, he was an emotional wreck.

Khari hovered nearby. Although he still hadn't spoken, he hadn't left their side, and Austin saw the boy's lips quivering as he looked upon the newborn.

"Do you want to hold your little brother, Khari?" Brooke asked.

Silent, Khari nodded.

Brooke beckoned him to the bed. Keeping the baby swaddled in his blanket, Austin helped transfer the child from Brooke's arms into Khari's. Austin showed Khari how to keep the child's tiny head supported as he cradled him against his chest.

The baby cooed. Khari grinned.

"Next, we'll show you how to change his diaper," Austin said, and Brooke chuckled. "Lord knows, I changed plenty of yours."

Khari looked from the baby to Austin. Although his eyes were glassy with tears, he held Austin's gaze.

"I heard everything you said," Khari said softly. "On the radio."

"Oh." Austin's heart stuttered. "I meant it. Every word."

"Can I . . . can I still call you Dad?"

"You're not calling me 'Austin,' or 'hey, you,' or 'old man.'" Austin smiled. "Yeah, I think that means you can call me Dad."

Khari bobbed his head, looked away. "I'm . . . sorry . . . for what happened. I wasn't really gonna . . ."

"I know."

"I couldn't stay there with them. I mean, I thought I wanted to, but . . ." Khari grimaced. "I can't live like they do." He sniffled. "I'm not like them. I don't *wanna* be like them."

"We don't need to talk about it, Son." Austin rested his hand on Khari's shoulder, squeezed. "I'm glad you're here. We'll figure out the rest, in time."

Khari whispered, "Thanks, Dad."

79

Austin awoke to Brooke's cry. He bolted upright, back aching from the chair on which he had fallen asleep.

"What's wrong?" Standing, he blinked in the muted light issuing from a lamp and glanced at the clock on the nightstand: it flashed 4:07 a.m.

"I'm okay," Brooke said in a raspy voice. Junior slept in a hospital bassinet within arm's reach, and she touched the baby as if needing to assure herself of his safety. "It was only a bad dream. I thought she was here with us."

He didn't need to ask to whom Brooke referred; there was only one *she* and always would be.

Brooke took the Styrofoam cup from the mobile bedside table and sipped water through a straw. Austin looked around the shadowed room.

Khari rested in a chair on the opposite side of the bed. His eyes were open in narrow, anxious slits. Austin gave his son the thumbs-up sign and the boy shut his eyes.

"It's only us," Austin said. "At this hour, no doubt we're the only ones awake in the entire hospital."

"Is the police officer posted outside?" Brooke asked.

Austin crossed the room and opened the door. The cop was gone, and no staff member occupied the nurse's station. The floor had an air of abandonment.

"Probably they're taking a break," Austin said. "Try to rest, babe, okay?"

"I'll try. Sorry I woke you."

Austin lifted a nearby chair and hauled it in front of the door.

"Maybe I'm paranoid, but a little barricade doesn't hurt," he said.

He scanned the room again. The bathroom door hung slightly ajar, as they'd left it. The curtains covered the big window that overlooked the parking lot.

Austin kissed Brooke on the forehead and settled back into his uncomfortable chair, adjusted the pillow the nurse had given him, and tried to find a bearable position.

Within less than a minute, he felt himself drifting off again, his gaze traveling around the room as drowsiness enveloped him. The curtains. The half-open bathroom door. Had it been half-open when he had looked earlier? He couldn't recall, but everything was quiet, and he was bone tired.

He fell back to sleep.

With a whisper, the bathroom door opened.

80

As silently as a resurrected spirit, Naomi nudged open the bathroom door. She wore a patient gown and an ID bracelet with a fake name. A bandage encircled her head from the concussion she had suffered when the RV had careened off the road and flipped down the embankment.

When she opened the door and saw Austin and his baby mama floating in a calm slumber, she felt her heart clutch.

They had taken away everything from her. *Everything.* Daddy, dead from a shotgun blast. Mama and Char, dead in their wrecked motor home.

Only Naomi had survived.

A passing driver had noticed the totaled RV at the bottom of the slope and called 911. Paramedics rescued Naomi; she was bleeding and half-conscious, dizzy with pain, crawling around inside the motor home and struggling in vain to save her doomed family. The team of paramedics loaded her into the ambulance and rushed her to the nearest hospital, Albany Memorial—which happened to be the same place to which her traitorous husband had taken his baby mama and her son.

Naomi learned of their presence there only because of the talkative staff. While they worked on her in the ER, attending to her scrapes and bruises and giving her a powerful painkiller, nurses chitchatted about a newly admitted family with a just-hatched newborn and their "crazy abduction story."

Naomi had suffered a concussion, but she remembered her purpose. When an assistant asked for her name, she had given them a fake one, Cleo Jones, the name of the badass lead character in her favorite old-school flick, *Cleopatra Jones*. The staff was so daft they believed her without question, and here she was wearing an ID bracelet with "Cleo Jones" printed on it.

You couldn't make this stuff up.

Fate, Naomi thought as she stared across the room and saw Brooke lying on the bed, her tender-faced newborn sleeping in the bassinet next to her. *Fate is a bitch, but she brought me here.*

Creeping upstairs to the maternity ward on the third floor had been easy. At that late hour, everyone was asleep. No one saw her or stopped her. She had searched until she found the room with the medical charts bearing Brooke's name. Slipping inside and finding the family resting, she hid out for a spell in the bathroom. Austin would be on edge after what he had been through, and she was wise to wait.

Now, at last, they belonged to her.

She flicked out her butterfly knife and approached the bed.

81

"*No!*"

Austin snapped awake. He had dropped into a vivid dream in which he occupied a vehicle of some kind with Brooke, Khari, and the baby. It seemed like an RV, with areas for sleeping and eating, yet it was impossibly long, like a train, and when Austin wandered along its length and finally entered the front cabin, he found Edward Xavier hunched over the steering wheel and glaring out of a shattered windshield at a stormy night. Edward turned and leered at Austin, his face studded with busted glass and his teeth painted blood-red. *Hey, son. Take a seat. We're on our way to hell . . .*

The shout yanked Austin out of his slumber. Khari had yelled. Khari was out of his chair and lunging toward someone.

He was throwing himself at Naomi.

Naomi wore a hospital gown and a head bandage. She stood beside Brooke's bed, but her gaze was focused on the bassinet. She gripped her butterfly knife.

She was lowering the blade to their sleeping baby.

The crazy thing was that Austin wasn't surprised to see Naomi in their room attempting to murder their newborn. Was she a patient? How had she gotten in there? None of that mattered then—he had expected she would show up, somewhere, sometime, if not at the hospital, then after they went home. She carried a grudge like no one he had ever known and had a predator's instinct for exploiting opportunities.

On his left, Brooke awoke with a strangled scream.

Khari slammed into his mother like a wrestler shot from a ringside rope. Naomi cried out as the boy tackled her. They crashed to the floor in a knot of limbs.

Feeling as if he were fighting through quicksand, Austin pushed out of his chair. He glanced at Brooke again and saw she was fine: she had snatched Junior out of the bassinet and clutched him to her chest.

Austin hurried around the foot of the bed.

"*Get off me, boy!*" Naomi growled, and Khari yelped like a kicked dog. He slipped off his mother and curled into a ball, face contorted with pain.

Naomi bounced like a gymnast to her feet. She glowered at Austin. She still had the knife.

Austin stood between Naomi and the bed. Behind him, Brooke turned away with the baby in her arms and fumbled with the nurse call button.

"*You.*" Naomi's glare seared Austin. "You took everything. Daddy, Mama, Char. *You* did it!"

"Stay away from us." He grabbed the serving tray off the mobile table. He held it in front of him like a shield.

Naomi charged him. She swung the blade in wild arcs, the knife whistling as it sliced through the air.

Austin raised the tray and deflected her strike. Swiftly, she flipped the knife to her other hand and swiped at him, getting past his guard, zipping the razor-sharp edge down his right arm in a bloody line.

Austin gasped, his arm feeling as if it were suddenly on fire.

Across the room, someone shoved against the door, unable to get inside due to the chair barricade. No help coming.

Naomi lunged at him again and swung the blade in a downward arc. He blocked the blow with the tray, but then it slipped out of his fingers and clanged against the floor.

Naomi pressed the attack. Shouting, he raised his arms and charged forward. The blade slashed his palm, opening a deep gash, but he grappled with her and seized her wrist, trapping the knife in midair, inches away from his face.

"Let go!" she shrieked.

Numb with pain, Austin twisted her arm and angled the blade toward her. Fighting him, she hissed and spat, her hair swinging in her face, hives glowing on her neck and cheeks. He was cursing at her, too, a stream of babble: "S*tay away from me and my family, dammit, stay away from me, stay away from me, stay away from me!*"

She was strong, high on adrenaline and hate, but he put all his strength into pushing back, all his determination, his resolve to finally end this propelling him to drive the knife toward her, and her resistance faltered. He had the steel against her neck. That neck he had once kissed with such passion. How had things come to this? Where had their lives gone off the rails? How had love turned to loathing?

Her slitted gaze locked on his and he knew the same thoughts played through her mind. But whatever love they once shared had fractured into rot and ruin.

Finish it.

He pressed the knife into her throat. Blood spilled over the blade. He drove it in further, further, and the honed metal slid into her flesh like a pin into a cushion.

"But I loved you," she whispered, tears tumbling down her cheeks.

She collapsed to her knees, into the crimson pool spreading around her bare feet. She reached for her neck, fingers fumbling around the knife's handle. Gasping and choking, she struggled to tear the blade out of her throat.

Austin backed away to the bed, leaving his own trail of blood. He reached behind him, found Brooke's hand, and held on like a man fighting against getting pulled overboard. She squeezed it, tugged him toward her.

Naomi finally pulled out the knife and tried to get up, but she lacked the strength. She dropped onto her side, blood puddling around her head. Her dying gaze fixed on Austin. He would remember that haunting stare for the rest of his life. Naomi's lips worked, but only a wordless wisp of air escaped her, and at last, the fire in her eyes flickered out.

She was gone.

Khari fell against him, sobbing, but thankfully, unharmed. Austin kissed his son's head and held him close. Brooke clasped the baby to her and squeezed Austin's bloody hand.

I'll never let them go, Austin vowed.

And he understood in his soul that they all shared that same purpose. They would hold fast to one another for the rest of their lives, through heartache and happiness. They were a family, assembled from trauma and love and fear, but they were a family, and they would survive, and they would survive together.

—

HEAR MORE FROM BRANDON

Did you enjoy this novel? Visit *www.brandonmassey.com* now to sign up for my free mailing list.

Mailing list members get advance news on the latest releases, the chance to win autographed copies in exclusive contests, and much more. I'll never share your email address and you can unsubscribe at any time.

ABOUT BRANDON MASSEY

Brandon Massey was born June 9, 1973, and grew up in Zion, Illinois. He lives with his family near Atlanta, Georgia, where he is at work on his next novel.

Visit his web site at *www.brandonmassey.com* for the latest news on his upcoming books.

ALSO BY BRANDON MASSEY

Thunderland

Dark Corner

Within the Shadows

The Other Brother

Vicious

The Last Affair

Don't Ever Tell

Cornered

Covenant

In the Dark

Frenzied

Nana

The Quiet Ones

No Stone Unturned

Made in the USA
Middletown, DE
19 July 2022

69690501R00172